The
Girl
in the
Midnight
Maze

The
Girl
in the
Midnight
Maze

Cathy Hayward

LAKE UNION
PUBLISHING

Text copyright © 2021, 2024 by Cathy Hayward
All rights reserved.

Published by Lake Union Publishing, Seattle

www.apub.com

Amazon, the Amazon logo, and Lake Union Publishing are trademarks of Amazon.com, Inc., or its affiliates.

ISBN-13: 9781662521737
eISBN: 9781662521720

Cover design by Emma Rogers
Cover image: © Melica © Davide Marzotto © kilic inan © Nature Design © ELLEN Daly © Chansom Pantip © Scisetti Alfio © Ortis / Shutterstock

Printed in the United States of America

For Hilda

We are shaped by our mothers, and, if we lack them, we are shaped by that loss.

Chapter 1

EMMA

JANUARY 2019

Emma's phone rang as she was peeling potatoes for mash. She glanced at the screen but didn't recognise the number so ignored it, cutting the peeled potato in half before adding it to the pan.

Her son James wandered into the kitchen, headphones clamped to his ears. He grabbed a carton of milk from the fridge and lifted it to his lips.

'James! Use a glass,' she said, nodding towards the cupboard.

He rolled his eyes but poured the milk into a glass and sat down at the kitchen table. 'How long till dinner?'

'Thirty minutes,' she said. 'How was college?'

James shrugged and looked at his phone. 'Same, same.'

'Best bit of the day?' coaxed Emma. She remembered asking the same question when she used to pick him and his sister Libby up from primary school. Best bit of the day? Worst bit of the day? What did you have for lunch? She learned that after receiving a standard response of 'fine', they would compete on who could describe the most outlandish things that had happened. Now they were both teenagers she was lucky if they answered at all.

James didn't look up. 'I scored a couple of baskets in practice and coach asked me to join the first team.'

'James, that's amazing.' Emma smiled and rested her hand on his shoulder. A faint blush crept up his neck. 'You must tell Dad when he gets in.'

James nodded and focused back on his phone.

'How many sausages do you want?' Emma asked, slipping them out of the packet on to the grill tray.

'Six?' he said hopefully.

Emma laughed and got a second packet out of the fridge. 'D'you want any help with revision later? I could go through those index cards with you, ask you some random questions?'

'Yeah, okay,' he said.

Really she should try to finish off the survey for the new development. She'd only got halfway through before she'd had to leave to pick up Libby and take her to street dance. That was always the challenge – trying to fit what was a full-time job into part-time hours. But Emma loved her afternoons off. Since James started school, she'd only worked from nine to three, meaning she could pick him and Libby up every day and spend the rest of the afternoon with them. Even now they both tended to do their own thing – James at basketball or out with friends, Libby hanging around in town – she still liked being at home when they arrived and they knew she was there if they wanted her. She could finish the survey after she'd helped out with the revision.

Libby came in and sat at the table. 'I saw you with that girl at lunch,' she said to James.

James narrowed his eyes and mouthed, 'Fuck off.'

'I saw that,' said Emma. 'It still counts as swearing even if you don't say it.'

James rolled his eyes again slightly and looked back at his sister mouthing something Emma couldn't interpret.

Her phone rang again and she glanced at the number. It was the same one as earlier and she still didn't recognise it. She was about to answer when Nick came through the door.

'Hi, gang,' he said. 'Nice to see everyone here rather than hiding in your rooms.'

'The draw of dinner rather than my company, I think,' laughed Emma as he pulled her into a hug. 'How was your day?'

'So, so.' He screwed up his face. 'Client meeting was a compete fiasco. I spent most of the rest of the day trying to sort out the mess.'

'Oh, darling, I'm sorry. Why don't you change? Then dinner will be ready.'

'Fab, I'm starving.'

'Libby, James, could you lay the table, please, while I serve up?'

There was a general grunt of disapproval but they both slowly got up and reached for plates and cutlery as Emma started putting pans of steaming mash, peas and beans on the table. Nick joined them and Emma dished up, making sure to put plenty on Libby's plate. She had been looking too thin recently.

They were halfway through dinner when Emma's phone rang again. She put her fork down. 'I know we say no phones at the table, but I just want to check it's not that number again. Someone keeps calling me.'

'One rule for us . . .' said Libby.

'Libby,' said Nick. 'Enough.'

It was the same number. Emma clicked 'Accept' and said 'Hello?' as she walked out of the kitchen, closing the door behind her.

'Hello, is that Emma Bowen?'

There was something official about the man's tone of voice that made her heart beat slightly faster. 'Speaking.'

'My name is Mr Eals. I'm calling about Margaret Chapman – your mother, I believe?'

'Yes?' Had she had a change of heart?

'I'm sorry to inform you that Margaret died earlier today. It was very peaceful.' The voice was soft.

Emma felt her throat constrict. She held the phone against her chest, unable to speak. Almost immediately tears spilled down her face. Mum was dead. She'd always thought they might reconcile. She'd rushed to her mother's bedside several times over the past twenty years of her illness, as she had gone in and then out of remission. She'd become so used to her recovering that she thought they'd always have time to make things up.

She swallowed with difficulty and raised the phone to her ear. 'Hello?' she said.

'Hello, Mrs Bowen.' The voice was quiet, understanding. Someone who was used to delivering bad news. 'I realise this will be something of a shock for you. May I suggest we talk tomorrow morning, once you've had time to digest the news. We can then talk about the official arrangements. Is there a good time for us to speak?'

'Any time,' Emma managed. 'Thank you, Mr Eals.' Emma ended the call. She opened the kitchen door again and looked at Nick and the children around the kitchen table. They were laughing. Three faces turned towards her.

'All okay?' said Nick.

'It's Mum,' said Emma, her voice broke. 'She died earlier today.'

'Oh, Em.' Nick was on his feet, holding her as her knees started to give way. He guided her back to the table. 'What a shock.'

Both James and Libby stopped eating. Libby got up and put her arms around her mother from behind. 'Sorry, Mum. We love you.'

'Thanks, Libs,' said Emma, wiping her eyes.

'I'm sorry too, Mum,' said James, frowning at her.

'I think I'm going to go upstairs for a while,' said Emma, getting to her feet. 'Leave you to finish off here.'

'I'll come with you,' said Nick.

'I just need a moment on my own,' said Emma.

'I understand,' he said, giving her another hug.

Lying on her bed, she let the tears come. But what was she crying for? She and Mum had never got on. She felt guilty that she hadn't been there at the end though – especially when she'd dashed up to be with her the other times they'd thought she was near the end. Had she died alone? No, Mr Eals had said it was peaceful so there must have been someone with her. *As her only child, it should have been me*, Emma thought, crying harder.

But their relationship had always been strained. Even as a young child. There was a feeling of slight relief that it was at an end, and it made Emma feel even more guilty.

Later, when Nick came up, she sobbed into his chest. 'I don't know why I'm crying so much. I didn't cry like this when Dad died and we were always so close.'

Nick stroked the back of her head. 'I think it's because you're mourning the relationship you never had.'

And that was it exactly, Emma thought.

Chapter 2

Betty

March 1937

Betty lay in the bath, her white legs flushing a blotchy pink in the scorching water. The passage light leaked around the edges of the bathroom door, merging into the glow from the streetlamp, fractured through the frosted glass window. The mirror perspired in the heat, dripping into the basin.

She took another gulp straight from the half-empty bottle balanced on the corner of the bath where the mould bred between the tiles. Her face twisted at the gin's bitter burn, but the bottle was cool against her cheek as she pulled a breath into her tight lungs.

Her mother's knitting needle balanced on the cloth used to wipe her sisters' faces. As she leaned forward to feel the pointed tip again with her finger, the water sloshed over the sides of the bath, on to the floor. The muffled sounds of her sisters finishing off their tea in the kitchen next door mingled with her mother's muted scolding.

There wasn't much time. *Not for me, not for it. He.* Betty was sure it was a he. *He would look just like him. But not grow up to be the coward his father was. He'd have a proper job where he'd have clean hands, a smart suit and a bowler hat. Live somewhere posh like Epsom, not in this tiny tenement.*

The hum of buses grinding up Battersea Park Road past St Saviour blurred with the shouts of the men clocking off, heading to the pub, and the yelling of the boys playing football by the dim streetlights.

She reached forward, over the tightness of her belly, and grasped the knitting needle, then let it float on the surface of the scalding water until it sunk beneath the water line, turning almost gaily downwards. The intense heat made her drowsy. It was difficult to move.

The pain won't be bad. Not as bad as standing there, looking the best I've ever looked, wearing that beautiful dress, waiting for him. Father pacing up and down. Then realising he wasn't ever going to come. That awful journey back home.

Angry steps sounded.

'You've taken all me bleedin' hot water. There ain't none left.' Her mother was at the door, shaking the handle.

'I won't be long, Ma.'

'Least you could do is be 'ere helping me with this lot, not dilly-dallying in there. Betty?'

'I'll be there in a minute.'

'What you doing in there anyway? Dolling yerself up? Got yerself another fancy man already, 'ave yer?'

'I won't be long, Mum.'

'Bloody hurry up. Cheek taking all that water. Nothing for yer pa when he gets home.'

The sound of steps moved away, and Betty imagined her mother, her thin, faded housecoat wrapped around her ample frame, stomping back into the tiny front room. There was a shout from next door, the sound of a child being slapped and then whimpering.

The knitting needle had settled, resting across the dark mound of her pubic hair. She stared at it. One small movement. Over. Quick.

She closed her eyes. She had no choice.

Chapter 3

Emma

January 2019

Emma yawned. It had been such a long drive to Morecambe to the solicitor's office. She wasn't used to driving that far and she felt guilty for leaving James in the middle of his mocks. And work. She'd never finished the condition survey. And it was due today. She sighed and looked around the small solicitor's office. The window ledge hadn't been dusted for years. A dried-out spider plant was caked with decades of grime. The reception area, which doubled as the secretary's office, was chilly. There was a heater under the desk of the woman who had only reluctantly glanced up from her pile of paperwork to welcome Emma. She didn't look much younger than the building.

Behind the secretary's desk, Emma saw a figure emerging from a narrow corridor. Mr Eals, her mother's solicitor, looked even more dilapidated than his office. His dark eyes were sunken into his face, barely visible below untamed eyebrows. The hand he held out to greet Emma was equally hairy. Already a short man, he was bent over, as if from the weight of people's troubles he had shouldered over the years.

He was smiling. 'Ah, Margaret's daughter, Mrs Bowen. I was hoping we would meet. It's a pleasure.'

'Good to meet you too, Mr Eals.' They shook hands and he ushered her back down the narrow corridor, years of spilled coffee staining the carpet tiles. The back door was open, the chilly draught riffling the stacks of paper lining the corridor and breezing into Mr Eals' small office at the back of the building. The windows here were high up on the wall, so there was no view of whatever lay behind the office. But even if there had been big windows, Emma suspected the old solicitor would have found a way of covering them. Every single surface in the room was buried under piles of manila files held together by elastic bands, labelled in the same spidery script. The top of a mahogany glass-fronted bookcase, which was full of impressive-looking legal tomes, was stacked to the window ledge, and even the chair opposite the old desk had several newer-looking folders on them. Mr Eals slid them on to a pile on his desk and indicated where Emma should sit. He eased himself past another tower of files and sat on a well-worn leather chair opposite her.

He was watching her, the tips of his fingers pressed together, his elbows resting on the cluttered desk. 'You do look like your mother. I suspect everyone says that.'

Emma smiled. 'Not many of my friends knew her.'

The contours around his eyes rippled as the old man returned her smile. 'Your mother was one of my longest-standing clients. I'm sad that this day has come. As a solicitor, you follow a client through their lives, intervening at the crucial points. Births, marriages, divorces, deaths of relatives, house purchases, and, then eventually, death. It's the natural order of my professional life.'

'So you had known Mum a long time?' Emma didn't recall her ever mentioning Mr Eals.

'Yes, since her twenties. She was one of my more interesting clients,' he said slowly. 'Now, have you got the death certificate we discussed on the phone yesterday? It is a relatively simple estate so, with a fair wind, we should secure probate in a couple of months.'

Emma drew the envelope out of her bag – she'd got the death certificate from the town hall that morning – and handed it over to the solicitor. He took out his glasses and put them on his nose before examining the death certificate closely. He nodded gravely. Then he raised his arms to the sides of the chair and used them to push himself upwards, until he seemed to judge that his knees would be able to support him. He moved slowly over to a pile of files in the corner nearest Emma and selected an enormous series of folders second from the top. It was held together by blue elastic bands, straining against almost a foot of paperwork. What on earth had her mother needed to discuss over the years?

Mr Eals dropped it with a thud on to the desk with the look of a man surveying a job well done. He rolled off one of the elastic bands and slid in the death certificate.

'Thank you for arranging to get this so quickly and for offering to sort out her possessions. As I said on the phone, the will makes a number of stipulations about certain items. I always think it's better for relatives to manage that. It saves unnecessary solicitor's fees and allows for what the Americans like to call "closure".'

'I think I'd have to go through years of therapy to get closure with my mother,' Emma said with a grimace.

She'd meant the comment light-heartedly, but Mr Eals paused and looked down at the file, stroking it.

'I'm not a religious man,' he said quietly, 'but I believe there's a phrase in the Bible about walking a mile in another man's shoes. Until we have done that, we will never understand what it's like to be the other person.'

Emma glanced down at her hands and realised she was twisting her wedding ring around her finger. She placed her hands on the desk and looked up at the old solicitor, who was watching her over his glasses. She nodded. Emma had no wish to walk in her mother's shoes. Their relationship had been difficult at best.

He eased a couple of sheets of paper out of the file. 'I have your mother's will here,' he said, passing it across the desk, 'so you can see what needs to be done.'

On the top sheet *Last Will and Testament* was printed in large bold letters across the top.

'*This Will is made by me Margaret Chapman of Flat b, 487 Marine Road East, Morecambe on this day Monday the 21st of January 2019*,' she read.

Emma looked up quickly. 'This will was made the day before she died,' she said, her eyes wide. 'Didn't she have a will before, or did she change it?'

Mr Eals hesitated. 'Your mother made some small changes to her will just before she died, but it was easier to make a new one than add them in as a codicil.'

Emma frowned and looked down at the document. Her heart started to thud. Why would Mum change her will just before she died?

The solicitor continued. 'Now, after the usual blurb about revocation, executors – that's me' – he looked up – 'and funeral directions, you'll see there's a section entitled "Specific Gifts".'

Emma traced her fingers down the page. There was a list of items that her mother wanted distributing to different people. Books, ornaments, jewellery, a coin collection. Nothing that Emma particularly remembered.

'All these items are in her property,' Mr Eals said, 'and I've arranged a courier to come to collect them later today to save you having to distribute them yourself. Some of them are going to other parts of the country, although a couple are local.'

Emma reached the end of the list and gasped. '*The Girl in the Midnight Maze*. She wants the painting to go to someone called Clare Richens. But—'

'Yes, your mother's friend Clare lives close by. I've included her address and phone number on this sheet,' he said calmly, slowly sliding another piece of paper across the desk. 'If you prefer, I can cancel the courier and you can deliver it yourself?'

'But *The Girl in the Midnight Maze* is ours. Our family's. It can't go to a stranger. I love that painting, it's beautiful,' Emma said, suddenly finding it difficult to swallow. She thought of the little girl dancing in the moonlight in the centre of the maze.

The secretary appeared at the door with a tray cluttered with a teapot, cups, and a milk jug. She laid it gently between them and set out the cups either side of the tray. Mr Eals reached forward and carefully poured milk and then tea into two cups, both covered in roses, and slid one across to Emma. She picked it up, her hands trembling, and took a sip.

With his fingertips once more pressed together in what she realised was his habitual pose, Mr Eals spoke quietly. 'I'm afraid that's what Margaret's will says. She wanted the painting to go to Miss Richens.'

Even though Emma hadn't seen the painting for years, for much of her childhood it had hung in the sitting room of their family home in Sussex, watching over her as she grew. When she was tall enough, she would reach up and follow the labyrinth with her fingertips, trying to find an escape route for the girl in the white dress locked within the shadowy prison of green hedges.

Her shoulders dropped and she looked back to the will. She hadn't thought there would be anything controversial in it. How naive. Mum had always loved any opportunity to be contentious.

'There is also the matter of her property itself. If you turn to page two, clause seven . . .' The solicitor paused and looked up at her.

Emma flicked over the page, scanned down and read out loud. 'To Elizabeth Margaret Bowen I leave my property Flat b, 487 Marine Road East, Morecambe.' She looked up at the old man. 'She's left her flat to Libby?'

Mr Eals smiled. 'Yes, to your daughter. Your younger child, I believe?'

Emma covered her mouth with her hand. 'But Mum hated Libby,' she said, rereading the text.

'Hate is a strong word,' he said calmly, slowly opening a drawer and extracting a set of keys. 'These are the keys to your mother's flat. I'm afraid it's been empty since she went into the nursing home a few months ago, but I've been keeping an eye on it.' He reached up and scratched his neck inside his starched collar. 'I think you'll find it all in order.'

Emma nodded, staring at the keys. Some had a carefully labelled tag, written in an unfamiliar hand: *communal door, front door, meter cupboard*. A small brass key was unlabelled.

'The residue of your mother's estate goes to a selection of charities, as you'll see on page four. If you can box it all up and label it, I will arrange for all of that in my role as executor. I can perhaps book another courier to save you taking it to the various charity shops she stipulated.'

Emma nodded blankly and then blurted out, 'What was it she changed the day before she died? The property going to Libby or the painting going to' – she looked down at the will – 'Clare?'

The old solicitor shook his head. 'I'm afraid I'm not at liberty to disclose the content of her previous will. I'm sure you understand.'

Emma nodded again, her foot tapping the floor.

'Now, this final document' – he slid a sheet of paper across the desk – 'details her funeral wishes. The music, readings and so on. Margaret had been in touch with a funeral home and made all the arrangements herself. You will just need to contact them and arrange a date.'

Emma scanned through a short list of music and the contact details for a humanist celebrant. *How very like Mum to want something different to the norm.*

'If you need anything else, do get in touch.' Mr Eals pulled himself up by the arms of the chair and stood. 'I will be in contact about the probate in due course.'

She also rose, clutching the keys. 'Thank you for your help,' she said automatically and followed him out of the room, her throat tight with repressed emotion.

Chapter 4

BETTY

AUGUST 1937

Betty's sickness never quite went away. The bleeding stopped, and the pain receded into a small knot in her stomach, but the nausea was always under the surface. Betty couldn't eat. She lay up on the top bunk bed in the room she shared with Winnie and Edie, dreaming of semi-formed babies being sucked into a bath plughole, swimming through the pipes and out to the river.

In the evenings, her mother sat in the front room knitting, her two knitting needles rhythmically smashing together. Betty watched her, unable to tear her eyes away, each new stitch looping her back to the pain and the blood.

But the swelling in her stomach didn't shrink as she hoped. It continued to spread. Betty's pale, unblemished skin stretched to accommodate it. The strange half-formed thing that she'd imagined long gone moved inside her, grasping at life. She saw its flesh torn apart, its features grotesque.

Betty hid its existence under cotton dresses and long cardigans throughout that long, wet summer. The tiny mewling creature was born in the same bathroom where it almost met its demise, slithering out into the bath, now empty and cool, but once again stained with blood. Betty smothered its cries in the dark, sleeping house.

◆ ◆ ◆

The knock made Betty start. She'd almost slipped into an exhausted sleep, despite the hardness of the bath against her back.

'Betty, you all right? I thought I heard something.'

Her eyes darted around the room, but she already knew there was nowhere she could hide the baby. It lay pink and still, warm where it touched her chest, but its back was already cooling. She'd been wrong all along. It had been a girl.

'Betty?' The voice was quiet but held a question. She wasn't going away.

Betty took a deep breath. 'I-I'm okay, Ma. But you'd better come in. Hold on.' Betty got on to her knees, holding the little body awkwardly with one arm. She used the side of the bath to lever herself up, her hand shaking so much it made her whole body tremble. Blood flooded down her legs into the bath. She watched it spin around and disappear into the plughole. *So much blood.* Her head swam and she used her free arm to steady herself against the side of the bath as she slowly eased out. There was still a memory of the pain between her legs but nothing like the vice-like agony that had gripped her through the night.

Betty adjusted the baby's tiny body in the crook of her left arm and used her right hand to crack open the door. It was even darker in the passage, and she could only just make out her mother's shadow. 'Ma . . .' she started, rubbing her forehead.

'Are you ill?' asked June, stepping into the room, her house-coat covering her nightdress. She glanced at the floor and gasped, covering her mouth with her hand. 'Oh, Jesus.' Crouching, she smeared some of the blood on her fingers as if testing it.

Betty realised she was still bleeding, blood pooling on the floor between her legs. In the early dawn light, it looked black and threatening.

June stood up and turned to Betty, putting her arm on her shoulder. 'Sit down on the bath, you've lost a lot of blood. I didn't know your monthly—' The baby shifted in Betty's other arm and let out a small kitten-like mewl. 'Oh.' June leaned in and seemed to see it for the first time.

Betty looked down at her rosebud mouth, barely visible in the darkness. She shuffled away from her mother to the window, feeling a trail of wetness stream down her legs. The first hints of dawn seeped into the room. The baby's dark blue eyes met hers. She was perfect in every way. There was no trace of what Betty had tried to do all those months ago. The knitting needle. She shuddered.

'What the fuck is that baby?' June hissed behind her.

Betty turned, her hair hanging over her face. 'I tried to tell you, Ma, but I didn't have the words. I'm sorry,' she whispered and took a deep breath. 'But look, she's beautiful.'

'It's yours?' said June, squishing her eyebrows together as if she didn't quite understand. 'But I would 'ave seen. I would 'ave known.'

Betty slowly shook her head. 'I 'id it, I thought it would go away,' she said quietly. She looked down at the baby still silently staring up at her.

June's eyes widened and the colour seemed to empty from her face, blending with the grey dawn light. 'That's why you was getting married, innit? I get it now. Why it was so quick. You knew you was preggers. No wonder the bleedin' idiot run a fucking mile.' She shook her head, her lips puckered as if she was eating a lemon.

Betty wiped a smear of blood from the baby's cheek. Despite the warmth of the room, the baby's body was cool to touch. She started to whimper. 'Ma, I need a blanket or something. She's cold.' She looked up at June.

'Pass the bastard here.'

Betty shook her head. 'Don't say that, Ma. It's not 'er fault.' Betty glanced between her legs. Blood was still trickling down her thighs, but less quickly now.

June reached for the baby and then stopped. 'Christ.' She knelt in front of Betty. 'The cord's still attached. Is she that fresh out?'

Betty nodded, the movement making her head swim again.

June took her arm and guided her towards the bath. 'Get back in there and keep that baby quiet. I don't want yer father knowing nothin'. I'll be back in a jiffy.'

Betty eased back into the bath, holding the baby tightly against her. She was opening and closing her mouth like a small bird in a nest. Betty slipped her little finger into the tiny opening and the baby sucked vigorously but just as quickly stopped and started to cry again.

'She wants milk, you silly thing.' Her mother had reappeared wielding a large pair of scissors.

'Ma, no!' Betty turned on to her side away from June, shielding the baby underneath. Her cries were getting louder.

'Don't be daft, I'm not gonna hurt her,' hissed June. 'I need to cut the cord and get the rest of it out.' She pulled Betty on to her back and then reached down and deftly snipped. 'You'll lose the bit inside and then the bleedin' will stop.'

Betty touched the cord where it disappeared into the baby's stomach.

'That'll fall away soon,' said June, clamping it with a wooden clothes peg. 'This helps it.' She laid an old blanket over Betty and the baby, tucking it under the baby's legs.

'How did you know how to do that?' asked Betty, staring at the blue rubbery hose lying between her legs like a dead snake.

'Most of us don't let things like this get this far.' June waved her hand at the baby. 'There are ways of getting rid of it long before it gets to a real baby.' She waved the scissors around. 'My sisters—'

The baby whimpered, more urgently this time, the sound bouncing off the tiles.

'Now you've got to feed it to shut it up. I'm not 'aving yer father woken at this hour just 'cause you couldn't keep your legs shut.' June reached under the blanket, her rough washerwoman hands grabbing Betty's taut breast. She gently brought the baby's head closer and pinched Betty's nipple hard with her thumb and forefinger.

'Ouch!' whispered Betty. A globule of yellow liquid appeared, and June pushed the baby on to it.

Betty looked down, her eyes wide as the baby's mouth clamped on to her nipple and started to suck, just as she had on her finger. She looked up at her mother. 'It works.'

'Of course it bloody works. That baby's got more brains than you 'ave, letting him get his way with you before you got that ring on yer finger. Stupid girl.' June stood with her hands on her hips, examining the room. 'Look at the state of this place. As if I 'aven't got enough to do.' She disappeared out of the room again.

The rhythmic sucking felt soothing. It was a strange mix of joy and pain. Dawn had broken and the muted morning light drifted over Betty. The baby's cheek was soft and flushed like the inside of a rose petal. Betty closed her eyes and leaned back against the bath.

June had come back into the room. Betty could hear her panting and wheezing, the sound of a bucket scraping along the floor. 'Jesus, so much blood. It looks like you got murdered.'

Betty felt a familiar squeeze inside her, screwed up her face and automatically pushed, grunting with the effort. June stood over and prodded at something dark at the bottom of the bath. 'That's the rest of it. God knows what I'm gonna do with that.'

The baby detached from her, and Betty opened her eyes, missing the warmth. Its mouth was still opening and closing expectantly. Betty looked up at her mother's pinched face. 'Shall I?' she asked.

June reached over the bath and turned the baby round, repeating the nipple squeeze on the other breast until the baby's mouth had latched on. The cheek that had been against her was warm and damp, like proved dough.

June rung out her cloth, pink liquid dripping into the bucket. 'Right, now just the bath to sort out. We need to get you out of there before your father wants to use it.'

Betty swallowed and looked back down at the baby. She had fallen off her breast and was sleeping in her arms, her mouth still working with the memory of the sucking. 'I'm going to call 'er Margaret, after Margaret Mitchell.' She looked up at her mother. 'The author of *Gone with the Wind*.'

June snorted, her hands on her hips. 'It don't matter what you call 'er, when you give her up they'll call 'er something else.'

Betty stared at her mother, her mouth open. 'What d'you mean?'

''Er new ma will call 'er whatever they want to, they won't keep the name. They never do, them people.' June started wiping the side of the bath. 'Now come on, let's get you out of there. Can't have yer father finding you like this.'

'You want me to give 'er up?' Betty whispered. She couldn't seem to focus on her mother. She was slipping out of reach. Betty slid further into the bath, curling up against Margaret, her eyes already full.

June stopped cleaning. 'You think you could keep 'er? 'Is bastard child? I'm not having no gossip about this family, thank you very much. Can you imagine the shame if you walked out of 'ere with that baby now? With everyone remembering that he stood you up at the altar. They'll know why now, won't they?' She dropped the cloth. 'Pass 'er to me. I'll sort it out. I know people who know people who'll keep it quiet. Find 'er a good 'ome.'

'No, Ma. Please, no,' Betty cried, her snot mingling with the salty tears. 'I want to keep 'er. I'll do anything, anything.' She stroked the baby's sleeping face, tracing the outline of her eyes. 'She's mine.'

June sat down heavily on the side of the bath, staring intently at Betty. 'Pass 'er to me, Betty,' she said, her voice hard. 'You have no choice. All we 'ave is our respectability. Without that we're no better than them families in the slums.'

Betty shook her head, choking on her tears. 'I've never loved anything as much as Margaret, I can't give 'er up.'

June stood and crossed her arms. 'You have no choice, Betty. It's either that or the workhouse. I'll leave you to say your goodbyes and then I'll take 'er. Be quick – yer father will be awake any minute and I want 'er out before then.'

The door closed silently behind her, and Betty looked down at Margaret, sleeping in her arms. The soft morning light bathed the baby's tiny chest as it rose and fell. A milk bubble formed at her lips and her next sigh blew it away. Betty followed the outline of Margaret's lips, feeling the moistness of her first milk, her own chest shuddering. She put Margaret against her nipple again. Instinctively the baby rooted around and latched herself on, took a few soft sucks and then drifted back to sleep, her mouth open.

Betty slumped over Margaret. 'Goodbye, my beautiful girl,' she whispered, through her tears. 'I've never loved anything more than I love you. You deserve more than I can give you. More than this.' She glanced around the small scullery bathroom at the chipped tiles and the mould growing in the corner. The bath was encrusted with dried blood, her legs streaked with it like the war paint the boys used to smear across their faces at school. 'You will have a better life without me.'

Her arms felt so heavy as she tried to stand that she thought for a moment she might drop Margaret. She steadied herself and stepped over the side of the bath, and wrapped herself in a towel, making sure Margaret was still covered in the blanket. Betty stumbled to the window, feeling dizzy. Her legs tingled with tiredness as if she'd walked a long way without stopping. She stood by the frosted window, the garden flowers a kaleidoscope swimming through the glass. Her eyes filled with tears again as she bent over and covered Margaret's forehead and face with tiny kisses. She turned her towards the light. 'Goodbye, my darling baby girl.' Her throat was thick, and she could barely speak.

At that moment, the sun broke over the line of the houses opposite and streamed through the window, wrapping Betty and Margaret in blazing sunlight. Betty blinked and felt a flutter in her chest as if a butterfly was battling its way out of her. She watched as Margaret opened her eyes and stared straight into her, her dark blue eyes unblinking.

Betty struggled to take a breath. Then the baby reached up and grabbed a piece of Betty's damp blond hair, pulling it towards her.

The door opened and June walked in. Betty turned around. Her mother was fully dressed in a hat and summer coat, holding the basket she used for vegetables. 'I've put a blanket in the bottom. She'll be very comfortable,' she said, tipping it up to show Betty. 'I'll go over there now, and no one need be none the wiser.' June stepped slowly towards her, and Betty felt her muscles tense and heart thump. She stuck her chin up. June held the baby's tiny fist and tried to open it and remove Betty's hair, but Margaret held on, still gazing intently at Betty.

23

Betty took a step back away from her mother. The windowpane rattled as she leaned against it. 'No,' she said. 'You're not 'aving her.' Her legs straightened and her fists tightened into balls as tight as Margaret's.

'Don't be a fool. You have no choice. Now give 'er to me.' June came closer, her hands reaching for the baby, the basket on her elbow.

Betty took a deep breath and thrust her shoulders back as if about to start a boxing match. 'I don't care what anyone says. I'm keeping 'er. She's mine. She's the only thing I've ever loved, who's ever loved me, and I'm bloody keeping 'er. Come what may.' Her voice had risen, and Margaret began to cry, small whimpers at first but then, as if she'd just discovered her lungs, great howls.

'Jesus Christ,' said June, waving her hands around urgently. 'Feed 'er again, for God's sake. Shut 'er up. She's going to wake the whole bloody building.'

Betty reached down and put her fingers in Margaret's tiny mouth, which stopped the crying. The door opened behind her, and Betty looked up to see her father standing in the doorway, blinking, and rubbing his eyes.

June turned and flinched. 'Now you've gone and done it,' she muttered to Betty. She dropped the basket by Betty's feet and turned towards her husband.

Edwin squinted at Betty, his head on one side. 'Is that a baby?'

'I'll leave Betty to explain,' said June, slipping past him into the passage. She glanced back at Betty. 'Put it in the basket, Betty, and I'll take it away in a minute.'

As her father approached her, Betty tightened her grip around the baby, drawing it even closer into her body. Margaret was still holding her hair. He leaned over, his eyes widening. 'You 'id it well,' he said quietly. 'I hardly noticed till the end.'

'Pa?' Betty looked up at him, wet rings around her eyes.

Edwin nodded at her. 'You was just like yer ma. A spark inside you. I thought you might be expecting but then yer ma said nothing so I didn't wanna ask.' He pulled back the blanket and looked at Margaret, his face softening into a smile. Margaret turned her head to stare at him. 'It looks just like you did. Those eyes—'

The silence spun across the room. Betty held her breath.

'What you going to call it?' he said eventually, pulling at his bottom lip.

'Her name's Margaret,' Betty said quietly, wrapping the baby up and carefully handing her over to her father.

'Like the princess,' said Edwin, his voice hoarse, taking Margaret. She looked impossibly small in his hairy, tattooed arms.

'She's your granddaughter, Pa, your first one.'

Edwin nodded and then looked at Betty. 'You shouldn't have let 'im touch you, you know, not before you was married,' he said, shaking his head, his jaw clenched. 'That bastard. I knew he was no good. We need to find 'im and make 'im marry you.'

'Don't, Pa. I don't want to ever see 'im again.' Betty closed her eyes and tried to push away the memory of his face.

Edwin stroked the side of Margaret's cheek and dropped a kiss on her forehead. Betty opened her eyes to see him looking at the basket June had left on the floor. He tugged on his bottom lip again and slipped Margaret back into Betty's arms. 'Where's Margaret gonna sleep then? In with you and the girls, I s'pose? It'll be cramped but they'll help, I'm sure.'

He turned away, put the plug in the basin and started running the tap. 'And we can get some money off 'er father for 'er keep.'

Betty closed her eyes and felt the tension slip away and warmth spread through her body. She looked down at Margaret and then at her father, busy shaving in the mirror. *Margaret, my beautiful, beautiful girl. You're staying with me. I promise I will look after you better than any mother ever could.* Betty touched her father gently on the shoulder. 'But what about Ma? She—' Betty glanced down at the basket and caught his eye in the reflection of the mirror.

'You leave your ma to me,' he said, holding his face taut for the blade. 'And for goodness' sake, clean out that bath. It looks like someone died in there.'

Chapter 5

EMMA

JANUARY 2019

The key marked *communal door* fitted easily into the lock but Emma struggled to turn it. Maybe it had always been as stiff, although she couldn't imagine her mother's arthritic hands twisting anything this forcefully. She balanced her bag on the top of the unmade boxes propped up against the door frame and tried again, grunting as she put all her strength on to the small Yale key. Nothing. Her thumbs, rough from childhood eczema, were red with the effort and icy from the January chill.

Emma tried the key marked *front door* instead, but it wouldn't even fit in the lock. She squinted through the door's frosted glass window, its distorted view of the hallway rippling before her eyes. Empty. She thought of ringing the downstairs flat – the name *Charnock*, listed next to the first bell, was vaguely familiar. But she couldn't bear the mixed sympathy and accusation. The look of 'we're sorry you lost your mother, but why haven't you visited her for years?'

Emma gazed up at the familiar house. White paint flaked off the eaves, while brown and green liquid oozed down the brickwork from the leaky gutters. The curtains were drawn in the bedroom of her mother's upstairs flat, but the sitting room's were open. Stepping back down the path, she could make out the visitor's armchair her mother kept in the window, its upholstery faded by the sunlight. The rest of the room was in darkness.

She made her way back to the front door. Reluctantly, she put her hand through the letterbox. She pulled the door towards her, simultaneously twisting the door key hard again. Something clicked, the key turned and the door swung open.

The shared hallway was just as she remembered. The same swirly carpet still protected by the transparent matting that led from the communal door to the entrances to the two flats. The same motion-sensing light flicked on as soon as she walked through the door, a dim glow flickering through a glass shade studded with insect carcasses. A radiator pumped heat into the narrow space.

The sprawling money plant had grown a couple of feet since she was last there and the plastic pot was straining to contain the roots. How long had it been since she'd seen her mother? Four, five years? A wooden cabinet held the electricity meters and fuse box and doubled as a counter for the post – the basket marked *Margaret Chapman* was empty. Presumably Mr Eals had been here recently collecting post.

Propping open the communal door with her bag, Emma brought in the boxes and stacked them in the hall. She selected the key to her mother's flat. It turned silently, but the hinges moaned as the door opened, narrowly missing the first stair. She squeezed inside, wedging the boxes behind the door. Her mother's faded Gore-Tex jacket hung from one of the hooks on the wall.

With the door shut, the temperature dropped and Emma started to shiver, despite her winter coat. She walked up the stairs, carrying a first batch of boxes into the sitting room. The air in the flat was sour. The heating had been turned off and the winter chill had permeated the furniture. Spores of black mildew had begun to attack some of the pictures.

Emma dropped her bag and the boxes, and immediately her eyes were drawn to *The Girl in the Midnight Maze*, hanging above her mother's desk. A huge oil, it was beautiful in its simplicity. An intricately painted maze in various dark green hues surrounded a girl wearing a white shift, her hands raised above her head, dancing, the light of the moon catching the tops of the hedges and her face and dress. The figure stared out at her laughing, untouched by the mould. Emma traced her finger across the girl's face and then around the maze, feeling tears prick her eyes. Soon this would be hanging in a stranger's house, the little girl witness to their lives. She shook her head irritably and looked away.

There was a lot more stuff than she remembered. Her mother had been a hoarder, but a neat one. Wall-to-wall shelves housed hundreds of books and knick-knacks. There was little chance of her sorting this out in one day, Emma realised, and regretted not coming better prepared.

She checked her phone to see if Nick had called back. Nothing. She checked her texts. He hadn't seen the message or the photos of the will she'd sent him.

Emma put her head round the bedroom door. Her mother's single bed was made, the blue flowery duvet tucked neatly beneath the pillow. When her mother had left her home for the last time, did she realise she'd never be coming back? Maybe it would've been easier if she hadn't known. Emma went into the cramped bathroom.

A steel frame perched over the toilet seat, giant handles to support someone getting up. There was also a seat in the shower astride a rubber mat and two large handles screwed into the wall either side of the shower controls. *Mum had needed help*, Emma realised, biting her lip as she looked at the aids. She glimpsed her reflection in the mirrored door of the tiny bathroom cabinet. Somehow she looked older, the faint lines at the side of her mouth deeper, the first hints of grey at her temple contrasting against her long dark hair.

In the tiny kitchen, Emma filled the kettle, switched it on and took a teabag from the tin next to it. Her mother's owl mug sat upside down on the draining board. Emma opened the cupboard with the other cups and looked for the familiar mug with a big letter E that she'd always used. It wasn't there. Emma's breath caught in her throat. She checked through the cupboard again and checked in the adjoining ones, but there was no sign of it. Had it been broken, or just thrown away? She put the teabag into her mother's owl mug, shivering again, and poured in the boiling water.

Emma opened the boiler cupboard and flicked a switch. To her relief, it immediately started to gurgle into life. She glanced around. Who had unplugged everything? Was it Mr Eals or had Mum known she was going to be away for some time? There was a rank smell coming from the fridge. If Mr Eals had been keeping an eye on the place, he hadn't done a very good job. She should have picked up milk at the petrol station.

Emma took the steaming black tea back into the sitting room and sat down in her mother's winged armchair. She couldn't recall ever having used it before; Mum had been very possessive about certain things. Emma had a panoramic view of Morecambe Bay – a glorious sight denied to anyone in the smaller guest's chair opposite, which she saw now had a broken spring waiting to stab unwary occupants in the thigh. As she sat cross-legged in her mother's chair and sipped from her mother's cup, she felt rebellious, as if she could return at any moment to admonish her.

Today the mist was low and even the lighthouse's flashing beacon couldn't penetrate the haze. She pictured her mother sitting here mesmerised by one of the fastest tides in the country as it swamped the sandbanks. It was hard to tear your eyes away. Like a game of Grandmother's Footsteps, you knew that as soon as you looked away, the incoming tide would be upon you.

She placed a hand on the cast-iron radiator next to the chair, and could feel the warmth seeping into it. The furniture was exactly the same as it had been all those years ago. The old desk where Mum had spent most of her time writing or studying was still there. But something had changed. When she had last visited there had been photos of Emma as a child – Mum had particularly liked a formal school picture of her, aged seven, with a large chunk of hair chopped out of her fringe above an angelic smile – and ones of James. There had also been the framed photo of Emma and Nick's wedding propped up on the desk. But that had been replaced by one of Mum in what looked like the Peak District and there were no photos of Emma, Nick or their children anywhere.

Emma got up and started opening the drawers. The top drawer in the desk was well organised. Stationery categorised in different sections. A large bulldog clip held scrap paper. The top sheet read *teabags, cheese, rolls, washing powder* in her mother's distinctive hand, but a line had been crossed through the page. The second drawer contained writing paper, envelopes and notecards. As Emma stood back, the light from the bay reflected off something shiny on the top shelf above the desk, catching her attention. She had to move one of the dining chairs from the fold-down table by the kitchen door and stand on it to reach what turned out to be another picture frame lying down flat.

She remembered the picture being taken. At Selfridges, maybe around 1979 or 1980. One of those formal portraits of a four-year-old Emma standing next to a life-size Jemima Puddle-Duck. Her scarlet tights had been horribly itchy and slightly too small, the crotch hanging mid-thigh however much her mother had yanked them up. She looked enviously at the little girl staring back at her – that innocence. That child hadn't known what was coming next.

My mug gone. Our photos banished. I wasn't even mentioned in the will. Despite their estrangement, Emma still had photos of her mum in her own home and talked to her children about her.

Emma looked at the visitor's chair. How many people had sat there since she was last here? How had her mother spent her time, apart from erasing her only child from her life? She sighed and got up, removing her coat. She took the copy of the will from her bag, laying it on the table. Mr Eals had carefully highlighted all the items Emma needed to find and distribute, together with the addresses where the courier he'd booked would take them. Her mother had accounted for everything she owned, down to stipulating that any rubbish should be recycled.

The will didn't make any sense. Her mother had loathed Libby, and had never been that close to Emma. She'd presumed the flat would have been left to one of her charities. The mobile trilled in her bag: Nick.

'Hi, darling. Thanks for calling back,' she said.

'How's it going there?' He had his work voice on.

'It's a bit weird, but okay. You'll never guess what, though.'

'What?'

'Mum left her flat to Libby.'

'What? But she hated Libby.'

'That's what *I* thought. Anyway I've sent you a photo of the will.'

Nick paused and she waited for him to read the document. 'I don't understand. She never liked her. Why would she do that?' he asked. 'It's so your mum though to use her full name Elizabeth and not call her Libby.'

Emma could hear Nick put his palm over the handset and say something to someone else in the office.

'Apparently she changed her will the day before she died,' she said.

'Bloody hell. So maybe she did have regrets about how she'd treated her – and you.'

'She's stripped anything about us out of the flat. All the photos, everything.'

'Even that one of you with the funny fringe?'

'Yep, and our wedding photo.' Emma could hear the slight crack in her voice.

'Typical. Poor Libby. But not "poor Libby" now, actually. It will give her a great start in life. Perhaps we can rent the flat out. Then she'd have the income.'

'No, I want to get rid of it. There are too many memories. We can put the money in trust for her or something. And, don't laugh, but this place is creepy. She's here. I can feel her here watching me.'

She could hear the background chatter from Nick's office as he went quiet and she could picture him working out what to say.

'You know, she threw out my mug, the E one,' she filled in.

'What?'

'Oh, never mind. I'm just being silly.'

'No, you're not, it's a difficult thing to do. I wish you'd let me come up there with you and help.'

'No, it's okay. You need to be there for James and Libby. And I need to do this myself.'

'Yes, of course. I understand.'

'I won't be back tonight. I don't know how I ever thought I could do this in a day. I'll get a hotel tonight – I'd feel weird staying here – and then come back tomorrow.'

'OK, that's fine. What shall I cook for the kids tonight?'

'There's some Bolognaise sauce in the freezer, and some garlic bread. You could do that with some pasta.'

'Good plan. We'll miss you tonight. We can tell Libby the news about her inheritance when you get back. I think it's important that we do it together.'

'Yes, I agree. But perhaps we need to decide what to do with it first, so it's settled when we tell her. I hope James will be okay with it.'

'Yes, it's an odd one, isn't it? Trust your mother. I love you, you know. Don't forget that. We all love you, even if she didn't.'

Emma held on to the phone long after Nick's voice had faded away. His cheeriness had temporarily lifted the gloom of the flat, but she felt it close in around her again. She turned quickly, sensing something behind her, but the only things were the flat-pack boxes propped up on the chair and *The Girl in the Midnight Maze* looking down at her. She set her shoulders back and started to hum as she picked up the brown tape.

Within half an hour the sitting room was full of a pile of thirty empty boxes, and she was on the second roll of tape. The books were going to the Oxfam bookshop, a short walk from the flat. Emma reached up and started to take them off the shelves. It was hard work packing the books in all the boxes and stacking them in the corner. Other than her breathing, the flat was eerily quiet. She kept seeing something out of the corner of her eye but when she turned, there was nothing there, just the painting.

To drown out the silence, she turned on her mother's portable radio and the soothing tones of *The World at One* drifted through the rooms. By the time the afternoon play began, there was only one shelf left to pack up in the sitting room – her mother's files of bills, bank statements and other official-looking documents – and Emma was leaving those for later for the solicitor to go through. The light was beginning to fade. Emma wandered back into the kitchen. The flat was warm now, but the heat intensified the rancid smell coming from the fridge.

There was a pair of ancient-looking rubber gloves lying over the side of the sink – as if awaiting her mother's arrival at any moment. Emma slipped her own hands into them.

Underneath the sink she found a roll of black bin bags and tore one off, shaking it open. So much for Mr Eals checking over the flat. With her jumper's soft wool jammed up against her mouth and nose, Emma opened the fridge. She was hit immediately by a putrid stench, which made her retch even though she'd been holding her breath. She started tipping the fridge's contents into the bin bag.

A wedge of ice had welded the glass butter dish to the back of the fridge. Determinedly, she prised it loose, cracking the lid with the effort. She recognised the dish: a cow made out of glass, guarding its now shrivelled contents. That was what she'd thought as a child when it sat on the dining room table, the butter solid in winter and liquid in summer. She felt the tears stinging the back of her eyes and blinked. She deposited the last few cling-filmed indefinable lumps into the bin bag and drew the corners together, tying them firmly, and immediately took it outside.

Back in the bedroom, Emma opened the bottom drawer and started to stack the jumpers into another of the boxes. There were six fleeces of varying sizes – the newest one far smaller than the oldest. Emma realised the cancer had slowly eaten her mother away. In the built-in wardrobe by the window a line of ironed shirts on matching hangers stood to attention, a few old coats and trousers at the far end. She could already imagine them hanging in the local hospice shop.

Emma brought over another box and started taking them off the rail. At the very back was a bottle-green child's wool coat. Emma would have recognised it anywhere. She drew the wooden hanger towards her. Somewhere among the dense threads clung the familiar institutional smell. She shivered. The coat was still as itchy as the day she'd first worn it.

Her parents had first left her with Auntie Angela. She remembered waking up on a summer morning and her elderly aunt, who she didn't really know, was in the kitchen waiting for her. What had she said? That her parents had left during the night? That they had to go away for a few days, that she was going to stay with her for a while? They'd taken a taxi to her aunt's house in Guildford because her aunt didn't have a car. She remembered being quite excited then. The seats were sticky in the heat and she had to keep peeling her thighs off them. She'd stayed at her aunt's for weeks and there was nothing to do but read and help around the house and garden. She'd lain at night in the little box room crying, wondering where her parents were.

At the end of the summer, she'd been fitted out in a new school uniform. She hadn't asked why. There was no point as Auntie Angela never gave any answers. It had been too warm for early September and she had sweated as she pulled on the blouse and wool kilt and slipped her arms into the heavy green coat.

Emma remembered Auntie Angela had packed the rest of the uniform – together with Blue Ted, Emma's books, and the few clothes of her own – into a battered old trunk that they had brought down from the loft. Even with so little in the trunk, they struggled to carry it out to the waiting taxi. It was too bulky to go in the boot, so her aunt and the driver, with much wheezing and gasping, slid it across the sticky rear seat, letting its sharp edges rub against the tan plastic. It took up most of the space in the back, forcing Emma to sit against the door with the window winder pressed into her side. She had gripped the handle on the side of the trunk, terrified that the door would spring open and she'd be thrown on to the road.

Emma had pressed her cheek against the window and stared as the parched Surrey countryside sped by. Soon the car slowed and Emma sat up taller, curious in spite of herself, looking at tall, dense fir trees and a gold-edged sign. She'd started to cry as the taxi stopped outside a stone building. Through her tears, she'd seen a miniature garden, with a maze of green plants clipped in the shape of crucifixes, leading to a central fountain where a moss-covered

Mary and a baby Jesus were worshipped by cherubs. Floors and floors of windows gazed down blankly, and Emma remembered craning her neck to see the weathervane against the blue cloudless sky. She could hardly breathe. The thick blouse had stuck to her skin under the prickly jumper.

A thin nun wearing a full grey habit had emerged from a side door and strode purposefully towards them. 'You must be Miss Bowen and Emma. I'm Sister Catherine, the matron. Welcome to Mount Carmel School for Girls.' There had been an edge to her voice.

'How d'you do?' Auntie Angela responded in her telephone voice. 'The family is very grateful that you could take Emma at such short notice.'

'I appreciate the very special circumstances in this case.'

Sister Catherine had patted Emma on the head and shook her aunt's hand firmly. 'The boarders always come back a day before the day girls to unpack into their new dormitories and settle into school before classes begin. We don't have any boarders as young as Emma, as I explained on the telephone. So I have decided to put her with a group of older girls at the top of the junior school, who can look after her until her own year group starts to board, two years from now.'

'Indeed. Thank you,' her aunt had murmured, rubbing her wrinkled hands together.

They'd carried the trunk through the grand entrance, passing under the words *Gaudeamus in Domino* carved into the stone. The smell of furniture polish had masked the deeper musky smell of seldom-used rooms. After the stickiness of the heat outside, the cool air had been a relief.

Away from the grand public entrance, the marble columns and parquet floors changed quickly into chipped plaster walls and stained lino. A warren of narrow corridors and steep stairwells led to a long room, filled with light from the huge metal-framed windows, with rows and rows of beds on each side, and a corridor down the middle separating the metal ends. Each bed space was uniform in its appearance with a blue counterpane covering a small bed, a wooden chair, a wardrobe, and a chest of drawers separating them from the next space.

The nun had walked them to the bed furthest from the door. 'This will be your bed, Emma. I'll leave your aunt to settle you in and see you for evening prayers.'

Emma nodded mutely.

Sister Catherine had strode back down the dormitory, her black rubber heels squeaking on the lino. After unpacking for her, Auntie Angela had sat down on the chair.

'Now, I'll try to arrange a tea with your father for half-term. That's in six weeks.'

'But you said it'd only be a—'

'This school is an amazing opportunity for you, Emma. One of the best in the country. You're extremely lucky to be here. Don't let your family down.'

Emma had realised that Auntie Angela was saying goodbye. For the first time since she had been living with her aunt she had wished she could stay with her and not be left alone. Her aunt had touched her arm briefly, before walking swiftly back down the dormitory, the click-clacking sound of her shoes gradually fading away. Emma had stayed on the bed holding Blue Ted and waited to see what would happen next.

Everything at Our Lady of Mount Carmel School for Girls had felt awful at first. Not just the coat and the scratchy kilts and tickly red knee-length wool socks, but the whole idea of living away from her family. It had been months before she'd stopped crying herself to sleep and had felt even slightly at home, thought Emma as she stuffed the green coat into a box.

Chapter 6

BETTY

OCTOBER 1937

'Betty's baby was born the other side of the blanket.'

Betty heard the stage whisper, as she knew she was intended to, dropped her chin, and focused on turning the hand of the mangle. Tiredness threaded through her arm as the grey water oozed out, dripping into the tin bath below. She pulled the shirt through the rollers and folded it carefully, still damp, before laying it in another basket.

A giggle rolled across the room. 'She was stood up at the church, my ma said. The father did a runner. And Betty was already caught out. Despite 'er looks, he couldn't stand the thought of being with that—'

'Shut up, Ada,' said Betty, not turning around. Ada had always hated her. He'd said Ada hadn't been sweet on him when he'd invited Betty on that first walk, but she knew that had been a lie. Just like all the other lies. And Ada had been determined to make her life hell ever since. She closed her eyes. Every time a new girl started at the laundry, Ada would go through the same routine of making sure the new girl would never go near Betty or even so much as talk to her. As if you could catch the sin of an illegitimate baby. There were other girls in the same situation as her but no one cared two hoots about them. It was Ada constantly bringing it up that made the difference.

Thinking of Margaret made her warm inside. Winnie was looking after her this afternoon. She'd be curled up on her bed, Margaret nestled in the blankets, singing to her. Margaret's dark eyes would follow Winnie, her pudgy arms reaching up to her. Winnie would lean over, covering her little body in kisses. Margaret would gurgle and laugh. She'd just started laughing – big belly laughs, surprising for someone so small. Betty's breasts ached, pushing against her apron, and she felt dampness. She pushed away the image of Margaret and put her arm across her breasts, pressing them in. The last thing she needed was another wet dress. The girls had laughed themselves silly about it last week.

Betty tucked a blonde curl behind her ear and grabbed a corner of the cloth from the basket and it kept coming – a huge greying sheet. 'Can someone 'elp me fold this for the mangle?' Betty looked around the room at the other girls, who, having been gossiping in one corner were suddenly all busy at other mangles, rinsing clothes or going into the bright autumn day to hang out the clothes in the yard. Helen – a girl Betty had been close friends with at school – glanced up, caught Betty's eye, and quickly looked away.

Betty's cheeks burned as warm as the flat irons on the range. She gathered all the corners of the sheet together and tried to fold it into the mangle, but a side brushed on the floor, the dirt sticking to it.

Mrs Eastbourne bustled in, her chest a good foot in front of the rest of her. 'What are you doing, Betty? You got that sheet all dirty, now you'll have to wash it again. And you can stay behind to make up the time.'

'Sorry,' said Betty, hanging her head. 'I asked the others to 'elp me fold it but—'

Mrs Eastbourne squinted around the room. 'And who can blame 'em? A girl like you. You'll have to learn to do it yerself. If you use one of them pegs, you can peg the sheet to this and then use your hands to feed it through.'

'But it would be so much easier if—'

Mrs Eastbourne raised a stocky hand, fat bulging around her gold rings. 'Don't answer me back, Betty.' She stood in the centre of the room, her hands on her hips, watching Betty try to fold another large sheet and feed it through the mangle – something that even two girls often struggled with. 'Ada, make sure Betty 'as all the sheets from now on. She must learn to do them 'erself. It'll be a good lesson for 'er.'

Ada looked up. 'Yes, Mrs Eastbourne.' Betty saw her give a small grin. 'Girls, whoever's got sheets, put 'em in Betty's basket.'

Mrs Eastbourne watched the girls sorting through their baskets. 'Who wants to do the deliveries today? I'll need two of you.' Everyone put their hand up. Pushing the trolley around the streets to deliver the bags of washing to the houses was much easier than hours spent inside washing, rinsing, mangling, and ironing. 'Not you, Betty. Edith and Helen. You can do it today.' There were groans around the room as Helen and Edith handed their baskets over to the others and followed Mrs Eastbourne out to start preparing the trolley. Helen turned back and gave Betty a sad smile.

Ada reached into her apron, drawn tight across her plump middle and drew out a cigarette, lighting it from the range. She leaned against the wall and puffed away, watching Betty struggle with the sheets. Betty turned her back on her, pegging one corner of the sheet to the ceiling hook and another to the other side of the mangle as she struggled to fold it, push it through the rollers and turn the mangle's hand. She'd managed to get into a good routine, and her basket was filling up with damp folded sheets when Mrs Eastbourne reappeared.

'What's that smell? 'As someone been smoking in 'ere?' She narrowed her eyes and peered at the girls. 'I can smell tobacco. Ada?'

Betty turned round to see Ada hanging her head. 'I don't wanna tell tales, Mrs Eastbourne.'

Mrs Eastbourne walked forward and took hold of Ada's chin. 'Tell me, child, I won't be angry. It's the Lord's wish that you tell the truth.'

'It was Betty smoking, Mrs Eastbourne,' Ada whispered. 'I told her that it would make the laundry smell but she said she didn't care.'

Betty dropped her head and felt the flush rise up her face. 'But I didn't—'

Mrs Eastbourne strode over to her, grabbing her arm. 'Get out. I'm done having a whore in my establishment. Your pa begged me to give you a chance, said you're a hard worker, but wasn't he wrong.' Betty dropped the sheet as Mrs Eastbourne dragged her across the room and attempted to throw her out of the door into the yard. 'You better go troll at Piccadilly where you belong.'

As she turned away, she saw Ada smirking, her eyes dancing with laughter. Betty slunk to the back gate, where Helen and Edith were putting bags on the trolley. Helen put her hand on Betty's arm and squeezed it slightly as Betty pulled open the gate to walk home.

Chapter 7

EMMA

JANUARY 2019

Emma let the courier out of the building for the last time and went back upstairs to her mother's sitting room. It looked bare now that most of the furniture and boxes had gone and the shelves were clear. She made another cup of black tea and made her way through the last few boxes – family bits and pieces to take home and the stuff she'd promised to deliver to her mum's friend Clare who lived nearby. She wanted to see where *The Girl in the Midnight Maze* was going. The only unboxed items in the room left to deal with were a few A4 files, a metal box, and the huge oil painting which dominated the room. Then the bedroom and kitchen to finish off.

Emma was sad that the picture was going – and to someone she'd never even met. She looked at it once more, although it was already imprinted on her memory. It was easy from the viewer's perspective to see the way out of the maze, but the girl was too short to see over the hedges and despite the moon it was too dark. Yet she didn't seem to mind. She looked delighted at making it to the middle, her hands flung in the air with joy.

When she was little, her mother had often put her on a dining chair so she could see the girl properly and find a way out for her – like those puzzles in children's books. But there was something funny about the maze. It kept changing. One day you'd think that the exit was in the bottom right of the painting. The next day that escape route seemed to have been covered by tall hedges and she'd struggle to find the new exit.

'How's the girl going to escape today, Emmie?' said her mother.

Emma put her head on one side and stared at the little girl. Then she reached forward, her mother holding the chair as it tipped slightly, and followed the paths until she found the way out – to the right-hand side of the maze, where the moon shone brightest.

'Well done, darling,' said her mother, lifting her off the chair and hugging her as she swung her to the ground.

'Who is the little girl, Mummy?' asked Emma, but her mother didn't answer.

'How does the way out change, Mummy?' she asked again, looking back up at the girl.

Her mother gave a slight smile. 'It's not that the painting changes, Emmie, it's just that you're looking at it differently each time.'

Emma would nod and look back at the girl who would still be laughing. But she didn't really understand what her mother meant. How did you look at a painting differently? A picture was just a picture.

Emma lifted the heavy canvas off its hook, and carefully stood it against the box destined for Clare. It felt like giving away a piece of her family history to a stranger.

When her mother had first become ill, the painting had disappeared from the sitting room and had been replaced with a landscape of the South Downs. Emma had found it in the spare room, above the little single bed with the scratchy blankets that

44

her mother had started to use after her illness. When her mother wasn't there Emma would stand on the bed and play the same game on her own.

She'd come upstairs one day to play and noticed the door to the box room was ajar. She'd walked quietly up to it and peered through the gap. The sunlight was shining through the thin orange curtains, creating a warm glow in the room. Her father was standing in front of the picture. She was about to go in when she realised his shoulders were trembling. Was he crying? She slipped away from the door and waited on the landing, shifting from foot to foot. He was ages but finally he emerged, wiping his eyes with his handkerchief. He had ruffled her hair, smiled a small smile, and had gone downstairs.

Maybe her father played the same game that she did. Maybe the escape routes changed for him too. She flung open the curtains so the girl in the midnight maze had a better view. It was sad for her to be trapped in this tiny room without any company. Especially in the dark.

Emma picked up a duster and wiped it across the top of the frame. After her mother separated from her father when Emma was a teenager, the painting had gone with her to Morecambe. Emma had missed its presence, only seeing it when she went up to visit. She was too old to be playing the escape route game by then. It was only as an adult that she discovered her mother had painted it, that it had won prizes and been displayed in a London gallery in the 1960s.

◆　◆　◆

Emma wasn't looking forward to handing over the painting to this woman called Clare and saying goodbye to it. God only knew what her mother had told her friend about her only child. Clare probably

45

resented her for being absent during her mother's difficult last years. Emma thought about the handrails in the bathroom.

When James was born, she and her mother had become close again for a time. Emma would take the train up to Morecambe with the baby chuntering at the scenery as it sped past them. Emma and her mum would walk along the promenade pushing James in his pram and have lunch at the beautiful Art Deco hotel on the front. Emma had felt close to her mother then.

But that chubby baby who had so endeared himself soon became a determined toddler, and a new baby arrived. A girl this time, and it was obvious her mother had never liked Libby.

It had been the start of the cooling of their relationship. When she and Nick had driven up to show the ten-day-old baby to her mother, there'd been an awful scene. And travelling with two children from Brighton was a challenge, so soon Emma found herself not going up as much. And then soon it became only once or twice a year. They had still exchanged cards and endured the odd strained phone call but then they hadn't been in touch at all. She should have made the effort to break the silence.

Emma took the files off the shelf and laid them on the floor. The solicitor had asked her to provide the household paperwork for probate purposes. She boxed up the slim black folder containing bank statements, then the carefully arranged utility bills. She flicked through, impressed by her mum's organisation.

The third file held records from Margaret's Open University courses. That could be dumped. The fourth was slightly larger and thicker than the rest. Emma recognised the pencil-drawn CND logo on the front in purple and orange – her own sixth-form doodle. Why had her mother kept this one? But then she reused and recycled everything.

Inside was her old home address in teenage bubbly handwriting, the dots on every 'i' made into purple hearts. *Make love, not war* was scrawled across the bottom. The file contained plastic pockets filled with official documents. The first held three old passports and a tattered driving licence. Emma took out the first passport – the old dark blue type – flicking to the picture page. Her mother's piercing eyes stared out from beneath long dark hair parted in the middle, just as Libby wore hers now. They looked so similar. The passport had expired in July 1973, its corner clipped away neatly. Her mother would have been almost thirty-six. Emma flicked through the pages. There were two stamps from her mother's stay in India during the 1960s. She took a deep breath, surprised by the sudden prick of tears.

In the next passport, expired in 1984, her mum's hair had been cropped down to just a few inches from her scalp, but that challenging stare hadn't changed. In May 1974 Margaret had been in Paris on her honeymoon, but the other pages were blank. The last passport was the newer burgundy type, but it had expired in 1998. At what stage did you stop renewing your passport? Did that feel like a sort of defeat, a recognition that you'd never travel again? That your next journey would be to another world entirely. Her father David had died with eight years left on his, still anticipating more foreign holidays. But his only journey after the diagnosis had been to the local hospice.

Emma stacked the passports and the driving licence beside the solicitor's box, wondering what to do with them. The solicitor wouldn't be interested but it seemed wrong to throw them away.

In the next plastic pocket was her mother's birth certificate, yellowed with age. 23 August 1937, Battersea. Betty Arnold was listed as her mother in the calligrapher's distinctive hand. There was no father's name. She pictured Granny Betty holding the tiny baby Margaret in a shawl, hanging her head as the registrar asked for the name of the father.

The story of her mother's arrival into the world had never been a secret. Granny Betty had crafted being stood up as a pregnant bride into a kind of warning to Margaret – and then to Emma – of the general dangers that men presented.

Emma had passed the lesson on to her two children. Nothing was worse than getting pregnant as a teenager – or getting someone pregnant. Fifteen-year-old Libby had laughed. 'Of course I'm not going to get pregnant. I'm not stupid.' Emma had smiled and hugged her. She knew Libby was sensible and told her everything. The other mums were envious that she got so much out of teenage Libby when most of her peers clammed up. But things had changed in recent months. Libby had retreated into her room and, when they insisted that she come and join them, into her own mind. She'd started going out in the evening more now too. Emma wanted her to have freedom but, living in a city, she was worried about the influences on Libby – drink, drugs, worse. It was so different from primary school where you knew all your children's friends and their parents. Emma didn't know who Libby hung around with at school. And Libby never said, however much Emma asked. Emma slipped the certificate back into the pocket and took a sip of tea, flipping past various school prizes for handwriting and artistic endeavour. Her mother had won several awards, but there was just one O-level certificate – for art. Despite her grammar-school education, her mum clearly hadn't fulfilled her promise. Emma couldn't remember her mother talking about her school days.

She laid the file on top of the passports, stood up and stretched, her shoulders aching from packing. These last documents were all destined for the loft at home – probably for her own children to find and clear out after her death.

Now for the metal box. She dragged it towards her by the thin handles welded to its edges. It was much lighter than she expected. Emma slipped her finger under the lid and lifted, but it didn't

budge. Then she spotted a small keyhole and remembered the unlabelled key among the set provided by the solicitor. It slotted easily
into the hole and turned soundlessly. As she lifted the rusting lid,
a sweet smell of lavender drifted up.

A small towel – white with pink and blue stripes – was on the
top. Beneath it was a cloth rattle and then a white wool shawl.
Emma smiled.

'My shawl,' she murmured. The towel and rattle she didn't
remember, but she'd seen lots of pictures of her mother holding her
in the shawl – at her birth and baptism. It had lain on top of her cot
for years. Emma picked up the shawl, breathed in its surprisingly
fresh aroma and folded it over the arm of the chair. The other two
items she placed by the passport pile.

At the bottom of the box was a brown envelope. Emma took a
sip of tea. She slid her finger under its long-dried flap and eased out
the contents. It was another birth certificate: *Elizabeth*. She froze.
What was Libby's name doing on it? And then she realised that
it wasn't *Elizabeth Margaret Bowen* – her own daughter – but an
almost identical name: *Elizabeth Margaret Bullman*. She traced the
name with her finger. Date of birth: *7 October 1953*. She scanned
across to the mother's name: *Margaret Mary Bullman*. Her mother.
Suddenly it was difficult to breathe.

The names were written in the same ornate hand as her mum's
own birth certificate. Again, no father was named. Place of birth:
Birdhurst Lodge. Emma mentally counted backwards. Born in
August 1937, her mother would have been just sixteen in October
1953. She ran her finger across the name. Elizabeth Margaret. An
exact mirror of her own daughter's name. Except they'd always
shortened it to Libby.

Emma looked out at the bay. A dark purplish bruise had spread
across the sky, meeting a charcoal stain in the west. The sky was
darkening as quickly as if it was on a dimmer switch. She wiped her

hand across her cheeks, smearing the tears away. Her own mother had been a teenage mum. Just like Granny Betty. But unlike her grandmother, she had never spoken about it. Where was that baby now? Emma did the maths. Her mother would have fallen pregnant in January or February 1953. Perhaps that would explain why such a clearly intelligent girl had earned a solitary O-level in the summer of 1953 – she would have been five months pregnant. And who was the father? Was he still alive? Emma imagined a handsome young man from the 1950s, a teddy boy perhaps, with her mum in Brockwell Park on a hot summer's evening. Wrong by the standards of the day, but romantic in retrospect.

Granny Betty must have been furious. No wonder they'd never got on. Her own daughter had been foolish enough to make the same mistake as her, despite all the dire warnings. Little surprise, then, that her mum herself had then drilled into Emma the dangers of becoming a teenage mum and the importance of contraception. She'd assumed her mother was referring to Granny Betty, but all the time it had also been about her own experience.

There was a sound behind her, as if someone was pushing something heavy and grunting with the effort. Emma jumped around, still holding the certificate. Darkness pooled in the corners of the room, spilling towards her. She heard the sound again and glanced up at the painting, half hidden in the gloom. The girl looked like she'd moved and was pushing at the edge of the frame.

Emma hurried to flick the main light switch. Nothing happened. And then she remembered her mother hated the harshness of overhead lighting so much that she would take out the bulb. Emma peered up through the lamp shade and, sure enough, there was nothing in the socket.

She found the switch to the table lamp near the other files, but it, too, didn't work. It was only when she'd crawled under the table to the wall and plugged in the lamp that the files were illuminated in a small circle of golden light. Emma went round the room, plugging in the other lights, dispelling the gloom from the sky outside. She could hear a rumble of thunder far away. It was not yet 4 p.m., but it seemed that the sun had already given up for the day.

The light on the desk reflected off the painting, illuminating the girl's dress even more. Her face looked different in the artificial light, contorted somehow. But she was still in the centre of the maze, where she always was.

Emma took a deep breath and sat back in the chair. She had a sister. Where was Elizabeth Margaret Bullman now?

Emma looked back down at the certificate. Her sister had been born somewhere called Birdhurst Lodge. Where was that? She picked her phone off the table, ignored the missed call from Nick, and googled the name. There was a link to a 2007 *Guardian* article entitled 'Houses of Shame' above a 'Sin and the Single Mother' headline from the *Independent*. Birdhurst Lodge had been what the Victorians called a 'house for fallen women'. She read a few lines. Emma could feel the tears coming again. She and Nick had been to see a film about mother and baby homes in Ireland. What was it called? Magdalene something. The girls had been treated like slaves, kept in the most appalling conditions, and forced to give up their babies. She had cried throughout. Perhaps her own mother had endured something similar at Birdhurst Lodge. Emma put the phone down, reached for her tea and found the mug on its side, the rug damp.

Her head ached and her eyes felt raw. She picked up the certificate again, her hands trembling. October 1953 was just a few months after the coronation, wasn't it? It was bold of her mum to choose the new queen's name for her illegitimate child, but maybe lots of people had at the time. Granny Betty had named her daughter after Princess Margaret. It all made sense now why she had been so distraught when Emma and Nick had named their own daughter

Elizabeth Margaret too. And to think they had done that to make her mum happy and keep her involved in their lives.

She looked out at the bay, little lights from fishing boats dotted across the water. Emma and Nick had brought their new baby up to see her mother when Libby was just a few days old. Emma remembered the horrific drive, either Libby or James grizzling all the way up the M1. The unscheduled stop at the service station after James had spewed semi-digested Weetabix all over himself. The hour-long tailback through Birmingham. Feeding and changing a screaming Libby on the hard shoulder of the M6. They'd all been exhausted by the time they pulled up outside her mother's flat. Her mum had been her usual offhand self, taking ages to come down and answer the door although she must have seen them getting out of the car.

Her mother was dressed in blue corduroy trousers and a striped cheesecloth shirt, her short grey hair unbrushed. She kissed Nick on the cheek, but barely acknowledged Emma.

'Leave the car there. It'll be fine for a few hours. The wardens don't come this far out of season,' her mum said, taking James's hand to lead him inside. 'Granny's got some lovely cakes upstairs for you. How was the journey, Emma?'

'Absolutely horrendous,' Emma said, pulling a face at her mother's back. 'I thought we'd never get here. James was sick all over himself and now the car stinks of puke.'

'Well, there's a washing machine here if you want to use it.'

They trooped up to the sitting room where her mum had laid out afternoon tea. Emma glanced up at *The Girl in the Midnight Maze*. She turned away but felt the girl's eyes on her. James bounded ahead, grabbing a French Fancy and cramming it into his mouth before anyone could stop him. Her mother laughed and ruffled his blond curls.

'You cheeky boy,' she said, sitting down and lifting him on to her lap. Emma stood watching her. She always seemed so affectionate with James, yet she couldn't remember her mother ever being like that with her. But grandparents always seemed to get on so much better with their grandchildren than their own children, didn't they? Something about the lack of responsibility, maybe. Or perhaps they didn't feel so resentful for sacrificing their own lives.

'This must be my new granddaughter,' her mum said, looking at Emma cradling Libby in a white shawl.

'I'd give her to you but I think she needs another change. Hold on.'

Nick flopped down into the visitor's chair and James wriggled from his grandmother's grasp to see what other cakes he could grab as Emma took the baby to the bathroom.

When they returned, Margaret sprang up again. 'All ready for a cuddle with Granny?'

Emma carefully handed her Libby. Her mother stroked the fair down on the baby's head.

'Do you still not have a name for her? Surely you've agreed on one by now?' said her mother, settling herself into her chair with the baby.

'We have, but we wanted to tell you in person.' Emma turned to smile at Nick. 'We're calling her Elizabeth – Libby – but with Margaret as her middle name after you. Elizabeth Margaret Bowen.'

Her mother stood up suddenly and thrust Libby back at her daughter without a word. She turned away, but not before Emma had glimpsed something in her eyes. Pain? Shock? Her mum tripped over the side of the chair as she rushed towards the kitchen. Libby started to cry.

'Mum?' Emma looked at her retreating mother and then quizzically back at Nick. He shook his head and got up to help her soothe Libby.

The girl in the painting seemed to be watching her. Emma turned and stood in front of the painting, cradling Libby. The girl almost seemed to be expecting her to say something.

'This is my little girl,' Emma whispered eventually.

'Are you talking to that picture?' said Nick, his arm around her shoulder. 'You're definitely not getting enough sleep.'

Emma laughed and turned around to cradle Libby between them. He kissed the top of her head.

She couldn't remember how long her mother had stayed in the kitchen. Not knowing what to say, she hadn't followed her. The tea was cold and the cakes almost all eaten by James by the time she returned quietly. The conversation had been stilted and they'd left quite quickly afterwards, for the long drive home.

Emma knew her mother had never held Libby since. Not once. And that had been the beginning of the end of their relationship.

Sliding her new-found sister's birth certificate back in its envelope, it caught on something else. She shook the envelope upside down. A photo slipped out, landing face down on the carpet. Emma hesitated. She sat back in the chair, eyeing the white square of stiff card between her feet, then she reached down and quickly flipped it over. Her mother's haunted eyes stared out from it. She was holding a tiny baby wrapped in the same striped towel from the metal box and half covered with the white shawl. They were standing against the stone wall of a building. Her mother looked like a child herself, but her eyes told an older story.

My mum and my sister. Her mother looked exactly like Libby did now.

Her phone rang. It was Nick. She stared at it for a long time, until his name stopped flashing and the screen went dark. She was still staring at it when the voicemail icon appeared. How could she tell him what she'd discovered? She didn't have the words.

Somewhere she had a sister. A woman named Elizabeth Margaret Bullman who was twenty-two years older than her. She picked up her phone, clicked on the Facebook app and typed in the name.

Chapter 8

BETTY

MAY 1940

Betty's arms ached as she lifted up the big can, tipping it carefully towards the shell so she didn't spill any of the hot TNT. She held her breath as it rose to the right level and then slipped into the tube that was going to contain the detonator. She could feel her manager behind her watching her cleaning and scraping it until it was exactly the right height inside the shell.

'Good work, Betty,' the woman said, resting her hand on Betty's shoulder before moving down the line.

Betty glanced sideways. All along the table, girls just like her were doing exactly the same thing. The work was hard, and the smell was terrible, but she loved working in the munitions factory. It was a long way from home. Nobody knew her here.

'Betty, could you give me a hand with the can?' Gwen was about the same age, a pretty girl with a shock of red hair that seemed to grow in all directions, however much she pinned it down. Betty slipped off the bench and joined her at the large cement mixer where she and Gwen held the can together while Joseph, the man behind it, tipped it to pour in the TNT.

'What you doing later, Betty?' He grinned at her through his moustache.

Betty watched the TNT, willing it to go faster. 'Just going 'ome to my ma.'

'How about a walk along the river after your shift?'

Betty shook her head. 'Sorry, I 'ave to look after me sisters.'

'Nuvver time, maybe,' Joseph said. She could feel his eyes on her as she and Gwen struggled back to the table with the can.

'He's sweet on you,' said Gwen, 'I can tell. What harm would a walk do? I think he's a nice man.'

Betty shook her head and picked up another shell. 'I don't wanna man, I'm 'appy as I am,' she said.

Gwen laughed. 'Well, I think he's handsome. I wish he'd asked me to go for a walk.' She sighed as she picked up the next shell.

Betty looked down the line at the other women and wondered for the umpteenth time what they'd say if they knew her secret. The factory job had come up two years ago and it was perfect because Woolwich was about as far as you could get from Battersea and still be able to get back in one day on the bus. No one knew her here, or her family situation.

What would Margaret be doing now? Edie would have her in the yard maybe, getting her to help with the washing. Margaret was good at handing over the pegs and folding some of the smaller clothes ready for the mangle or the iron. But she wanted more for Margaret than just a laundry maid. Her girl was bright – she had that look in her eyes. But she wasn't interested in books in the way Betty was – she loved drawing. Betty thought of the tin of watercolour paints she'd seen in the shop. She'd save up and get it for Margaret's birthday rather than her having to always draw in chalk or pencil.

Edna, the girl on her other side, nudged her. 'Can you give me a hand with this one, Betty?' Betty finished her shell and then helped Edna to steady her own while she poured in the TNT.

At the end of the table, their superior clapped her hands. 'Girls, ladies, we have a new recruit. Please everyone welcome Ada Kirby who's joining us today.'

Betty's hands jolted, spilling a tiny amount of the TNT on the table. She looked up into Ada's sharp eyes and could tell from her smirk that Ada had seen her.

'Betty, perhaps you could you come here and show Ada the ropes.'

Betty slowly put down her empty shell and climbed off the bench. Her legs felt like lead as she walked down the line.

'Ada, Betty is one of our most experienced workers so you'll be in good hands with her. I'll leave the two of you to it.' Her superior walked away down the line.

Betty confronted Ada's smirk. 'I wondered where you'd got to, Betty, where you were going when you got up so early for the bus,' she murmured. 'And here you are after all this time.'

Betty hurried along the wet pavement. A bus hissed by and she glanced up to check the number.

It was so bloody unfair. Ada wouldn't say anything straight away, but Betty knew that slowly she'd butter up the other girls and spread her poison. Betty didn't have any real friends at the factory. She'd kept herself to herself and she knew that some of the other girls thought she was stand-offish because she worked hard, kept her head down and didn't gossip. It wouldn't be difficult for Ada to turn them against her.

She began to sob and she covered her mouth to stifle it. Her job paid well and meant she could give her mother enough and still have a little bit left over for luxuries for her and Margaret. Now she'd have to find something else again and it would never pay the same. She heard another bus coming and stopped abruptly to see the number. The person behind her walked straight into her.

'I'm so terribly sorry,' said a warm, well-to-do voice.

Betty glanced up. A handsome face. He was lifting off his hat.

'No, no, it was my fault. I wasn't paying attention. I'm sorry.' She cast her eyes down to the wet pavement and turned back to check the bus.

'Are you hurt? I did rather bash you.' The man had his hand on her arm.

'No, no, I'm fine. Please don't worry.' She tried to move away.

'You've been crying, haven't you? Are you all right?'

Betty looked up into eyes the colour of chocolate. They were wrinkled with concern. She felt her lips rise into a smile. 'I'm fine.' But she didn't move away this time.

'I practically assaulted you. Look, there's a Lyons teashop just here. Can I get you something by way of apology? A pot of tea? A Chelsea bun? It's starting to rain again.'

It had been a long time since her break and she was hungry. The man still had his hand on her arm. What harm could it do? She bobbed her head and he grinned.

'Marvellous. It's the least I can do.'

The bakery counter was laden with scones, Bakewell tarts, swiss rolls, and currant buns – the warm, sweet aroma making Betty even hungrier. She'd never seen so much food, especially since rationing had begun. She slipped into the seat opposite the man. He really was very handsome. And very posh. She tried to remember what her mother had said. About minding her Ps and Qs. And to speak properly.

'I don't even know your name.' He was smiling at her.

'Betty Arnold,' she said quietly.

'I'm Jack Bullman.' His lips were like the bow of a ship, perfectly shaped for a kiss. She felt herself blushing and looked down at her hands on the table. Her nails were ragged and her palms rough from the factory. She self-consciously slid them under the table.

'I didn't hurt you, Miss Arnold, did I? When I fell into you?'

She glanced up at him, trying to avoid his lips. But his eyes were just as seductive. Betty shook her head. 'It was my fault. I was rushing to change bus to get home.' She deliberately pronounced all her Ts and Hs.

'And where's home for you, Miss Arnold?' He tipped his head to one side and she could feel his eyes on her, travelling from her face down her uniform. She suddenly wished she was wearing something other than her overalls. And anything but trousers.

'Battersea,' she whispered.

'Ah, I'm not far from you. In Streatham.'

Betty nodded.

The waitress appeared, red buttons down the front of her uniform. Betty couldn't understand what the waitress was asking her – she'd never been to a restaurant before. Jack ordered for her in the end.

'I hope you like it. It's always difficult choosing food for someone else, isn't it? In case they don't like it.'

Betty smiled but wondered what it would be like to turn food away, to say you didn't like it. In their house, they fought over every scrap, whatever it was.

'Where were you coming from on your way back to Battersea?'

'From Woolwich. I work in a munitions factory there, making shells.' She held her head up. 'War work.' She smiled.

'You look beautiful when you smile,' said Jack, his face softening around the edges. 'I-I mean, you look beautiful all the time, but

especially when you smile. It makes your whole face come alive.'
She looked back at her hands cradled in her lap, but not before
she'd spotted the start of a blush creeping up his neck.

'What are you doing for the war?' She felt bold asking him a
question like that.

'I'm a cook in the Navy,' he said as the waitress reappeared with
the pots of tea and the largest Chelsea buns Betty had ever seen. She
set them all out on the table, her starched hat bobbing to and fro.

'You never thought of being a nippy?' Jack said, indicating the
waitress.

Betty knew very little of the Lyons nippies, except that they
were never married and were seen as wholesome and proper. They
certainly wouldn't take unmarried mothers. She shook her head.

'Why not? I reckon you'd sell a lot of cakes. I'd certainly queue
up to buy one if you were serving them.' He winked at her.

She looked up, her throat thick.

'May I ask something?' he said.

Betty nodded and took a sip of the scalding tea.

'Is your hair real? I mean, the colour? I've never seen such fair
hair. It's so golden.'

Betty smiled. 'Yes,' she said. 'It comes from my mother.' She'd
hoped that Margaret would inherit her hair but she was dark, after
her father.

Jack reached his hand across the table and she thought he was
going to try to touch hers, but he pushed the plate towards her.
'Taste your bun. They really are so delicious.'

She took a bite and the sweetness flooded her mouth. He was
right, it was probably the most delicious thing she'd ever tasted.
Betty took another bite and looked around. The room was full of
couples sitting either side of tables, laughing, gossiping. Some wore
factory uniforms like hers, or army uniforms. Others were in civ-
vies. Everybody seemed so bright. So confident. So loud.

'You know, you're the most beautiful woman in this room,' said Jack, his thumb touching hers against her teacup. She felt a shiver go through her and suddenly wanted him to touch all of her hand. She moved it from her teacup and put it back in her lap. This wasn't her world. These people, this laughter. Her world was Margaret. What was she thinking, sitting here with this man when she could be almost home by now, almost holding her little girl in her arms?

Betty held her chin up. 'You're very kind, Mr Bullman. But you don't know who I am. I'm not the type of woman you should be seen having tea with.'

Jack's smile spread across his face and made him even more handsome, and then he began to laugh brightly. 'And what sort of woman are you, Miss Arnold, that I shouldn't take you for tea? I'm intrigued.'

Betty dug into her bag and brought out her purse. She wasn't sure how much this cost, but she didn't want to leave in his debt. She took a few coins out and put them on the table. She'd been hoping to put them towards another dress for Margaret, but it would have to wait. She needed to pay for her folly.

Jack reached across the table and took her hand. 'What are you doing? You don't have to pay. I asked you here.'

Betty pulled her hand free. 'I'm sorry but I came 'ere on false pretences.' She felt her accent slip. 'I'm not who I said I was.'

'Who you said you were? You didn't say you were anyone. Just that you worked in a munitions factory. And that's honourable work.' His face was creased together.

'I have a daughter, a beautiful little girl. But I was never married to the father.' Betty rose from the table. 'I'm sorry, I should never 'ave come. I'm not the sort of person you should be seen wiv.'

Jack rose with her, slinging some coins on the table. 'And I'm not the sort of person who listens to what other people think. I make up my own mind.'

They stood looking at each other across the table, Betty on her tiptoes, her heart hammering.

'Come on, let's get out of here,' said Jack firmly. 'The rain looks like it's stopped. We can go for a walk in the park and you can tell me all about this beautiful little girl of yours.' He came around the side of the table and put out his arm.

Betty looked up into his face and felt warmth spread through her. She'd told him the truth – the first man she'd ever told – and he hadn't run away. She smiled and slipped her arm into his.

Chapter 9

Emma

January 2019

There were hundreds of Elizabeth/Lizzie/Lizzy/Liz/Beth/Eliza/ Libby/Elsie Bullmans on Facebook in the UK, let alone anywhere else in the world. Most though were too old or too young to fit the profile. Some were Black, or Asian, or had been born outside of the UK. Her sister could easily have emigrated, of course, or taken on her adoptive parents' name. She could have got married and taken her husband's name. Or decided that social media wasn't for her.

The battery alert on Emma's phone flashed up. Five per cent. She needed a power cable. She stretched out her back, hearing her bones creak. Her shoulders ached. The boiler must have switched off and she was cold again. And she was hungry – the petrol station sandwich felt like years ago.

For the past few hours she'd scrutinised the faces of people at weddings, birthday parties, and christenings – people she didn't know but hoped might be her sister. But she'd seen no one who bore a resemblance to her mother.

Emma retrieved the charger from her bag just in time to keep her phone alive. With it now plugged into the socket, she lay on the floor of the sitting room in her mother's flat and flicked through the screenshots of her shortlist. Eliza Bullman from Donegal was in the right age range and looked a bit like her mother but her profile was protected, so she couldn't delve too deep. Lizzie Bulman from Durham looked quite like Mum, but the surname was missing an L. Ellie Bullman from Seaford fitted the bill but again her profile was protected. It seemed that everyone who Emma wanted to investigate further had wisely shielded themselves from prying eyes.

She went back to her own Facebook feed. Libby's primary school friend Rosie had posted a couple of pictures of the two of them on the beach from last weekend, both bundled up in huge hoods, fighting the wind. They looked older somehow, worried. She hesitated over the picture, which didn't have a caption, and then clicked on Libby's name. Emma's eyes widened as she realised that Libby had defriended her. And changed her profile picture to a very provocative pose, her hair flicked back, her chest thrown out, barely covered by a thin vest top. Emma sighed. Even six months ago, Libby would have tagged Emma in posts and photos. Now with her fifteen-year-old independence she'd defriended her and spent more time on Instagram and TikTok. Every day they seemed to be growing further apart. How could she change that? Everything she did seemed to be wrong. James was a bit grumpy but he seemed so much more straightforward in comparison.

It was too late now to get a hotel room. Out-of-season Morecambe had little to offer. She glanced at her mother's bed and quickly looked away. Instead, she got the old blanket from the car and bedded down on the floor of the sitting room, using her coat as a pillow. The curtains open, she watched the lights on the sea and cradled a final cup of tea and the remains of an emergency chocolate bar she'd found in the car. Her empty stomach growled gratefully.

Emma tried to get comfortable on her side. Even with her eyes closed, she could feel the girl in the painting looking out at her from the canvas on the floor next to her. She shifted on to her other side and screwed her eyes shut. She was tired, but sleep didn't want to come. The occasional car hissed along the damp street. A couple of drunk young men on their way home serenaded each other all the way up the road. She was convinced that she could hear the swish of the girl's dress as she twirled in the centre of the maze.

Emma turned on her phone's torch and illuminated the painting. The girl was stationary, fixed in her celebratory position. Emma got up and touched its rough surface, stroking the girl's pale face, and moved even further in, their noses almost touching. She'd always thought the girl was laughing – her hands thrown up in the air in delight at making it to the centre of the maze at night. Now she thought she saw again that the child's face was contorted in fear, her hands raised in a call for help. Emma shuddered. Who was she? She looked more closely at her face but her long dark hair partly obscured her face. Maybe that was why she'd never realised the child was terrified. How could she not have seen that? What was she even doing in the middle of a maze all alone in the middle of the night? Was the painting her mother as a child? Or maybe it was the daughter her mother had given up. Elizabeth Margaret Bullman. Emma squinted at the little girl but her face seemed suddenly blurred, holding its secrets.

Sleep must have come, because the dust cart woke her just after five. The painting was still there, leaning against the two boxes. The girl trapped. Emma looked at her closely again. She had looked a little like her mother herself at that age. She'd seen the pictures of her mum as a child with long dark hair. The painting was beautiful, a perfect symmetry. She traced the maze with her fingertip. After creating it at nineteen, her mother had kept it with her throughout her life.

Emma knew very little about her mother's life before she'd met her father David in the 1970s. It was full of gaps, unlike her father's. He'd mapped out a steady existence of Sunday football games in the winter and cricket matches in the summer in the spare time from his banking job where he worked for forty-five years. Emma knew that her mother had left home at sixteen after disagreements with Granny Betty – and now she understood why – but her knowledge of her mother's activities after that were sketchy. How she had got to art school and what she'd done between that and her trip to India in the late 1960s was a mystery. Emma wondered why she'd been so incurious before about her mother's early years. Perhaps all children were. The painting, she realised, seemed to be the one source of continuity. Emma imagined it hung above different fireplaces, propped against a wall, lying wrapped up under a bed.

She traced her fingers along the top of the gilt frame, shifting the dust that seemed to have appeared overnight. Emma put the painting face up on the brown parcel paper on the floor. She quickly covered it over, obscuring the girl's scream, and lay back down on her makeshift bed. Contemplating the day ahead, she didn't know what she was dreading most: visiting the solicitor again, meeting Clare, or giving away part of their family history.

Clare's house was much grander than she expected. Mr Eals had said that Clare had been her mother's yoga teacher and then become a friend, so Emma had imagined a modest home. Instead, stone lions guarded wrought-iron gates behind which a mock Tudor house stretched over a double garage. There was room for her little Fiat next to the red MG outside the garage, but the gates were shut and Emma drove down the street before finding a space.

She awkwardly lifted the large painting out of the back of the car, catching the edge of the frame and tearing the brown paper to reveal the gilt. It was heavy to carry up the street and she wedged it against her stomach, resting her face against the canvas where the girl would be, hiding underneath the paper.

As Emma stood outside the gates, looking for a button to press, she sensed she was being watched. She glanced up in time to see a figure step back from an upstairs window. Emma waited, and a few moments later the gates began to soundlessly open. She slipped through the gap. Her feet crunched across the gravel and she felt herself walking in an exaggeratedly careful way. Everything was immaculate. The pink and yellow primroses perched perfectly in varnished wooden pots bordering the porch. The boxed hedges were closely clipped into uniform squares around a polished bird table which no bird had probably ever dared stand on. The front door remained firmly closed although, through the frosted glass panels standing sentry-like on each side of the door, Emma could see a human shape in the hallway.

She pressed the doorbell lightly. But only after the trilling had ceased to reverberate through the house did the blurred figure start moving towards the door. Emma's arms were shaking, partly from the effort of holding the painting, shield-like across her chest. The door slowly cracked open.

'You must be Emma. I'm Margaret's friend, Clare.' The voice was hard and cold. Clare turned around before Emma had a chance to respond, her long dark hair almost touching the top of her leggings as she walked along the thickly carpeted corridor.

'Hi,' Emma said to her departing back, tempted to just leave the painting in the hall and run. But she could feel the weight of the birth certificate in her handbag. Clare might have answers.

She stepped into the house, struggling down the hall with the package. The huge kitchen-diner looked like something out of a magazine. She and Nick had wanted to extend their kitchen to create something similar but had never had the money.

A panting black Labrador got up from where it had been sprawled in front of the wood-burning stove and sniffed Emma. The room was stiflingly hot. Clare was looking out through the huge bi-fold doors into the January gloom, her hands firmly on her hips, her shoulders set.

Emma caught her eye in the reflection of the window, but if Clare saw her, she gave no sign. Emma's soles squeaked across the kitchen tiles as she walked towards her.

'Take your shoes off, will you.'

The voice was remarkably similar to Sister Catherine's and Emma felt like she was six years old again and muttered an apology. She propped the painting against the kitchen island and slipped off her trainers. She lined them up next to the painting, looking at the chipped coral nail varnish on her bare feet.

'Is that my painting?' Clare had moved across the room and was standing near the parcel, her hands resting on the island.

A warmth flushed across Emma's face. She knew she needed to be building bridges rather than digging trenches, but she heard herself saying, 'If what you mean is whether that is my mother's painting that she left you in her will, then yes.'

Clare moved around the side, advancing into Emma's territory, touching the side of the parcel where the paper had been torn away. 'It's damaged,' she said, picking at the paper and making the tear worse.

'It's fine. I just ripped the paper taking it out of the car.' Emma smoothed the torn area down. 'My father bought this frame second-hand years ago especially for that painting. It hung above our fireplace for all of my childhood.' She was suddenly glad her father wasn't alive to see the painting go.

'I know.' Clare unwrapped it and began making the tape into a ball. She lifted the painting and moved over to the wall opposite the wood-burning stove, where a picture hook was already waiting. She struggled to lift it into place and caught the wall with the side of the painting, denting the plasterwork slightly. But eventually the mounting wire caught the picture hook and the painting slid into place. It filled the space perfectly, as if she had already measured it and prepared the space. Emma wondered if she had a key to her mother's flat.

Clare stood in front of the painting, motionless.

Emma remained by the island, watching Clare watching the girl. From this angle, the girl's scream seemed joyous, the tears that had been in her eyes earlier, invisible. What could Clare see?

Emma walked towards her until they were standing almost side by side. 'My mother painted this for her foundation degree when she was nineteen. It helped to secure her place at art college.'

'I know.' The tone was less harsh than before. 'She told me about that. It was one of the works that she was most proud of.'

How could this woman tell her about what her mother thought? 'Really? She always told me that she thought it was dreadful.' Four or five years ago, when Emma was last in touch with her mum, no Clare had ever been mentioned. And yet now her mother's painting was hanging in this interloper's house.

From this angle, the girl's terror was again clear, the dark of the night such a contrast against the white of her dress. She wondered why she had never seen it before.

Clare moved forward to adjust the painting. Then she turned to Emma, a proprietary hand on the frame. 'Margaret knew how much I admired this painting and she wanted to give it to me as thanks for my support over the past few years.'

Emma winced. She hesitated, choosing her words. 'My mother was not always an easy woman to live with.' It sounded weak.

'No one is easy, but no one should die alone.'

'She died alone?' Emma bit her lip. She hadn't thought that her mother would have been alone. Her father had died surrounded by her, Nick, and their children.

'Well, her solicitor was by the bed. But he was paid to be there.'

Emma had had enough. 'Her death was predicted, I believe. Were you not able to be there?'

Clare looked hard at her. 'I was teaching. I couldn't take unspecified amounts of time off to sit with her. It wasn't as if we knew exactly when she was going to die.' She turned away, muttering under her breath. Emma thought she heard the word 'hypocrite' but couldn't be sure.

'I think there were some other things which are mine. A sculpture and some books?'

'They're in my car. I couldn't carry everything in one go,' said Emma, trying to breathe evenly. The silence smothered the room, sucking out the air. She took a breath. 'Before I get them, there's something I need to ask you.'

'Yes?' Clare turned towards her but didn't otherwise move.

Emma slipped the handbag strap over her head and walked towards the island, taking out the birth certificate and spreading it across the surface. 'When I was going through my mother's things to give to the solicitor, I found something. And I wondered if you knew about it.' She pointed to the certificate.

'What is it?' Clare moved back to the island, her head to one side, her arm outstretched.

Emma gave her the certificate, scanning her face for a reaction. Clare held the certificate at arm's length and squinted at it. She then moved so one of the spotlights was shining directly on the paper. Her face was blank.

'Did you know?' Emma was unable to wait.

'Hold on.' Clare rummaged in one of the island drawers and brought out a pair of reading glasses. She perched them on the end of her nose, reminding Emma even more of a teacher.

Clare flattened the document on the worktop and traced her fingers across the columns, frowning. 'She had a baby as a teenager?' Clare looked up at Emma, her eyes wide.

'It seems that way,' said Emma. 'Did you know? Did she ever mention it, the baby, to you?'

'No, never.' Clare sounded hurt. 'She always referred to you as her only child. Margaret Bullman. Is that her maiden name?' Two lines scored into the bridge of her nose. Emma nodded. Clare was still holding the certificate. 'It doesn't say who the father was.'

'I thought you might know. She might have confided in you. I didn't know anything about this until I found the certificate last night.'

Clare walked over to the painting and looked searchingly at it, glanced down at the certificate and closed her eyes. Then she looked up and turned towards Emma. 'Do you want a cup of tea? I know I could do with one.'

Truce. 'Yes, please.' Emma smiled. She took off her coat and hung it on the back of the high stool and perched on it awkwardly. She hated chairs where you couldn't touch the floor. It was like being a child again. Clare put the certificate in front of her and Emma reread the details she'd already imprinted on her mind, as if they would reveal further truths. There was a silence, but a more companionable one than before as Clare filled the kettle and prepared mugs.

'Peppermint or chamomile? I don't have any caffeine in the house.'

'Peppermint's great.' She thought of her mother again and her love of herbal tea.

Clare placed the steaming mugs between them. 'So where did you find it? Margaret said she'd prepared for the end and that everything was in order. What an awful expression.'

'I don't think I was meant to find it. It was tucked away in a locked box of baby things. I thought they were mine, but then I saw the birth certificate and the photo.'

'There was a photo? Did you bring it?'

Emma slid the envelope out of her bag and gave it to Clare.

Clare covered her mouth with her hand. 'My God, she looks so young.'

'Too young to have a baby.'

'Yes. Do you know what happened to the baby? To Elizabeth Margaret?'

'No, but I know where Mum had her. Birdhurst Lodge was a mother and baby home. I don't think they would have let her keep her even if she had wanted to. I looked into it. They weren't nice places.'

'I saw that film about the mother and baby units in Ireland.' Clare winced. 'Was Margaret raised Catholic?'

'Yes, she was. It's likely that the baby would have been adopted at a few weeks old.'

'That's just bloody awful. To have to give up a baby that young. How could you ever get over it?'

'I don't think Mum did get over it. I think it coloured the rest of her life.'

'What d'you mean?'

'She was never like my friends' mothers. She was always different. Odd. Angry and odd—' Emma trailed off. 'Did she mention her childhood to you much? I know patchy details – that she didn't get on with Granny Betty – but there are huge gaps.'

'She hated Betty, I know that. Couldn't stand her.'

'But why?'

Clare rubbed the lines between her brows, smoothing them out. 'Margaret never said much about her family, but she did mention that her mother had betrayed her. That was the actual word she used. She refused to elaborate when I asked her how – it was still too upsetting for her to go into, I guess. I knew that she married twice and had you – and that you didn't get along either . . .' Emma looked down and squeezed the teabag with her spoon. 'But I never really asked more. She was very keen on her grandson. She talked about him a lot.'

'James, yes. She doted on him, but not her granddaughter, Libby.' Emma picked up the certificate. 'The really awful thing is that I gave Libby the formal name Elizabeth Margaret. What were the chances?'

'Christ, that is unfortunate. How did she react when you told her?'

'Badly. She just walked out when we told her the name.'

'But you can imagine the shock of another baby called Elizabeth Margaret, after what she'd been through. I guess it just shows that the wound was still very raw. Even after all that time.' Clare cradled her mug, peering into the liquid.

'We just thought she was being her usual angry self. After that we didn't see much of her because it became too difficult. She was so awkward with Libby.'

'I've seen the will.' Clare waved her hand towards the painting. 'She left Elizabeth, your Libby, the flat and only small amounts to the others. Was that some sort of apology?'

'Or leaving her worldly goods to one Elizabeth because she couldn't leave them to the other Elizabeth? Who knows. I'm meeting the solicitor after this so I'll see if he knows.' Emma shook her head. 'What was she like at the end? Was she . . . *compos mentis*? Is there a chance that she thought she was leaving the flat to the other Elizabeth, her first daughter? God, it feels weird to be saying that.'

'She knew exactly what she was doing at the end,' Clare said firmly. 'The will was changed to give the flat to Libby the day before she died. I don't know what the old will said, but she definitely knew what she was doing. Margaret knew she was dying and she was ready.'

'So she was thinking of Elizabeth at the end.'

'I think she probably thought about her every day.' Clare sighed. 'Thirty years ago this May I lost a baby at seven months pregnant.' Her voice caught on the words. 'He just stopped moving. Despite having two more children after him, I never stopped thinking about him. I'll be thinking about him as I die, I'm sure.'

Emma closed her eyes. 'I'm sorry. That must have been awful.'

'Yes . . .' Clare got up abruptly and brought her laptop over to the island. 'So would you want to meet her? If you had the chance?'

'Yes, I would, very much. Just to see what she's like.' Emma took a sip of the cooling tea. 'It was lonely as an only child. I think that's why I wanted more than one child. So my children would never be lonely.'

'Have you searched for Elizabeth online?'

'Yes. There's no Elizabeth Bullman on Facebook that properly matches her age, race, and location. But Elizabeth is a name with hundreds of derivatives. It's one of the reasons we chose it, so Libby could decide.'

'That's true, she could be hard to track down,' said Clare, tilting her head to the side.

'I wonder if Mum ever tried to trace her, or if she ever tried to trace Mum?'

'Possibly. We may never know.'

'She's twenty-two years older than me. She might be desperate to have some answers now.' Emma tapped her fingers on the table.

Clare leaned over and touched Emma's arm, just above the wrist. She flinched. 'She might well have a very established, happy life. She might not want that to be disrupted. All of this is a long time ago for her.'

'It's just weird thinking that I have a sister somewhere.'

'A half-sister.'

'A half-sister,' Emma conceded. 'She still might want to meet me.'

'There are ways to do this. I've seen it on the TV.' Clare opened her laptop and started typing. Emma watched her manicured fingers flitting across the keys. 'Look, there's a thing called an Adoption Contact Register where you can leave a letter for your birth parent or adopted child in case they want to get in touch.'

'Surely, that's for the parents though?'

'No, it says here that you must be a birth relative,' said Clare, reading from the website. 'That is any person who is related to the adopted person by blood, including half-blood, marriage, or civil partnership. That's you. You're her half-sister.'

'Okay, what do I need to do?'

Clare slid the laptop over to her and Emma began typing. It took twenty minutes to fill out the form and send it into the ether.

'I'd better head off and grab some lunch. Thanks for today, Clare. I appreciate that this isn't easy for you either.'

'No, it isn't.' Clare looked straight at her. 'But I do know that Margaret wasn't always easy. And there's something about one's family. They know the buttons to push.'

Emma laughed ruefully as she struggled to get her shoes back on without untying the laces properly. 'If you want anything else of hers, then just shout. I've distributed everything that was mentioned in the will but there are a few bits left.'

'Thanks, Emma, that might be nice. I wouldn't mind a couple of her books on Buddhism. She had such a diverse library, and such a diverse knowledge. There were basic, common-sense things that she knew nothing about, but then she had an in-depth knowledge of some really obscure concepts.'

'That's so true.' Emma laughed, picking up her bag. 'Did you know she loved backgammon and back in the early 2000s started to play it online. I kept trying to explain to her how dial-up internet worked but she ignored me. And then she ran up a two-hundred-pound phone bill.'

Clare led the way out of the kitchen. 'I'll give you a hand getting the other bits from your car now,' she said, slipping on some ballet pumps. 'If you've still got stuff to do, I'll help if you like? I've done a couple of house clearances like this myself, so I know how tough they can be.'

Chapter 10

BETTY

JULY 1942

Jack looked even more handsome than he had on their wedding day the year before. The same beautiful smile, and she loved seeing him in his Navy uniform. It brought out the colour of his eyes.

She bit her lip, and then worried she'd smudged the lipstick on to her teeth, as she signed Margaret's adoption forms next to his scrawled name. She felt him watching her, and turned and smiled, her eyes bright.

'Thank you.'

'I love you,' he mouthed behind the registrar's ramrod-straight back.

Outside the registrar's panelled office, a stern-faced woman sat next to four-year-old Margaret at a desk, playing what looked like noughts and crosses with her.

The child scrambled up as they walked out arm in arm, her knee-length white socks already crumpled around her ankles. She ran towards Betty, hiding her face in her red dress.

'Now Father is your real father, Margaret. He's adopted you formally,' Betty said, bending over and stroking the child's dark pigtails, threaded with red ribbon.

Margaret said nothing, but she looked at Jack and half-smiled.

'Say "Thank you, Father",' instructed Betty.

'Thank you, Father,' parroted Margaret.

'Congratulations, Mr and Mrs Bullman,' said the woman, the registrar's assistant, her mouth twisting into a smirk, reminding Betty momentarily of the laundries. She'd never have to put up with that again, not now Margaret was officially Jack's daughter.

'Thank you.' Betty gave her a small nod before turning to the main door. Jack swung Margaret up by the arms on to his shoulders, tucking her dress behind his hat. She put her hands across his high forehead.

'Watch her head,' Betty said.

They went through the door and Jack dutifully ducked. Jack and Betty linked arms again to walk the few hundred yards from Somerset House to the Strand Palace Hotel, past the new bridge.

'Are you sure the restaurant's still open? I heard that American airmen are staying there now,' said Betty, struggling to keep up with him. Her red heels were new and pinched slightly.

'Of course it is. Some of my old pals work there. We can use up those coupons you've been saving. I only have a few days before I have to go back.'

Betty smiled up at him.

She looked in the shop window, watching the reflection of the three of them as they walked down the Strand. They were a proper family now. And she knew Jack wanted his own children. They'd have lots of beautiful children running around Pullman Court soon.

Chapter 11

EMMA

JANUARY 2019

The solicitor's secretary asked Emma to wait, and so she sat on a high-backed chair near the door of the cluttered reception area. She took out her phone and started rereading the 'Houses of Shame' article on the *Guardian* website. The huge communal dormitories where the pregnant women stayed sounded like her boarding school Mount Carmel, though even the nuns hadn't made the children help with domestic duties and attend daily prayers. She remembered *The Magdalene Sisters* film she and Nick had watched. It had been hard to stomach seeing the beatings the mother superior had inflicted on the girls, some of whom had become pregnant as a result of being raped by family members. It had seemed a million miles from her own life. In comparison to the Magdalene Laundries, Birdhurst Lodge sounded almost benign, but the picture of the prams with smiling babies lined up while being inspected by what was presumably a respectable married couple was heartbreaking.

She gazed out of the small bay window and imagined her mother standing at the window of the ivy-clad manor house, watching as a couple approached the pram and examined her own daughter.

Such couples couldn't have children, and that would have been awful. Nick and she had tried for years to have a third child after James and Libby, but nothing had happened. All those tests only to be told that her infertility was unexplained. Perhaps in those days you weren't told, they simply didn't know and one day you gave up and found yourself looking along a line of babies born to single teenage girls.

A register was apparently kept of the 'removals' – the ominous-sounding word for adoptions. Women who gave up their babies 'cried and cried for weeks afterwards' the article said. Once their babies were taken away, what did the women do? Had her mother gone back home? Or stayed with friends? Where was the father during this time? Had he stuck with her or disappeared at the first sign of trouble?

After everything that Betty had been through with Margaret as a baby, it seemed so awful that Margaret should also have been a teenage mother. Emma had in that way been different from both her mother and her grandmother. And Libby was far too sensible for anything like that. At least she hoped she was.

It was the sort of cough designed to politely intrude on another's thoughts. Not too loud, but enough to bring you back to the present: the sweltering radiator, the icy blast under the door.

The solicitor was standing a few feet away, his arms crossed. 'Mrs Bowen, I didn't expect to see you again so soon.'

Emma stood up. 'Thank you for agreeing to see me at such short notice. I just have a few questions about my mother.'

'I see.' Mr Eals paused and pursed his lips. 'I'll help you if I can. Come through.'

She followed him down the narrow corridor into the same room as the day before. He slowly eased himself into his chair and looked at her, his fingers creating a steeple.

'How can I help?'

Emma focused on a brown mark on the wall just past the solicitor's head. 'I met up with Clare Richens to give her the things mentioned in the will.' Emma paused, her mouth dry. 'She said that the change leaving the flat to my daughter Elizabeth – Libby – was made the day before my mother died. You said she made some small changes. Do you know why she did this?' She glanced directly at him and then quickly looked away.

'Unfortunately client confidentiality extends beyond the grave. I'm not at liberty to talk about her matters specifically.' The solicitor smiled obliquely. 'But I will help you in any way I am able.'

Emma unzipped her handbag and took out the envelope. Despite its age, it looked stark against the array of old files on his desk as she slid it across to him. 'I found this among my mother's things. It was well hidden.' She could feel her stomach fluttering.

Emma watched him closely as he opened the envelope, the birth certificate and photo slipping on to the desk. With practised patience, he slowly took out his reading glasses and slid them on to his nose, the hairs temporarily flattening under the thin wire. There was not even a flicker of astonishment on his face as he examined the certificate carefully for several moments and then turned his attention to the photograph. When he finished, he methodically took off his glasses and put them back in a brown leather case, placed both documents back into the envelope and passed them across to Emma. With his fingertips once more pressed together, he finally spoke.

'She was very young to have a child. It was different in those days, of course. People beget children when they're still children themselves now.'

'So you know about Elizabeth? Did my mother tell you?' Her heart started beating faster.

Mr Eals examined his fingertips meticulously. When he looked up, his eyes were melancholy.

'I first met your mother in her very early twenties when she was living in London and I was a pupil at the Inner Temple. She needed advice about a rogue landlord who was attempting to illegally evict her, and I was recommended to her as someone who could give informal assistance, as a friend, rather than actual legal advice, which I wasn't then in a position to give. We struck up a friendship and over the years she consulted me from time to time about all manner of matters. I became aware at some point in our friendship that she had had a baby at a young age who was subsequently adopted.'

He was looking almost apologetically at the pile of files in the corner of the room. Emma suspected the solicitor felt he had already gone too far.

'Do you know where, to whom?' Emma leaned forward in her chair. 'Did my mother ever try to trace her . . . her . . . other daughter?'

'I can appreciate that this is something of a shock.'

Emma waited, picking at her nails, but the solicitor remained silent. She looked at him, but his face stayed impassive with no apparent urge to break the silence. He would be very good at poker.

'I've approached the Adoption Service about trying to trace her, my sister. Apparently there's a way that they can put adopted people back in touch with their birth families.'

Mr Eals pressed his lips together. 'Indeed. Although they do not offer a tracing service. Their service acts like a dead letter box. One party leaves a letter for the other to find. And if both parties want to be in touch then they are introduced.' He took a breath as if weighing up what to say. 'You have not formally asked for my advice. Indeed, my client is your mother's estate, so I am not in a position to offer you formal counsel. But I would caution you against investigating, against delving into the past. The past is often best left exactly where it is. There may have been reasons why your mother did not share her past with you.'

Emma shook her head. 'But this woman, Elizabeth Margaret Bullman, may have been searching for my mother. She may want to meet her.'

'Even if that is the case – and it's by far from certain that she herself wants to dig into her past – you will be contacting her to inform her that the mother with whom she spent only a short time, has recently died. She will never now have the chance to know her and develop a relationship with her. You need to consider what impact that might have on her.' He was so measured, it was infuriating.

'I agree. But she has a sister she knows nothing about, surely she deserves to know that?' Emma realised she was waving her hands around and quickly slipped them on to her lap.

'She may have her own siblings in her adopted family and be perfectly happy. Given her age, she may have her own children and grandchildren.'

'Yes. But in that case, she won't have got in touch with the Adoption Service and we won't be able to find her anyhow.' Emma could hear the petulance in her voice.

Mr Eals began to speak and then paused, his eyebrows drawn together reminding her of a long furry caterpillar stretched across his forehead. 'I can only reiterate my recommendation. The past is best left alone. There may be reasons why your mother chose not to trace her or to let the matter be more widely known.'

Emma looked at him closely. 'You know something, don't you?' She could feel her heart beating faster. 'You knew about Elizabeth all along and you know something more.'

Emma had a sudden urge to grab the file and run to her car and lock herself in until she had read through the papers. She felt the solicitor knew a great deal more than he was prepared to reveal. And perhaps some of those secrets were locked up in the documents on his desk.

Mr Eals smiled, and the caterpillar separated. 'I appreciate that this is a very difficult time for you, Mrs Bowen. It's easy to see intrigue when there is none. I urge you to take an old solicitor's advice – an old man's advice.' He paused. 'Margaret told me that you have a good life, a good marriage, good children. Focus on that and leave this matter be.'

'Did she say that?' Emma's eyes glistened. 'About the children?'

'Indeed, indeed.' Mr Eals nodded. 'How are you getting on with the clearing of your mother's property?'

Emma sighed and her shoulders dropped. 'Good, thank you. I've boxed up all the items mentioned in the will and the courier has taken them away. It's just the stuff for charity now, and some stuff for the bin. I should be done by tomorrow.' She took a deep breath. 'We'd like to put the flat on the market and then we can decide what to do with the proceeds. My husband is looking into setting up a trust for our daughter. I was wondering if you could recommend a good local estate agent?'

'Naturally, I'd be delighted. If you drop the keys back to me once you're finished, I would be happy to make the arrangements.'

'As long as I don't find out any more secrets in the meantime.'

Mr Eals raised his head just a little too quickly and looked at her. 'Indeed.' He nodded and smiled distractedly, and then looked at the pile of files in the corner.

Emma was sure at that moment he knew more than he was saying. The challenge was how she could find out what that was.

Emma couldn't face another night on the floor of the flat, nor did she fancy taking up Clare's offer to put her up for the night. The impersonality of the Morecambe Travelodge suited her well. Lying on the starched bed looking at the cheap sea-view print which she was sure was in every room, she phoned Nick and talked about the last two days, before she realised he hadn't spoken for a long time. 'Sorry, darling. I've just yakked on and on. Is everything okay there?'

'Don't be daft. I know it's tough for you. Yes, it's all fine here. Everyone's missing you.' Emma could hear the sound of the TV in the background.

'How did James get on with his chemistry mock? I messaged him but haven't heard back. I was worried that meant bad news. And how's Libby? What time did she get home last night?'

'Oh, his exam was postponed. The teacher was ill or something. Libby was a bit past curfew but she did answer her phone when I called, so that's something. They've both been out of their rooms more than usual, hanging around downstairs. I guess it's just a change in their routine – they're used to you being here all the time.' Whatever he was watching was now on an ad break. 'But they miss you, we all do.'

'I'll be home tomorrow.'

'Good, I've run out of ideas of what to cook.' Nick laughed. 'I'm only joking. Well, I have run out of ideas, and the freezer's empty, but it's not the same without you here.'

Emma felt herself welling up again. It was the longest she'd ever been away from them. 'I miss you all too.'

'I'll leave you in peace. Sleep well and safe journey tomorrow.'

She could hear the TV again.

'Night.'

But sleep proved just as elusive between the stiff white utilitarian sheets as it had in her mother's flat the night before. She had just drifted into a light sleep when Mr Eals came dancing into her dreams, waltzing with her mother's file through the maze from the painting, his light feet tripping down the paths in the moonlight. At one point, there was another person with him – Emma couldn't see their face – and they were throwing a baby between them over the top of the hedges as they danced, the baby's terrified screams sounding above their raucous laughter. She woke up, her heart pounding, the sheets tangled around her.

The room was stiflingly hot, the heater wedged on high. Emma got up and went to the steamed-up window. She couldn't open it, but her hand felt the coolness of the pane, and she leaned her feverish forehead against it, breathing in the slightly cooler air. She looked out at the street, where a drunk couple were making their way down the road, supporting each other as they walked unsteadily home. It was just after one o'clock. The girl's heels caught in the cobbles, her white legs walking awkwardly. She looked like Libby. At the corner they avoided a teenage boy throwing up into the gutter and crossed out of sight.

Calmed, she went back to the bed, the sheets now a twisted pile in the middle. She remade it, making sure not to tuck the sheets in, and slid back inside.

What did Mr Eals know beyond the basic facts about Elizabeth's existence? Had her mother tried to trace her daughter? Had Mr Eals helped? Was he the father even? What was he so anxious to keep secret? She felt trapped in a maze of secrets, the more she looked for answers the more lost she became. And just as she thought she could see over the maze and work her way out, the hedges only became higher and denser, the moon hid behind a cloud and she was plunged into darkness.

Chapter 12

Betty

February 1946

The raindrops ran down the train window, blurring the fields as they sped past. They'd been lucky it hadn't rained like this for the send-off. The clouds had threatened as they'd stood on the quayside at Southampton waving Jack off to New York. He'd been offered a job advising on a kitchen layout at one of the new hotels there and the money was too much to refuse. She'd tried to hold his gaze until the boat was a small dot on the horizon and she wasn't sure what she was looking at any more. Betty slumped into the train seat. He'd be gone for weeks.

If her mother had looked after Margaret, she'd have been on the boat right now, bound for New York with Jack, instead of on the train. *'I'm not 'aving your bastard child while you go tripping off round the world.'* The memory of her mother's words made her wince.

Betty closed her eyes. She loved Margaret, she loved Jack. It was just that she was constantly torn between the two of them – a perpetual tug of war.

There was a sharp tap on her shoulder. Betty opened her eyes and swivelled round. A plump lady in a two-piece tweed suit and matching hat was leaning across the aisle, her pink neck folded over the top of her blouse, almost entirely covering the collar.

'Would you mind stopping your daughter doing that? It's terribly irritating.' She waved a veiny hand heavy with rings in the direction of Margaret who was drawing patterns in the window's condensation, her fingers squeaking against the glass.

'Margaret, do stop,' said Betty, reaching forward to smack her hand away.

Margaret looked up, pouting. 'It's not fair. I wanted to go to New York.'

'So did I,' said Betty, a tightness around her eyes.

'Why didn't you go then? I would've,' said Margaret, crossing her arms.

Betty spoke through a pinched mouth. 'Because I have to stay and look after you, Margaret.'

Margaret rolled her eyes and flicked her head, her dark hair falling forward over her eyes. She looked up at her mother, her eyes sulky.

The expression was so familiar; Margaret did it all the time when she was cross. But it also reminded Betty of someone else. Betty closed her eyes and there *he* was. Standing there in the park with her, the day she'd told him she was expecting Margaret.

He'd rolled his eyes and flicked back his head, his black hair falling over his eyes again almost immediately. 'You should 'ave been more careful, Bets. I thought you were taking care of fings.'

Betty had nodded at the ground. The funny little rubber cap that Ruth had loaned her had fitted okay, although she could always feel it when it was there. But there'd been the time in the park when it had come loose and fallen out. He was supposed to be pulling out too but there'd been too many times when he'd misjudged it and she'd felt him explode inside her. Then it leaked through her knickers all afternoon.

'So what you gonna do wiv it?' He had sounded angry, impatient. Her shoulders dropped. Betty thought of the tiny creature growing inside her. Their baby. Part of them. Her baby. She felt her heart beat a little faster.

She looked up at him through her lashes and put her head on one side, her blonde curls bouncing. 'I know it's not what we planned, but it's not all bad news. We could marry quickly and be free to have fun whenever we wanted.' She put her hand on his hairy arm and drew her lips into a smile. 'All the time.'

He looked down at her, his expression softening. 'You're a beautiful girl, Bets.' He stroked the side of her cheek. She recognised the look in his eyes – he always looked like that before he slipped his hand into her blouse or up her skirt.

'Whenever we wanted,' she repeated, thrusting her chest forward, so her brassiere pushed her breasts up and together.

He glanced down and she heard his breath quicken. He stroked the side of her breast through her blouse. She licked her lips and kept her lips parted. He flushed.

'I'll come to yer house tonight and speak to your pa,' he said, his eyes glazed. 'We'll need to marry quickly before anyone suspects.'

She nodded, smiling up at him. Their baby. Warmth spread through her body and her fingertips tingled.

He reached down and pinched her bottom hard.

'Ow,' said Betty, leaning into him.

'Come on, you tease. Let's consummate our engagement. There's no one in the yard at this time of day. We can go there.' And he'd led her away to the tiny yard off his workshop. It was one of the last times she ever saw him. She hadn't been there that evening when he'd asked her father permission to marry her. And she'd only seen him fleetingly when they spoke to the priest about the ceremony. On her wedding day she'd waited at the altar for more than half an hour before they realised he wasn't coming.

Betty sighed and covered her face with her hands. It didn't get any easier, remembering it all. Thank God for Jack.

'What's the matter, Mother?' Margaret flicked her hair back and it fell forward again.

Betty leaned across the table and smacked her face, the sound ricocheting off the train window. 'I've told you not to flick your hair like that. You'll give yourself a crick in the neck.'

Margaret's chin and lips wobbled and she started to cry.

Betty swallowed. 'Oh, Margaret.' She jumped up and moved around the table to sit next to her. 'I'm sorry, I didn't mean to.' She hugged Margaret violently, clinging to her.

'Ow, you're hurting me.' Margaret pushed her away, and Betty sighed and leaned back in her seat. She stared out of the window. Margaret started drawing on the glass again, the squeaking sound echoing around the carriage.

Chapter 13

Emma

January 2019

'I know her stuff isn't really here, but I can still feel her.' Clare stood in the centre of her mother's empty sitting room, looking around.

'Yes, I can too,' said Emma. 'When I was packing up her stuff on Monday, I could almost feel her watching me.'

'She probably was. To make sure you did it properly.' They both laughed.

'So what needs to be done? How can I help?' Clare asked, hands on her hips.

'I've packed up everything that was mentioned in the will. What's left needs to go to the charity shop – unless you want anything?'

'Aren't you taking anything for yourself?'

'There's the odd thing that I remember from my childhood – the biscuit tin, this Eskimo thing, a mother of pearl box. I've put those in this box. But most of this stuff is new.'

'It must feel strange, now that both your parents have gone.'

'Are yours still alive?' Emma asked, then regretting sounding so surprised.

But Clare smiled. 'Yes, I was something of a happy accident. My mother was only eighteen when she had me so they're in their seventies.'

'And they stayed together?'

'Oh yes, neither of them have even kissed anyone else.'

'How lovely.'

'Yes. But a hard example to live up to.'

Emma nodded. 'You're right. It does feel strange that both my parents are gone. There's nobody I'm in touch with who knew me when I was a child. We have no other family. And I met my oldest friend when I was in my teens. That's a strange feeling.'

'It sounds quite lonely?' It felt like more of a question than a statement.

'Not really. I have a great life, a lovely husband, two wonderful children. A good job and they allow me to work part-time so I can be around for the kids more. I've really missed them these last few days. It's been so odd being away from them all.' She paused and picked at the skin on the side of her thumbnail which was already raw. Emma sighed. 'Do you know if Mum ever had any therapy or counselling or whatever?'

'Not that I know of. But don't forget, I didn't know about her other daughter or any other stuff like that.' She looked around the room. 'She may have done, I guess, but it wasn't as popular as it is today. And it's expensive too.' Clare walked into the kitchen and started opening cupboards. 'How's the planning for her funeral going?'

'Okay. I've been in touch with the funeral home. She had very specific requests – a sort of Buddhism meets Wagner funeral.'

'Wagner?'

'Yes, she's chosen "Ride of the Valkyries" to end with. The music from *Apocalypse Now*.'

'Gosh, that's not very Buddhist, is it?'

Emma shrugged. 'No, but then she was a master of contradictions. Despite leaving the south all those years ago, she wanted the service to take place at our local crematorium in Brighton. It's next Thursday. Are you going to be able to make it?'

'I'm sorry, I can't.' Clare looked down. 'It's a long way to go. And I'm not very good at funerals.'

'Oh, don't worry. I think it's just going to be family.' Emma gave a small smile. 'I don't know of anyone else to ask.'

'Lots of people are lonely at the end of their lives. Everyone they've known has died, or—'

'They've fallen out with them.' Emma regretted saying it because Clare immediately crossed her arms and frowned.

'Let's get this lot sorted.' She walked back into the sitting room, took a couple of flat-pack boxes and disappeared into the bedroom.

Emma could hear the familiar screech of the brown tape. She wandered into the kitchen and started wrapping in newspaper anything she thought the charity shop could sell. A few boxes later and with all of the kitchen cleared she went back into the sitting room and sat on the floor in front of the antique desk, its lower drawers flung open like a gaping mouth. It was the only place in the room that she hadn't yet tackled. Countless folders labelled with various correspondence courses cluttered up the two shelves. For someone who had left school with just one O-level, Margaret had had a passion for learning.

Emma started tipping the paper out and throwing it into recycling bags. There was also a turquoise Clarks shoebox. Emma remembered new school shoes in those boxes in the 1970s and 1980s. She flipped open the lid, thinking it might contain more family secrets, but inside were just some old ration books, some more photos – of her mother in India – a few postcards, and some old letters in what looked like Granny Betty's handwriting tied together with string. She'd go through it all later at home.

'Look at these fantastic shoes. Original patents!' Clare's voice drifted through the closed bedroom door. Emma went to help her.

Chapter 14

BETTY

JULY 1947

Betty could hear the low hum of them chatting in the kitchen. It was a relief they were getting on. Jack and Margaret always seemed to be griping at one another. She lay back on the pillows and took a shallow breath.

The bedroom door opened and Jack appeared with a wooden tray, Margaret following with a glass of water. Jack set down the tray on the side table. The smell of the sausages, mashed potato and creamed swede made her gag.

'Darling, try this, it'll make you feel better.' He drew the tray towards her. She looked up at him.

'It keeps coming back to me when I wake up,' she whimpered, covering her mouth.

'What's the m—' Jack held his hand up to silence Margaret.

'Shh, darling. It'll be all right,' he said, helping Betty to sit up. Jack put the tray on her lap and gestured at Margaret to bring the water.

'What's wrong, Mother?'

'I told you Margaret, it's noth—'

But Betty shook her head at Jack. 'No, we should tell her.'

'Betty, it's a private thing,' he said.

'But she's my daughter. Our daughter,' she corrected. 'She deserves to know. To understand.'

Jack raised his eyebrows and withdrew from the bed, standing by the window.

'Father and I want to have another child,' she said, reaching to hold Margaret's hand. 'But I can't seem to have one. I did have a baby inside me, but it just died.' She heard her voice crack. 'It was a little boy.'

What would their son have looked like? What would he have grown into?

'But aren't I enough?' Margaret asked, her brows drawn together, eyes cross.

'Of course you are, darling, you're everything to me. But we thought it would be nice to have another child. A brother or sister for you.' Betty stretched her face into a smile, drawing her daughter to her.

'Our own child,' mumbled Jack, walking out of the room.

Chapter 15

Emma

January 2019

Through the glass-paned front door, the solicitor's face was more wrinkled, his eyes more hooded, than the previous day. He was leaning over the secretary, looking at some files, his hands rubbing his temples as she came through the door, the little brass bell rattling against the frame. Mr Eals looked startled, as the secretary's smile automatically broadcast across her face. 'Hello, how may I help you?'

'I'm here to see Mr Eals. It's Emma Bowen.' She spotted a look of unease pass across the woman's face.

'Oh . . .' She looked anxiously up at Mr Eals, who smiled back reassuringly and patted her shoulder. He squeezed through the gap between the desks and shook Emma's hand, gesturing her to once again follow him. As she walked past the desk, she saw her mother's death certificate on top of a pile of other paperwork. And in front of the secretary was a faded document titled *Certificate of Adoption* in large letters. She stopped and scanned down and saw the name Elizabeth. As she leaned in further to see, narrowing her eyes, she realised Mr Eals had stopped and was watching her.

Emma blushed as she turned and followed him down the corridor. His office was unchanged and she sat in the same chair as the previous day, watching as he eased slowly into his. She waited for him to speak, but he was busy observing her over his fingers pressed together in his habitual pose.

'I have the keys,' she said awkwardly and placed the small bunch on the desk. Mr Eals smiled and took them, and then opened a desk drawer to extract a luggage tag. He laid it on the desk and, taking a fountain pen from another drawer, wrote her mother's name on it before attaching the string to the central silver ring.

'How is Margaret's flat?'

'Tidy at least. I've left the furniture there as the estate agent you recommended said it would make the place look better.' It had been an exhausting three days and Emma was glad there was no reason to go back. Soon strangers would be poking around, sizing it up for furniture, curtains, and carpets. It made her sad to think of the place being gutted, but at the same time the secrets the flat had held were now free.

'I'll liaise with the agent and keep you informed. I would imagine it will take a little while to sell.'

Emma had no doubt that Mr Eals would be straight round to the property, but for what she couldn't say. She imagined him slowly climbing those steep stairs, surveying her work. Had he visited her mother there much? Had he been in love with her? It seemed unlikely, but he'd admitted to being fond of her. There was a chance Elizabeth was his child. Perhaps he was protecting his own secret.

'Did you know Elizabeth's father, the boy who got my mother pregnant?' She was watching him carefully for a reaction and was satisfied to see the slight recoil, the drawing together of the eyebrows.

'The boy, no.' He paused and looked over her shoulder. 'It all happened a long time before I met your mother. And a long time before you were born,' he added pointedly.

'I thought it could have been a boy at her school. Someone who charmed her enough but then didn't hang around to face the consequences.'

'Hmmm, possibly.' Mr Eals' gaze remained fixed on the wall behind her, his fingertips pressed together, resting on his top lip.

'I saw an adoption certificate out there. It's Elizabeth's, isn't it?'

'Emma, you know that I cannot let you see your mother's file.'

'I do want to meet her, my sister.'

'I know you do, and I'm sure you'll be persistent enough to find her.'

'But you don't want me to.' Once again, she felt like a petulant child pushing a strict father to change his mind.

He took a deep breath, and sighed, looking at her directly. 'You are so very much like your mother. You will do what you will whatever I counsel, just as your mother did. There were times when she didn't take my advice.' He blinked. 'But I think she came to regret it. And I think you might too.'

Chapter 16

BETTY

OCTOBER 1948

Betty had never been to the main doctor's surgery on the corner of Streatham High Road, preferring the less intimidating and cheaper local surgery. But now that visiting the doctor was free through the new National Health Service, Jack had said there was no need for such restraint. He strode into the imposing Victorian building with his hands clasped behind him, his head high. Betty followed behind him, her heart hammering.

The receptionist was what her mother would have called 'mutton dressed as lamb'. She sat, her red nails flicking through patient records, ignoring the growing queue of patients. By the time they'd got to the front, Betty was feeling sick with nerves.

'May I help?' she said, her voice bored.

'My wife and I are here to see the doctor,' Jack said.

'Which one?' Her lips pursed, the lipstick leaking into the wrinkles above her mouth.

'Which what?' Jack asked.

'Which *doctor*?' Her lips were now pressed into a thin line.

'Which doctor did you book the appointment with, darling?' Jack looked down at her expectantly.

'I . . . hadn't realised there was more than the one,' she stammered. 'I just booked an appointment with a doctor, like you said I should.'

The woman raised her eyebrows. 'What's your name?' she drawled.

'Jack Bullman. And Betty Bullman,' he said.

'Have you been to the surgery before?'

The questions, and then the forms she had to fill out when her writing wasn't that good, drained the little confidence she had. By the time they were sitting in front of Dr Tucker's desk, she wished they'd gone to the local surgery instead where they knew her and her lady problems.

Dr Tucker's desk was cluttered with files and notepads. A bottle of Quink sat next to a pen stand, waiting to write out prescriptions. Between the files, the desk pad was stained with coffee rings. Dr Tucker had the look of a man who'd sat behind the same desk for forty years, heard every type of problem, and been well-paid for doing so. Did he resent that patients like Betty and Jack could now visit for free? His grey moustache was neatly trimmed, his eyes seemed kindly enough, his waistcoat struggling to contain his stomach. How he managed to put on weight with rationing was anyone's guess, Betty thought. Even chefs like Jack were thin. Perhaps people paid him in food.

Thank goodness Jack was taking charge of the conversation. She wouldn't have known what to say.

'It's about my wife, you see. Betty,' he said. 'We're keen to have a baby and it's not happening.'

She looked down at her hands and realised she'd been twisting her hankie into a rope.

The doctor smiled at them. 'I understand. How long have you been planning a family?'

'About eight, nine years. Since we got married.'

'Ahh.' The doctor sucked his pipe and looked at her. 'Mrs Bullman, you look young and healthy.'

'Yes, sir,' she said, keeping her eyes downcast. There was a pulled thread on her skirt. She must mend it when she got home.

'And you, Mr Bullman, all functioning normally?'

'Yes.'

'Any success in becoming pregnant at all?'

'Yes. We have a daughter, Margaret. But my wife lost a daughter earlier this year, quite late on.' The memory of the tiny, still creature that she had eventually delivered after hours of labour still felt very raw. How they'd sat there with it in their arms, wrapped in a white shawl until the nurses took it away. 'And she lost our son last summer . . . before he was due.'

'How old is your daughter?'

'Margaret's eleven.'

She saw the doctor mentally counting and the small frown as he reached his conclusion. Betty's shoulders slumped. She hadn't wanted to go, but Jack had insisted. He wanted answers, he'd said, however embarrassing it was going to be. He wanted to be a proper father, he'd said, to have his own child. It was like Margaret didn't even exist for him.

'Is Margaret your daughter, Mr Bullman?'

'I adopted Margaret not long after we married.' Betty inched down further in her chair.

'Your wife was presumably widowed in the war?'

'No, she wasn't married to Margaret's father.' She saw Jack's face flush.

'I see.' Dr Tucker swivelled in his chair and focused on her. 'Mrs Bullman, did the doctor who treated you for the recent lost pregnancy give you any idea of what the problem was?'

'No, sir.'

'And your first successful pregnancy, Mrs Bullman, no complications there?'

'No, sir.'

'How old were you when your daughter was born?'

'I was sixteen,' she whispered.

'Did you receive proper treatment throughout that pregnancy?'

'No, sir. I didn't tell anyone about the baby . . . until she arrived, sir.' She focused on the pulled thread. It wouldn't be too difficult to mend, so long as she was careful not to make it worse on the way home. There was always the temptation to fiddle with it.

'I see. It wasn't a planned pregnancy?'

Betty shook her head. The room was roasting. A buzz of bored conversation from the waiting room drifted through the door. The doctor's pen scratched against the paper.

'Mr Bullman, I appreciate that this is a sensitive issue. But may I ask your wife a very personal question?'

Betty slid further down into her chair.

Jack crossed his legs. 'Yes, of course. We both want to get to the bottom of it and have a family. We'll both do anything we can to make that happen.'

'Good. Mrs Bullman.' The doctor had turned round to face her again. 'Do you believe anything happened during that first pregnancy that would affect your ability to have another child?'

Betty turned her wedding band round and round on her finger. She didn't look up as she nodded.

'I see,' the doctor said. 'Did you bleed for a time afterwards and suffer any ongoing pain?'

Betty nodded again.

'Hmmmmm.' The doctor scratched on his pad. There was a red mark on Betty's finger where she was twisting the ring.

'Mr Bullman.' The doctor turned to Jack. 'I think we need to refer your wife to a specialist for further investigation. I suspect that what happened in her first pregnancy caused a genital tract infection or pelvic inflammatory disease, or something of that sort, which has caused secondary infertility. It's fairly common after that sort of . . . occurrence. The fact that she was able to fall pregnant is positive, but we need to know why she lost those babies so late. My secretary will write to you with a date and further details.'

'Right,' Jack mumbled. He sounded uncertain now. 'Thank you, Doctor.' They stood, and Jack opened the door for Betty.

Back on the pavement, Jack turned to her, gripping her shoulders too tightly. 'What the hell was that all about? You've never said anything about that before. What happened while you were pregnant with Margaret that the doctor thinks is stopping us having a baby now?'

Betty started to cry. She couldn't tell him, she just couldn't.

Jack shook her again, harder this time. 'Tell me, for God's sake. I've got a right to know!'

Chapter 17

BETTY

FEBRUARY 1950

''Ow old are you, Betty? Twenty-nine, thirty?'

Betty looked at her mother across the dining table, her loaded fork paused before her open mouth. She knew what was coming.

'I'm twenty-eight, Mother, you know that,' she said as calmly as she could.

'If you want more children, you better 'urry up. You'll be drying up inside soon. And Margaret's what, twelve now? That's a big gap.' Her mother ladled the food into her mouth and managed a small smirk at the same time.

'Mother, for God's sake.' Betty looked past her mother to the sideboard where Margaret's school photos stood, and the picture of Winnie and her new baby.

'Winnie's preggers again, and 'er baby's only nine months old. And she's much younger than you.' As her mother chewed, small flecks of partially ground food flicked on to her chin.

'Yes, she wrote and told me.' The letter had made her cry all day. She was happy for Winnie – the girl was a born mother, she'd been wonderful with Margaret when she was small. But why could it not happen to her too? They were so desperate for a baby.

'Auntie Winnie's having another baby?' Margaret put her fork down and looked at her. 'You never told me. I love babies. I'll do a painting for her.'

Her mother turned towards Margaret, all smiles. 'You'd love a brother or sister, wouldn't you, Margaret? Must be so lonely 'ere all on your own. No one to play with, just your boring old ma and *step*-pa.'

Her mother always emphasised the word 'step'. It made her blood boil. What did she know? She couldn't have guessed the truth. Jack was the only person she'd told. And she'd kept the secret from him for more than a decade. She hadn't wanted to ever tell him, but he'd forced her eventually, standing outside that posh doctor's surgery after that awful appointment.

'I've got a right to know, Betty.' He'd gripped her too tightly, hurting her. 'Stop crying,' he shouted at her, grasping her face firmly between his hands.

'Oh, Jack. Jack, I'm so sorry.' She was sobbing properly now. 'I didn't realise it would mean I couldn't have another baby. I was just terrified of what Mother would say—'

'What your mother would say about what?'

Betty's lip quivered. 'What Mother would say if she found out I was expecting. So I tried to get rid of the baby,' she whispered.

Jack let go of her. 'How?' he said.

'I'd heard what the other girls did, so I did the same,' she whispered. 'Mother's kn-n-itting needle in the bath with some gin.'

Jack gasped. 'Oh, Christ.' He turned away from her and wrapped his arms around himself. She couldn't hear what he was saying.

She ran round in front of him, pulling at his arms. 'I'm so sorry, Jack. I know I should have said before. I was just so ashamed.' She realised her hands were wet with tears as she pulled at his arms.

'You could have killed yourself, Betty. Women die from *abortions*.' He hissed the word. His body was trembling. 'You should have told me before.' His voice rose and a red flush began to rise up his neck. 'I had a right to know that you might not be able to give me my children.'

'But I didn't know that then, Jack. I thought it would be fine. I'd had one baby, Margaret turned out well, despite that, so I thought it would be okay.' Her voice was shaking. She felt sick. Would he now leave her? Would she be back where she'd started?

He opened his eyes. She was looking up at him, her own eyes pleading. He held her gaze for several seconds, then he turned.

'Where are you going?' she asked.

'Home,' he said grimly, striding away. She ran to keep up with him, her heels click-clacking on the pavement.

Margaret's fork clattered to the floor and Betty automatically reached down to pick it up for her, pulling her from her memories.

'Are you going to have a baby, Mother? I'd love to have a sister.'

Margaret's very existence probably meant that she could never have Jack's child.

'I'm not having a baby, Margaret. Granny's getting confused.' Betty stood up abruptly and went into the kitchen.

There she leaned against the counter and focused on breathing. Her mother was impossible. Why did they invite her for Sunday lunch? It always upset her. And Jack would be bad-tempered all day. And take it out on her and Margaret.

'Lovely beef, Jack. Where did yer get it?' She could hear her father trying to make the peace. 'We don't get nothing like this at home.'

'I brought it back from the hotel especially. We're not really supposed to, but everyone does.' Jack had always got on well with her father. But then everyone did.

'We get lovely meat at 'ome, don't be ridiculous,' said her mother, an edge to her voice.

'Yes, dear, you do your best with the coupons, but it's nothing like this.' Her mother would be furious about that. Good. Betty walked back into the dining room.

Her mother was pursing her lips.

'You did well on Thursday, didn't you, Jack? Better than everyone expected,' her father said.

She knew Jack didn't really want to talk politics with her father who was proudly left-wing. But anything was better than goading her mother. 'Yes, quite a swing to the Conservatives. Attlee was lucky to keep his job.'

'I can't see them government lasting long.'

'No, not with such a small majority. But we need stability not change.'

She started to clear the table. Her mother, having lost her audience, got up to help. Just the pudding to go. How long would they stay after that? Not more than an hour surely?

In the kitchen, her mother was standing with her hands on her hips, staring at the pie. 'What's this, Betty?'

'It's a fruit pie, Mother, for pudding. As you well know. The custard you made is warming on the top there.'

Her mother watched as Margaret stacked the dishes near the sink, looking for something else to criticise. 'You know, you need to use a little more vinegar on them windows.'

Betty picked up the pie, ignoring her, and walked back out to the dining room. Her mother followed with the jug of custard.

'C'mon, everybody, let's tackle the pudding,' her mother announced. 'Fruit pies never were Betty's strong point, but I've made my famous custard so that'll cover a multitude of sins.' She smiled around the table.

'It looks lovely, Betty,' said Jack. 'I love all your puddings.'

The room was silent except for the sound of spoons scraping bowls.

She felt her mother's eyes on her again.

'Of course, when you 'ave another baby at your age, you'll find it 'ard to get that figure back again. *If* you 'ave another baby, I mean.'

Chapter 18

Emma

January 2019

It was a slow drive back to Brighton. Every time she thought the traffic was easing, another log-jam appeared. Seven hours after leaving her mother's flat, Emma finally drew up on her street.

Emma left the boxes with the bits and pieces she'd collected from the flat in the boot of the car and picked up the certificate file and her handbag. The skeleton frames of the hornbeam trees were etched against the wintry sky. Shrieking seagulls wheeled overhead or perched territorially on rooftops.

At the edge of her path, Emma stopped and looked at her house. Everything else might have changed in her life, but the house looked exactly like it always had done. Solid. Comforting. She felt it reach out and draw her in.

As Emma put the key in the lock, she could hear shouting on the other side. Libby telling James he was a pig – a fat, ugly pig. She opened the door and saw Libby and James slouched further down the hall staring daggers at each other.

'Hi, Mum. Thank God you're back. Dad's cooking is crap,' said James.

'Thanks a lot.' Nick came out of the kitchen, looking flustered, a tea towel over his shoulder and grease stains down his white T-shirt. Emma smiled at the sight of the three of them. She was home.

'Hi, Mum,' said Libby, a small smile making her pale face even more beautiful.

'Hi, darling, how's school?'

Libby shrugged.

'Hello, Em, you look worn out.' Nick drew her into his arms. 'Come on, you two, truce. Go and lay the table.'

'How was your physics mock, James?' asked Emma to his retreating back.

He turned and shrugged.

◆ ◆ ◆

Later, when they'd all had supper together, and James and Libby were in their rooms, she and Nick sat on the sofa together cradling large glasses of red wine.

'What a crazy few days,' Nick said.

'You or me?' Emma laughed.

'Both. The kids were unsettled with you being away. Funny how your mother managed to upset them even in death.'

'It was only three days, but it feels like so much has happened. So much has changed.'

'Show me what you found.'

Emma picked up the CND file and flipped through the pockets. She'd added a new one for her half-sister Elizabeth's birth certificate and slotted it in place. It seemed right that it should be part of the record of her mother's life, after being hidden for so long.

Nick studied it and sighed. 'I wonder who the father is . . . whether he's still alive,' he said, tracing his finger along the blank line. 'If he was the same age as Margaret, he might be.'

'Clare and I thought it was maybe someone from school. Mum got really bad O-levels after being quite a promising pupil – if all these school awards are anything to go by. Something happened in those last few months, and maybe that was it. She was seeing a boy from school and was distracted.'

Nick frowned. 'Do you think that's it? When people are in love, they might work less hard at school, but I don't think she would have neglected it entirely . . . Did something else happen to make her grades slip?'

'Well, she was pregnant. But even I was pretty distracted at that age and I wasn't having sex with anyone.'

'I suppose . . .' Nick flicked through the file.

They sat together in silence looking at the certificate and the photo, trying to picture her mother in 1953. What had happened that summer?

'Mum was just a bit older than Libby when she had Elizabeth. Imagine Libby pregnant,' said Emma.

'I'd rather not,' said Nick, pulling a face.

They sipped wine, and she moved into him, fitting her body against his while still cradling the glass. She felt herself properly relax for the first time since she'd found out her mother had died.

'Maybe Margaret wanted to give up the baby,' Nick said hopefully. 'Maybe she wasn't forced at all.'

'Yes, I wondered that too. How could she cope with a baby at sixteen, especially in those days?'

'Did your Granny Betty know – did she put her in that home? Did the father's family know? There are so many questions.'

'And not many answers,' Emma said.

'But you said you'd seen an adoption certificate among the solicitor's files?' Emma nodded. 'And you're sure it's not your step-grandfather's adoption of your mother? There was no "Jack" on there?'

'No, it definitely had the name Elizabeth on it.'

'Okay, then if the solicitor can get hold of a copy, it must be on public record. We should be able to find it.'

'I tried while I was up in Morecambe, but I don't think you can just access adoption certificates in the same way you can with births, marriages, and deaths.' She paused. 'I suspect he already had it on file. Maybe my mother gave it to him.'

'Well, let's try.' Nick disappeared out of the room and came back with his laptop, and the rest of the bottle of wine. He set both down on the table and googled 'find an adoption certificate'. They read and clicked in silence.

'I get why they'd be closed records,' Emma said at last. 'And I've already filled out the form, so there'll be a note on the Adoption Contact Register in case Elizabeth wants to get in touch. She may already be on there, so we could get an answer really quickly.'

'There are lots of "maybes", Em.' Nick put his arm round her shoulders. 'She may not want to be contacted. She may not be in the country. She may be dead.'

Emma wrenched her shoulders away from him. 'Don't say that.'

'I just wonder if the solicitor is right. This is a real can of worms, and we don't know what we're going to find. You're dealing with a lot just with your mother's death, let alone all of this.'

'Not you too. This is my can of worms and I'm bloody well going to open it. Out there is a child my mother rejected. I always wanted a sister and now I can have one.' She realised she was crying again and wiped her eyes angrily with her sleeve, leaving black mascara streaked across the cuff. 'All of this helps to explain why my mother was the way she was.'

'You know I fully support you doing this. I'm just worried what might happen. I can't help thinking there's something else going on here.' Nick slugged the rest of his wine.

'What's going on is that my mother had a baby by some boy at sixteen, put her up for adoption, and then when she had me felt full of regret for what she'd done first time round. She must have looked at me every day and thought about Elizabeth. No wonder she hated me.'

'Oh, Em.'

She was still crying and he pulled her towards him.

'How do you feel about her death now – not about all of this stuff, but about her dying? It's been an awful few days for you.'

'I've been thinking about that too. I think I miss most the relationship that we didn't have. And perhaps the realisation that her death means that can never change now. It can never be put right.'

'But your relationship with this new half-sister can be?'

'Yes, exactly.'

'I know it's your can of worms to open, but it's also your half-sister's,' Nick began tentatively. 'She may want it firmly shut. When people are adopted it's not always a happy story. She may not want to go back.'

'That's true, but I want to try.'

Chapter 19

MARGARET

FEBRUARY 1952

Margaret wandered into the sitting room, flicking her long dark hair over her shoulder. Her stepfather was sitting at the dining table, his newspaper spread across it. 'Where's Mother?' she asked.

Jack glanced up from the paper. 'She's gone to Westminster Hall to see the King.'

'I thought the King had died.' Margaret sat herself down in the dining chair opposite him and started to file her nails. She wanted to get them just like she'd seen in that magazine, the perfect oval shape. Then they wouldn't snag so much.

'There's no need to be rude, Margaret.' Her father looked up at her in that angry way of his. 'You know perfectly well that the king has died. Your mother has gone to pay her respects.'

He was so easy to goad. 'I think it's a waste of time. He's dead; he won't know whether she's gone or not.' She started blowing the nail dust off each nail on to the table. Her father loved that table. He was always going on about not putting anything on it without a cloth underneath.

He ignored her and returned to the paper but then muttered, 'That's not what your mother believes.'

'But it is what you believe, isn't it? You don't believe in all that church . . .' She searched for the right word. 'Crap.'

He looked up again, his eyes narrowing. It was hard not to smile. 'Please don't swear, Margaret,' he said, giving one of his sighs and going back to his paper.

'But you don't, do you? You never go to church with Mother, only at Christmas and Easter and stuff.' She took a small pot of red nail varnish out of her pocket and put it on the table. Then she carefully wiped each of her nails with the flannel. Slowly, methodically, Margaret started to paint the nails on her left hand. She watched his reaction to the smell. He wouldn't be able to help himself, he'd say something. He coughed.

'Does your mother know that you're doing that?' he said, looking up again and then glancing at the jar. 'Isn't that polish hers?'

'She won't mind.' Margaret smiled at him confidently. 'She always lets me try her stuff. We're the same shoe size and everything, size four.' She put her head to the side and looked at him pouting, just as she'd been practising in the mirror. The boys at school always seemed to melt when she did it, and offer her chocolate. She wondered casually whether it would work on him too. 'Don't you think we look alike?'

He examined her face for a long time, his eyes travelling from her lips to her eyes. He glanced down at her chest, none of the boys seemed able to resist doing that either. He took a deep breath and let it out slowly.

'You do look very alike,' he said eventually, and then focused back down at his paper. She watched him. She could tell from the way his eyes were moving – darting around the page rather than moving along line by line – that he wasn't really reading it. He was thinking about her chest. How funny that it wasn't just boys her own age, but it worked on men her father's age too.

When her breasts had started to grow a couple of years ago, she'd been embarrassed. It had been excruciating strapping them down to play tennis and hockey. The other girls had stared at them and asked to touch them, comparing them with their own flat chests. But she was beginning to realise they could be a benefit. And while it was inconvenient they were there, they gave her a power she'd never had before. And they worked on men of all ages.

She went back to painting her nails. Mother really did have the best nail polish.

Suddenly her father stood up, jogging the table and making the brush slip on to her finger. Damn. She wasn't sure there was any polish remover.

'I wish you'd do that in the bathroom,' he said irritably. He walked out of the room. Then she heard the front door bang.

Margaret used another nail to remove the extra polish and started to paint her other hand. They were going to look very pretty, just like the girls in the magazine.

Chapter 20

Emma

January 2019

Nick had left for work by the time Emma's phone alarm trilled her awake the following morning. In those few moments of floating consciousness, she was back in the Morecambe flat, sitting in the visitor's chair, asking her mother about Elizabeth, the girl in the painting watching over them.

Seven a.m. The usual mad hour getting the children to have breakfast, making packed lunches and then getting them out the door to school and college on time. At least she had compassionate leave and wasn't due back to work until next week.

Emma helped James with some last-minute revision for his next physics paper and slipped an extra chocolate bar into Libby's packed lunch. She looked exhausted at the moment.

◆ ◆ ◆

Emma's Thursday catch-up with her friend Ruth in the local cafe was a key part of her week and, even though she was still off work, she was glad of the distraction of thinking and talking about something other than her mother's death and her new half-sister.

'How's everything going?' Ruth's sympathetic face made her want to walk out.

'I'm okay.' She smiled the tight-lipped smile she'd got used to over the past week and sat down in the threadbare ornate chairs that Metrodeco specialised in.

'The usual, ladies?' The waitress with the tattoo sleeves and the facial piercings had come over.

'Yes, please. Thanks.' Emma's smile was genuine this time.

They were at risk of being as much an institution on Thursday afternoons as the place itself.

She'd known Ruth since they'd qualified as surveyors at the same time, both working for Grosvenor, a big property firm in London. All those late nights studying, and then the even later night celebrating afterwards when they'd passed first time. Their lives had mirrored each other's after that with weddings and babies happening within a few months of each other. Ruth had moved down to Brighton a few years before Emma. So when Emma and Nick began to get tired of the grime of the capital and worried about schools for James and Libby, it was an easy decision to swap their pokey south London flat for a bigger place by the sea near where Emma had grown up.

Despite her initial reluctance, it suddenly felt good to talk about everything with someone else.

'Blimey, Em, that's a real head-fuck. But you know that finding your half-sister, if you do find her, could create more problems, not solve them.'

'I know,' Emma said, through a mouthful of cake. 'You're not the first to point that out. But it might help me to understand the past. Why my mother was like she was.'

'True. I know you had a hard time with her.'

'I feel robbed.' She'd never said it before. But realised it was true. For years, she'd been witness to all her friends' idyllic childhoods and found hers didn't match up. She could feel herself welling up again. When would she be able to talk about her mother without crying?

'Robbed?'

'Of a different childhood. A better one. Mine was very lonely, especially after Mum disappeared for a while. I was dumped in boarding school – or at least that's what it felt like. To have had a sister would have made all the difference.'

'Very few childhoods, very few lives, are perfect. They might look that way, but behind closed doors no one really knows what another person's life is like.' Ruth drained the last of her tea and signalled to the waitress for another pot. 'And Elizabeth would never have been a real sister to you because she was so much older.'

Emma took another sip of the tea.

'I had a friend at school who had a really difficult relationship with his father,' said Ruth. 'He was always so off with him and definitely favoured the younger brother. It was obvious even when I went round there. And he could never understand why. It upset him all his life – well into adulthood. He still lives locally now.'

'Oh yes?' said Emma, a twinkle in her eye.

'A few years ago both his parents died in quick succession – it was really sad. He was going through his mother's things with his younger brother and they came across loads of old photos. One of them was his mum with a man's arm round her waist. They looked very close, very intimate. On the back, it was dated eleven months before he was born. And the man looked exactly like Charlie – my friend. It became obvious to Charlie and his brother that there had been some "overlap"' – Ruth mimicked little inverted commas in the air – 'between this man and their dad. And the chances are that the man in the photo was actually Charlie's biological dad – not the father who had brought him up.'

'And?'

'And Charlie's dad knew that – or at least suspected it – and that's why he treated Charlie so differently to the younger brother who was born two years later.'

'So what did Charlie do?' Emma's teacup was hovering between her saucer and her mouth.

'He went looking for this other man.'

'And? What happened?'

'He didn't want to know him, the birth dad. They were the spitting image of each other apparently. But he didn't want to know. Just as the dad who brought him up didn't want to know. The birth dad denied being close to Charlie's mum, even though by then they'd unearthed tonnes of evidence to show they'd been together.'

'How did Charlie take that?' Emma poured a cup of tea from the new pot.

'He was devastated. He'd wanted answers and thought that he'd found them.'

Emma slumped back down in her chair.

'Going back and digging up old history isn't always the answer, y'know,' added Ruth, leaning forward and putting her hand on Emma's knee. 'Surely the story shows you that. You might not find anything positive. You could risk ending up like Charlie: disappointed, let down, and wishing you'd never started the whole thing.'

Emma looked away towards the waitress, who was busy doing complicated latte art on top of two enormous cups of coffee.

'Your mother kept Elizabeth secret for a reason. Just as Charlie's mother never let on about his biological father. Some things are best left.'

'But you don't understand. How my mother treated me affected my whole life – my confidence, my relationship with Nick, my relationship with my own children. Just as it affected Charlie.' Emma realised she was talking too loudly and the cafe had gone quiet. Even the tattooed waitress was listening. She dropped her voice. 'I've always wondered why, and now I think I know. And I want to meet my sister.'

'I know you do, Em,' Ruth said, touching her hand. 'But I'm worried for you, that's all.'

Emma smiled at her and gripped her hand briefly. 'I just wish I could find Elizabeth before Mum's funeral. She has a right to be there.'

Chapter 21

Margaret

June 1952

Margaret always loved their family days out. Her mother and father would decide where to go and they'd get the train up to Waterloo, or sometimes the bus. Every year around this time, they went to Buckingham Palace. They'd walk down the Mall arm in arm, Margaret in the middle. When she was young, her mother and father had swung her between them. She remembered screaming as she was flung in the air. Sometimes her father had carried her on his shoulders. She had a vague memory of being in Trafalgar Square looking at Nelson and a pigeon landing on his head and her swatting it away. But she was far too grown-up for swinging. She was the same height as her mother now.

Outside Buckingham Palace, they waited for the Changing of the Guard, their family custom. Although it was June, a slightly chill breeze was blowing. Margaret stood next to her mother, peering through the black railings at the figures in red tunics and bearskin hats standing rigidly outside the building. They always came early, to make sure they got a good position. She hopped from foot to foot to keep warm, regretting wearing the patent shoes with the slight heel, although they went so well with the stockings. She tried to see over her shoulder to make sure the back seams were even. They were her mother's and she was wearing the same type of shoes too, but a longer skirt. Suddenly a gust of wind caught her skirt and it ballooned up.

'Argh,' cried Margaret, grabbing it from behind, and keeping her hands on her bottom to keep it in place.

The Old Guard started to form up in front of the palace. 'Where's your father?' her mother said, looking either side of them.

Margaret swivelled round to look for him. He was standing some distance behind, watching, an odd expression on his face. The breeze shifted again and tugged at Margaret's skirt.

'What are you doing waiting over there? Come and join us.' Margaret smiled and called him over.

Betty had also turned around and was watching him, her expression unreadable.

As he strode towards them, they moved apart so he could squeeze in the middle. He slipped his arms around both of their waists and drew them to him, just as the group of new bearskin hats and red tunics from the Wellington Barracks appeared. Margaret felt his thumb creep under her waistband as the Household Division stood to attention. She shivered.

Chapter 22

Emma

February 2019

Emma stood outside Woodvale Crematorium, her arms wrapped around her coat against the biting February wind. The celebrant had come out a few minutes before the service was due to begin and was chatting to Nick, who had put on his work suit and a black tie. James and Libby stood around on their phones. James wore his black tie as if it were a noose, looking permanently uncomfortable. Emma had been worried that Libby would wear one of her too-short skirts, but instead she looked demure in a knee-length loose-fitting black dress, which Emma took a while to realise was from her own wardrobe.

Emma knew so little about her mother's final years, she hadn't known who to tell about her funeral. She'd enclosed short notes with the various bequests and had asked Mr Eals to spread the word. He seemed to know more about her mother than anyone else. But Emma hadn't heard back from anyone.

The sea mist had been low all day, the gravestones outlined spookily in the murkiness. It had hardly seemed to get light at all, which was why she missed the grey Jaguar coming up the drive to the chapel until it was almost upon them. She peered through the windscreen as it came to a halt, but could only see her own family's awkward reflection.

They waited to see who the driver was, stamping their feet and breathing into their hands. She should have brought gloves. Even the celebrant stopped his professional funeral small talk to watch as the driver slowly eased out of the car. She'd only ever seen Mr Eals in black, so she wasn't ready for the flash of red waistcoat. He walked carefully towards them.

'Margaret hated black,' he said, 'so this is my small homage to her.'

Emma smiled. 'Hello, Mr Eals, I wondered if you'd come.'

'I like to see my clients safely on their way.' He shook Nick's hand and smiled gravely at the children. 'Shall we go in? Are you expecting anyone else?'

'I had hoped that I would have been able to track Elizabeth down in time . . .' Mr Eals looked at her sharply. 'But no luck yet.'

The chapel was big enough for at least fifty people. It was dominated by the wicker coffin – her mother's last attempt to reduce her impact on the environment – lying on a plinth at the front. The five of them spread out across the pews: James and Libby together towards the back, Nick and Emma sitting in the front on the left, Mr Eals on the right. He coughed as he settled into the front pew, the sound echoing around the empty spaces.

Emma's father's funeral had been so different. He'd been a popular man and died while he still knew a lot of people. The church had been packed and the funeral sad but joyous. It had seemed so straightforward. She'd loved her father and had been devastated by his death. The children had felt the same. There was nothing left unsaid. No complications. Funerals were supposed to be the concluding chapter of someone's life, but her mother's story was still such a mystery – whole chapters had been ripped out and she'd never spotted that they were missing until it was too late.

Over the years, Emma had sat through many funerals. The familiar rituals were calming and comforting. But this was different. The service wasn't in a format Emma recognised – her mother had chosen a humanist service. It started with a recorded clanging of bells and some sort of Buddhist chant. She could hear James and Libby stifling giggles.

As the bells faded away, the celebrant reappeared. 'Welcome, everyone, to our celebration today of the life of Margaret Bullman. I never met Margaret but she left specific instructions for her funeral which we'll carefully follow today as we honour her life. I'd like to start by asking you to share a happy memory you may have of Margaret.' Emma sighed. She would have much preferred the traditional Christian service where you could just sit and listen.

The celebrant was looking at them all expectantly. A voice came from the back of the chapel, making Emma jump. 'I remember visiting Granny when I was little and she always had really lovely cakes.' James. Emma smiled. Her mother had started his lifelong obsession with Mr Kipling's French Fancies.

Mr Eals rose slowly to his feet, gripping the front of the pew. 'I first met Margaret in the 1950s in London. She was working at Liberty. She really was more full of life than anyone I've ever met. She had an enthusiasm for life, for trying new things, for learning, that was quite extraordinary.' His voice was faint and he seemed transported back by his own memories, gazing into the space above the coffin.

It was so at odds with her own memories of her mother. Angry. Bitter. Stubborn. Difficult. After that first year at boarding school, when she'd only seen her aunt in the holidays, her father had finally picked her up at the end of the summer term. She hadn't known what overjoyed meant until she saw his old Austin Allegro pull up outside the school, when she was expecting her aunt's taxi. He looked much older than she remembered, with more grey hair and deep lines either side of his mouth. His eyes looked sadder. But he still swung her up in the air and caught her.

'Oh, Emmie, I missed you.'

'I missed you too, Daddy, so much.'

On the journey back through the lush Sussex countryside in the full bloom of summer, they talked non-stop about school, the house, the cats, and the dog. But when they pulled up the drive to their house, he stopped the car and turned to face her.

'Emmie, Mummy hasn't been very well. She's still very poorly, so don't expect too much from her. She's got a long way to go to recover so she's staying in the spare room.' He spoke quietly and seriously and looked her directly in the eye.

'What's wrong with her?' Emma copied his tone, trying to be grown-up.

But David just shook his head. 'I know I can rely on you to be sensible and not make too much noise.' He turned away, opened the car door and lifted out the trunk from the boot. She skipped up the garden path to the front door and rang the bell, but no one came to the door. Instead her father fumbled with his keys while tipping the trunk on its side. Emma tumbled into the house and threw herself at the dog before rushing off to her room.

It was exactly the same as she'd left it last summer. The same covers on the bed. The same toys on the shelves. It all looked frozen in time, the sunlight showing the layers of dust. She ran along the corridor to the spare room and opened the door with a flourish. Despite her father's warning, she didn't think to knock. She was immediately plunged into darkness, even the light from the window on the landing failing to penetrate the shadows.

'Mummy?' She could just about see a shape lying on the bed underneath the painting of the girl in the midnight maze.

'Go away, will you. I'll be down later.' It wasn't like her mother's voice. It was tense and irritable. Frightened. She closed the door quietly, her hands shaking, and ran back along the corridor into her bedroom where her father had left the trunk. Emma spent the rest of the afternoon unpacking and rearranging her room, erasing memories of boarding school and thinking about a long summer at home. She went downstairs and found her father in the kitchen, preparing supper.

'I didn't know you could cook, Daddy.' She jumped up and down next to him, keen to help.

'You mustn't expect too much, I'm still learning, Emmie.' He sat her up next to him on the counter as he chopped.

'What's wrong with Mummy? She was really horrid to me.'

'Oh, Em, you didn't go and see her did you? I told you not to disturb her.' Her father's face looked tense. 'She's very poorly. But she will get better. I know she will.'

Dinner was strained. Emma came into the dining room to find her mother already sitting at the table. The lights were off and the blinds pulled halfway down the windows making it hard to see. Emma automatically switched on the overhead light and her mother groaned. Emma switched it off quickly.

'Mummy doesn't like the lights on, darling,' her father said, walking into the room with a pie dish. 'It affects her nerves.' They sat around the table in silence, eating a quite nice fish pie with peas. Much better than the ones at school.

'Your father's peas have done well this year,' her mum said quietly. Emma looked up at her, unsure how to respond. Her mother was looking at her father. 'Thank you for making supper and collecting Emma. Now we can be together as a family again.'

Her father had nodded and smiled encouragingly.

Had her mother been happy then? She couldn't remember any time that her mother had been what you'd traditionally describe as happy.

Nick nudged her. 'Emma, darling . . .'

She looked up and realised that everyone was looking at her expectantly. 'Do you have a memory of your mother that you'd like to share, Emma?' the celebrant asked again.

Emma thought about her mum and how little she'd known her. How now she would never really know her. She bit her lip. 'I remember—' She faltered, unsure of what she was going to say.

'Maybe the time we came up to Morecambe with James as a baby,' Nick prompted gently.

They'd walked along the front to the Midland Hotel and had tea. Her mother had pushed the pram for a bit, Nick and Emma walking behind sharing a surprised look with one another. She'd appeared to be the perfect grandmother.

'Yes, that. The tea at the hotel on the front. It was sunny. James slept all the way through it, even when Mum took him out of the pram to—' Emma's voice cracked and she couldn't continue. Then the tears started to slip down her cheeks and she found she couldn't swallow. Libby slipped into the pew beside her and handed her a damp tissue. Nick finished the story before 'Ride of the Valkyries' drowned out all her thoughts.

They emerged into the fading light, blinking, Nick's arm around her shoulders, Libby at her other side. Emma was still crying, dabbing at her eyes with Libby's now sodden tissue. There were three wreaths displayed on the ground outside the chapel. The traditional white lilies that Nick had ordered the day before, a circle of white chrysanthemums, and a spray of exquisite white roses tied with simple raffia. Emma bent down to read the labels.

Margaret, you were a great friend and confidante. You're forever in my heart. Clare.

Emma could imagine Clare sitting in her kitchen, looking at the painting of the little girl in the maze and ordering chrysanthemums. They were very her. Tidy, delicate flowers. She leaned towards the roses. Who were they from?

No matter that our hands cannot entwine

For all these days I hold you in my heart.

The tears came quicker now, dripping down her face and on to the label, obscuring the beautiful words. It was suddenly hard to breathe. Who had written these lines? Who would have described holding her mother in their heart? Her mother had been single after splitting up with her father. But someone had loved her. She touched a petal, as cool and soft as a silk sheet. Had she known she was loved? Had she loved them back?

She picked the card up from the roses and stood to see Nick helping Mr Eals back into the old Jaguar. The door closed quietly and the car moved smoothly off down the drive. Nick strode back over to her.

'You know he drove all the way from Morecambe to be here, in one stint? That's some client support. Our solicitor doesn't even want to come to our office round the corner.'

'Maybe he was more than just her solicitor,' Emma said, remembering Clare telling her that Margaret had died with her solicitor at her side. She'd presumed it was for the last-minute changes to the will, but maybe it was more than that. She looked down at the card.

◆ ◆ ◆

That evening, they all sat around the table eating lasagne.

'Thank you all for coming to Granny's funeral, and sharing your memories. And for giving me that tissue, Libby, that was kind.'

Libby spoke through a mouthful of garlic bread. 'Why were you crying so much? You didn't get on with Granny anyway, and you hadn't seen her for years.'

Emma sighed. 'No, but sometimes when you lose someone you didn't get along with, it's harder than when you lose someone you loved unequivocally. You realise that you can never put it right.'

'I liked Granny,' said James. 'Why did we stop going up to see her?'

'I don't know really,' said Emma. 'It was just such a long journey when you were both little, I suppose. And then you get out of the habit.'

Emma glanced at Nick and he nodded.

'We have something to share with you both. It's about Granny and her will,' she started.

Both James and Libby looked up expectantly.

'We wanted to wait until after the funeral, until things were a little more settled,' added Nick.

'Did Granny leave us something?' asked James.

'Yeah, she left you a lifetime's supply of French Fancies,' scoffed Libby. James gave her a look.

'Granny left you both something,' said Emma. 'But it's more than that. When I was clearing out her flat, I discovered that Granny had had a baby as a teenager, when she wasn't that much older than you, Libby.'

'What?' said Libby. 'But who? Not you.' Both children's eyes were wide, listening to her intently, just as they had when they were small and she was reading them a story.

'No, not me. This baby was born in October 1953. A little girl that Mum called Elizabeth Margaret.'

'That's my name,' said Libby immediately.

Emma nodded. 'Yes, we realised that too. It must have been quite a shock for Granny when we gave you the same name as her own daughter.'

James leaned forward. 'But isn't that what happened to Granny's mum too? Didn't she have her as a teenager?'

'Yes,' said Emma. 'History repeated itself.'

'So where's this person now? Do you know her?' asked James.

Emma shook her head. 'I've no idea where she is or what happened to her at all.'

'But we are trying to find out,' said Nick. 'Your mum is keen to meet who would be her half-sister.'

Both children were quiet as they digested the news.

'And this leads us on to the will,' said Emma softly. 'It's a rather odd situation. Usually I'd expect a grandmother to split a gift equally between her grandchildren but that's not been the case.'

James and Libby glanced at each other and then looked at Emma. She turned to James. 'Granny left you a gift of one thousand pounds.'

'I can go away with my mates . . .'

'Hold on. To be invested for you for when you're twenty-one.'

'Oh, OK,' he said. 'Great twenty-first party, though.'

Emma laughed and turned to Libby. 'Granny left you her flat, darling. Dad and I are going to sell it and invest the money for you. Again, for when you're twenty-one.'

Libby's mouth fell open. 'That whole flat?' she said. 'Mine?'

'I thought I was Granny's favourite,' said James, crossing his arms in front of his chest.

'We're not sure why Granny chose to do this, but we think it may be linked to the baby that she had when she was young – the fact that Libby has the same name as that baby.'

'That's insane,' said Libby. 'It's like I'm rich suddenly.'

'What did you get, Mum?' asked James.

Emma gave a small smile. 'If it's any consolation, James, I got nothing at all. My name wasn't mentioned in Granny's will.'

Nick covered her hand with his and squeezed it gently.

When the call came through in the early hours of the morning, they didn't even realise Libby wasn't at home in her bedroom. An unfamiliar female voice told Emma she'd found Libby at The Level, high or drunk or both – but *compos mentis* enough to give them Emma's mobile number. Nick and Emma both rushed to Libby's room only to discover the sleeping Libby was just some screwed-up clothes.

Emma pulled on jeans and a jumper and was in the car within minutes. She'd heard of friends of friends having to pick up their drunk fifteen-year-olds from parks after dark, but she'd never dreamed that could be Libby. And not at two in the morning. And at The Level, a well-known local dealing spot.

'I'm fine,' slurred Libby, when Emma eventually found her half passed out in the skate park with the policewoman. 'Just the pill I took was a bit stronger than usual,' she whispered to her mum. With the help of the police, they got her home and into bed. Afterwards, Emma and Nick lay in their own bed wide awake.

'How could we not have known she was taking drugs?' said Emma, rubbing her eyes. 'And why did her friends just leave her at The Level on her own?'

'We need to come down hard on her,' Nick said. 'We need to show she can't behave like this.'

'I'm not sure that will work,' Emma replied. 'She'll just rebel even more. Remember what she was like as a toddler. And she still needs to know she can talk to us.'

'Every teenager needs strong boundaries. It makes them feel safe. And she has GCSEs next year. It's an important time,' Nick said.

Emma woke the following morning feeling bleary. She laid in bed fretting about Libby. Nick was still asleep and she left him, hoping he didn't have a morning meeting, but the smell of bacon made her get up. Downstairs, Libby, looking as if she'd had a full twelve hours' sleep, was busy making two bacon bagels.

'Morning, Mum,' she said breezily, swigging direct from the orange juice bottle.

'Libby, what on earth are you doing?'

'Bacon soaks up hangovers, you know that.'

'I didn't think you'd be up.'

'I've got another full-day art assessment – counts towards my GCSE coursework.'

'And you chose last night to go out?'

Libby shrugged. 'I've been leaving the house at night for ages, Mum,' she said, stuffing half the bagel into her mouth. 'Everyone does.' And she walked down the hallway, and out of the front door.

Emma stood watching the space where she'd been.

Chapter 23

EMMA

FEBRUARY 2019

The following Sunday, Emma's mobile rang and she answered it without thinking.

'I found something.' She could hear the excitement in Clare's voice.

'Clare?' *Hold on*, Emma mouthed to Libby, sitting next to her on the sofa. 'I still want to talk to you.' Libby picked up her own phone and started scrolling.

'Yes, it's me. I've found a letter from your half-sister Elizabeth.'

'What? Where?' Emma had become almost accustomed to Clare's random phone calls, started as if midway through a conversation.

'A letter from Elizabeth to Margaret, dated 1981. It was in a book I took from her flat.'

'What?' Emma's mind jumped back. 1981 was the year it had all gone wrong. The year she went to boarding school and her mother disappeared. She would have been five, six. Emma stood up and walked into the kitchen to look for headphones. They'd decided Nick was going to prepare lunch so that she could have a chat with Libby.

'Elizabeth had tracked Margaret down. She wrote to her at a place called Greystones—'

'My home.' She'd loved that house, with the huge garden backing on to farm fields. Nick looked up at her questioningly and Emma whispered, '*Clare.*'

'Saying that she'd discovered she was her birth mother and she wanted to meet.'

'My God. Where was Elizabeth living then?'

'Bizarrely not that far away. In Steyning.'

'Bloody hell. That's, what, five miles from Greystones – only fifteen miles from here. I wonder if she's still there?'

'That's what *I* thought.' The voice grew more distant but at the same time seemed to reverberate. Emma realised Clare'd put her on speakerphone.

'So I looked on Facebook. Hold on, I'm just getting the laptop. The thing is, she had a different surname from the one we were looking for. Not Bullman. But what must have been her adopted name or even married name.'

'And?'

'It's Penn. Elizabeth Penn. P-E-N-N.'

'Sounds American. Pennsylvania.'

'Yes, it does, doesn't it? But if she went to America to get married or whatever, she came back. She's still in Steyning. According to Facebook.'

Emma's heart skipped a beat. She opened the odds and ends drawer and started rifling through it. Nick was noisily chopping vegetables.

She found the headphones and plugged them into her ears, and went back to the sitting room. Libby had disappeared. *Damn*, she thought. It had been hard enough to get her to sit down in the first place. She shouldn't have answered the call.

Emma touched the Facebook app on her phone.

'Okay, I'm on Facebook. Oh God. There are tons of Elizabeth Penns.'

'You need to search by area. There's nothing for Steyning, so try Worthing. It's the local major town.'

'I know Worthing. I went to school there when I was very little.'

'Once you've searched there, she's the . . . one, two, three, four . . . ninth one.' Emma couldn't help feeling irritated with Clare at times. She had completely taken over the search for Elizabeth.

Emma swiped down her phone. 'How did you work that out?' She clicked on the tiny image, and her mother's dark, challenging eyes stared out at her, framed with a silvery fringe and bob. Emma almost dropped the phone. Elizabeth had her mother's cheekbones, which Emma had also inherited. But there was also something else she recognised in the face but couldn't place.

'It's her, isn't it?' Clare's voice was quiet.

Emma's voice broke. 'It is,' she whispered.

'And it's not just her face. She lists herself as coming from London, and we know she was born in London.'

'Loads of people are born in London,' Emma said automatically.

'And her home town as Steyning.'

'There must be lots of people who move from London to the Sussex countryside.' Emma's heart was beating faster. Did she want this woman to be Elizabeth? She wasn't sure.

'There's more. Have you clicked on any of the photos?' There was a jubilance in Clare's voice.

Emma was still staring at the face, transfixed by its resemblance to her mother and trying to piece together what else it was about Elizabeth that looked familiar to her. She reminded her of someone

139

she knew. It was something about the high forehead. She'd covered it well with the fringe, but you could still tell. She was an attractive-looking woman, someone her mother would call 'handsome'. Not beautiful, but handsome.

'Emma? Are you there? Have you clicked on the photos?' There was definitely a triumphant edge to Clare's voice.

'What? Sorry?'

Clare sounded impatient. 'Click on the photos tab.'

Emma slowly touched the photo icon. She saw it straight away. The same picture that she'd seen for the first time less than a fort-night ago. Her teenage mother Margaret holding a baby on the doorstep of Birdhurst Lodge. She pressed on the image to enlarge it even though her mother's anxious smile and too-tight holding of the baby were now burned into her brain. The enlargement brought up the picture caption.

> *Do you recognise this woman from 1953? This is my birth mother who I've been searching for. I was born in a mother and baby home in 1953 and adopted by my parents soon after. I would dearly love to meet my birth mother and any other birth relatives.*

The photo had been shared more than one hundred and fifty times.

Emma slowly put the phone down on her lap, but she could still hear Clare's voice through the headphones.

'It's her, isn't it?' Clare's voice was ecstatic. 'It took me hours to find it. You wouldn't believe the number of Elizabeth, Liz, Liza Penns around aged sixty-six-ish. But it's definitely her. That's the same photo you showed me.'

Emma looked again at Elizabeth's profile picture and visualised her own face alongside it.

'Emma?' Clare sounded slightly annoyed.

'Can I call you back?' Without waiting for an answer, Emma pressed the red button, ending the call. She scrolled through the five other Facebook images on Elizabeth's profile which were public. One showed a younger Elizabeth, her arms around two teenage children, flanked by two elderly people. A classic family pose. Was there a husband? Or perhaps he was behind the lens. Another showed a sheepdog in what could be the Sussex countryside. Another was perhaps Elizabeth as a child. She had long dark hair like their mother. Emma enlarged the photo. It looked a little like the girl in the painting. And the final one was the profile picture, which was so puzzling to Emma. She clicked on it again, mesmerised by Elizabeth's eyes but disturbed by the familiarity she couldn't place.

She pressed on her phone's photo album and started scrolling through her own memories. There were the old family images of her as a child that she'd scanned in for her father's funeral. She flicked through them until she found one with her father, mother, and her together. She looked about eight. She flicked between the three images – the present day, her childhood, and Elizabeth's profile picture.

Elizabeth, she and Libby had inherited her mother's dark eyes, while Elizabeth and she had her mother's cheekbones. But neither Emma nor Libby had Elizabeth's high forehead or pointy ears. Maybe they belonged to her father, whoever he was. Her mother's teenage romance.

There was nothing else visible to the public on Elizabeth's profile. Emma's finger hovered over the 'Add Friend' button. She could message her now and tell her who she was. She could even comment on the baby picture. But no one would want to find out something like this through Facebook. The phone rang again and she accepted without meaning to.

Clare's voice came flooding through, a tumult of noise. 'Are you okay? Sorry, this must have been a terrible shock. But it's definitely her. Did you read the caption to the image?'

'Yes, I did.' Her voice felt weak.

'I've added her as a friend but she hasn't accepted yet. Maybe she doesn't go—'

'You've done what? For Christ's sake, Clare. You had no bloody right to do that.'

There was silence on the line. 'I thought you wanted to meet her. Don't you?'

'Yes, but not like this. Not through Facebook. I need time to think. To know what to say.'

'Oh, Emma, you don't need more time, darling. You just need to drop her a note, say who you are and what you've found out.'

'But, Clare, Elizabeth is searching for a mother – a mother who died two weeks ago, who we just cremated. I can't go blundering in.'

Clare hesitated. 'True, it needs to be handled sensitively.'

'And that means not through Facebook. She wrote to Mum in 1981, yeah? What did she say?'

'Let me read it out, hold on.'

'No, just take a picture of the letter and text it to me.'

'How do I do that?'

'Oh, never mind, read it out then if that's easier.'

'Okay.' Clare cleared her throat. '*Dear Mrs Randall, There's no easy way to say this, but I believe you're my birth mother. I was born on 7 October 1953 in Birdhurst Lodge and was adopted ten days later. After my mother died when I was twenty-six, my father encouraged me to search for my birth parents. I approached the Adoption Service but they said there was no letter on file for me, and no contact details for you. I left a letter with them for you, but maybe you didn't realise that you can now trace adopted children?*

Clare paused. 'Poor Elizabeth, it must have been awful to discover that her mother hadn't left a letter for her and didn't want to be in touch.'

Emma found she couldn't speak.

Clare continued. '*As the years have gone by, I've wondered who you are and what your life has been like since those days at Birdhurst Lodge. Have you had a good life or has that experience troubled you? Did you go on to marry and have other children? And I've wondered who my father is.*

'*I've been very lucky. My parents are wonderful people, who couldn't have children of their own but adopted me. They told me all along that I was special and different and loved especially because of that. But there's always been a feeling that I didn't truly belong with them, that I was lacking something, that there was a hole inside of me.*'

Clare's voice broke. 'Sorry,' she said and blew her nose loudly, the sound echoing down the phone.

'*Five years ago I got married, and then last month I had a baby of my own. Holding Emilia made me realise what it must have been like for you to give me up. And it made me all the more determined to find you. And it turned out it's not so difficult at all. I can hardly believe that you are close by. It seems that we are both drawn to the Sussex countryside. I'd love the chance to meet you and introduce you to my daughter – your granddaughter. I hope you feel the same.*

'*Love Elizabeth (née Bullman, adopted as Allen, now Penn).*'

Emma could picture her mother unsealing the letter with her brass letter opener, standing by the hall hat stand. Did she look at the signature, or did she just read the first line and know? Or did a sixth sense tell her who the letter was from? Had she been waiting for Elizabeth to get in touch?

Emma could imagine her slumping into one of the dining room chairs. Perhaps she couldn't read the whole letter. Once she realised who it was from, she might have put it down, unable to continue. Did she sit at the table and cry? Had she ever written a response? The fact that Elizabeth was still searching for her on Facebook two decades later suggested that she hadn't. She'd hidden the letter.

'So which book was this letter in?' Emma asked Clare.

'It was in the middle of a children's book that I took from her flat. *Mistletoe Farm*.'

'God, I remember that book. Blue cover with white writing. A tree on the front.'

'At least we know now that Elizabeth was adopted at birth,' said Clare, 'and not months or even years down the line. That must have meant a better start for her. To be with adopted parents right from the beginning of her life.'

'True, yes. From her letter it sounds like she had a good life too.' It suddenly dawned on Emma that she'd been worried and already feeling guilty that her adopted sister would have had a very different experience from her.

'So what are you going to do? Write her a letter?' Clare's voice had an urgency to it.

'I think so. I just need to think about it. I don't want to scare her off. And obviously she'll be upset that Mum has died. What's the address on the letter? There's a chance she's still there.'

Clare read out the address and Emma scribbled it down. She said a quick thanks and goodbye to Clare, then picked up her laptop and looked up the electoral register for an Elizabeth Penn in Steyning. She'd moved since she sent the letter but was still in the town, just off the high street. Had she ever walked past her in Worthing? Or stood next to her in a queue at the big out-of-town Tesco?

Before she could talk herself out of it, Emma picked up the photo of Margaret and the baby Elizabeth, and Elizabeth's birth certificate, and put them in her handbag. She called to Nick that she was popping out. She thought of Libby, hiding away in her room, saved from a difficult conversation by Clare's phone call. She'd sit down with her when she got back.

As she drove, her mind was blank. She couldn't allow herself to think. She had no plan. She just wanted to see Elizabeth in person, to see if she looked like her photo. Eventually she was off the main roads and driving through a series of postcard-pretty villages.

She passed the *Welcome to Steyning* sign as the satnav warned her to take the third exit at the roundabout. The route took her away from the high street to a more residential area. She turned left on to Mill Lane.

'You have reached your destination, which is on the left.'

Emma pulled up behind an old Land Rover, parked outside the house next door and gazed up at Elizabeth's home.

Wisteria Cottage might once have been covered in wisteria but right now it was bare and the modern red brick blazed uninterrupted into the street. The garden was well kept. Neat flower beds, stocked with plants even in the dead of winter, bordered the path to the white front door. The windows stared blankly at her, no sign of life behind the dark opaque panes. Maybe Elizabeth was away. Or having lunch out with her family or friends? Did her children still live here? But they would be grown-up themselves. If she was midsixties, her children would likely be in their twenties or thirties. She could be a grandmother. Emma imagined James and Libby at that age. They would one day move out – James was already looking at universities and Libby had talked about going travelling.

She was so deep in thought, staring unseeing at the house, that she didn't notice the car pull up behind her. The doors banging shut startled her. A man and a woman walked past her car, the man catching the flowers he was holding on her wing mirror as he squeezed between the house's front wall and Emma's car. The woman went round the other side. She was laughing and walking awkwardly.

Then it all happened so suddenly. As the couple walked down the garden path, the front door to the house opened and an older woman – with the same silver bob from the Facebook photos, and wearing a faded apron over dark trousers – was framed in the doorway. She ushered the couple into the house. The door quickly closed and they must have moved to the back of the house because the front windows remained dark. Emma sat paralysed, trying to take it all in.

Her phone trilling jolted her out of her daze.

'You okay, darling? Where are you? Dinner won't be too long. Another hour or so.'

'Okay, thanks. I'll be back in thirty minutes.'

'Where are you?'

'I'm in Steyning. Elizabeth lives here. I've just seen her.'

'Christ. Why didn't you say anything? How did you find her? Are you OK? You should have let me come with you.'

'I'll tell you later,' said Emma, gazing intently at Elizabeth's house. 'I'm on my way back.'

Chapter 24

Betty

July 1952

Some of her happiest times were when it was just her and Jack in the flat. Margaret seemed to bring so much tension with her these days that Betty could never relax when she was around. But when it was just the two of them, it reminded Betty of the early days of their marriage, when Margaret had been small. And they had been happier.

She wiped down the Formica top and started taking cutlery out of the drawer to set the table. Betty went through into the dining room, her heels click-clacking on the wooden floor. Jack was sitting at the dining room table, his copy of *The Times* spread across it. He always read it from cover to cover, telling her about any interesting stories he came across. He'd always educated her, explaining how the world worked, right from the first day they'd met.

He glanced up and smiled.

'What are we having, Betty?' he called.

'Pork chops, your favourite, followed by tinned fruit,' she said, laying out the knives and forks. 'I'm just waiting for Margaret to come home so I can serve up. She should have been back by now,' she said, looking at her watch.

'Come here.' He held out his arms towards her, and she hurried across the room and squeezed on to the dining chair beside him. He kissed her neck, and she was pleased she'd used the new bath oil he'd bought her. She turned her face and kissed him on the mouth.

'Errr, hello?'

She hadn't heard Margaret come in, but she stood framed by the doorway, looking at them.

'You two are disgusting.' Her school uniform was too small for her. She seemed to be bursting out of it everywhere. She must see if it could be let out any more. The poor girl with that chest. Betty had hated her breasts when she was young. They were such a constant source of embarrassment.

'Margaret, where have you been?' Betty sprang up. 'I've been worried about you. School finished ages ago.'

Margaret shrugged. 'Just hanging out with my friends, doing some painting.'

'You know you have to come straight home after school, I've told you that before. You're not yet fifteen.'

Betty felt so tired being a parent to Margaret. It wasn't just the challenge of dealing with her. The girl oozed life whereas she felt just so rundown all the time.

'Next month I will be, and then I can do what I like.'

She wondered if she had a boyfriend. Was that why she was always late? She'd said so many times to her to keep away from boys, not let them so much as wink at her. That was where it had all started for her. *He*'d winked at her one afternoon, and a wink had become a smile, the smile an excuse to stop and chat, and then before she knew it, she was pregnant and he'd stood her up at the altar. But Margaret just ignored her when she tried to talk to her about the dangers men presented.

'You will do no such thing,' said Betty. 'And say hello to your father, please.'

Margaret flicked her hair over her shoulder provocatively and smiled at him. 'Hello, Father.'

'Margaret.' Jack glanced at her briefly and then looked back down at his paper.

Margaret sauntered out into the hallway and Betty followed after her.

Chapter 25

EMMA

FEBRUARY 2019

It was an almost impossible letter to write. How to strike the right balance between being joyful that she'd found a long-lost sister and sad that the mother her sister wanted desperately to find had recently died?

Emma sat cross-legged on the bathroom floor with her laptop – the only place she could lock herself away from the family – for a long time before she started drafting the letter.

She tried to ignore the drum and bass pounding from James's room. Focused on her task, she chewed the side of her thumbnail as she wrote.

Dear Elizabeth or was that too formal? *Hi Elizabeth* felt too casual.

> *I know this letter will come as a shock, and be difficult to read, and I apologise in advance, but I'm keen to get in touch with you.*

She'd been told in a management course once that if you were going to deliver bad news to someone, it was best to come straight out and say that it was going to be a difficult conversation.

My name is Emma Bowen, I'm the daughter of Margaret Chapman, née Bullman.

Once she read that she'd know what it was all about.

I believe I have recently discovered that she is also your own mother.

Or did that sound too formal too? It was so difficult to get it right.

I'm sorry to say that Margaret died recently, at a nursing home in Morecambe after a long illness.

Best to just come out with it. She didn't want Elizabeth reading the letter thinking there might be some huge reunion only to discover at the end that her mother had died.

I found your birth certificate, together with some items from the first few days of your life among her things when I was clearing out her flat.

Did she need to explain how she'd got her contact details and her married name? She wouldn't have got that from the birth certificate.

I understand from a letter that we found in a book of Mum's that you got in touch with her many years ago. So

the news of her death will not be what you'd hoped. I'm
sorry to have to tell you this.

It all sounded so false, so fake. But how else could she say it?
I'm sorry I had a life with our mother, but you never knew her? Of
course not.

It was hot in the bathroom, the towel radiator pumping out
the heat into the tiny space. Emma took off her jumper and hung
it over the bath.

She shouldn't ramble on too long. She should come to the
point and suggest meeting up and then leave it to Elizabeth to
decide.

I live quite local to you – Brighton – and would love to
meet up and chat.

No, that sounded too trite.

Share my experiences of our mother if that would be help-
ful. I'd also be really interested to hear about your life.

That was the real truth. She was curious about Elizabeth and
desperate to meet this new half-sister that she'd known nothing
about, but always wanted.

Until recently, I thought I was an only child so the news
that I have a half-sister has been an exciting discovery,
and I'd like the opportunity to get to know you, if that's
not too painful a prospect.

My address and mobile are above. If you'd like to get in
touch and arrange to meet, then I'd love to hear from you.

Best to give her both the address and phone number, so she could decide how she got in touch.

Love? No, too cosy. She didn't even know her. *Yours sincerely?* She wasn't a bank. *Best wishes, Emma* sounded about right.

She read it through again and imagined the letter arriving at the little cottage, Elizabeth's puzzled face as she read the unknown handwriting. She wouldn't put her address on the back, so as not to give away the truth too quickly. Not that Elizabeth would recognise her name, but she might guess.

Finally Emma was as satisfied as she was ever going to be, and she hand wrote out a neat copy on her writing paper. Libby's previous letter to her grandmother, thanking her for a day out, was still faintly imprinted into the paper. *She was a good girl for writing to her*, she thought, and always without asking. It was hard to marry that Libby with the one she'd found out in the middle of the night. They were like two different people.

How long might it take Elizabeth to get in touch? In the next day or so, as soon as she received it? But, more likely, Elizabeth would think about it for a while and then she wouldn't get a call or a letter for a week or so. Maybe she wouldn't get in touch at all. It was going to be difficult just waiting, not knowing.

If she posted it now, it would be picked up first thing tomorrow. She walked to the letterbox on the corner and then let herself back in the house. Her stomach rumbled at the tantalising smell of roast beef.

'Em, Libs, James – dinner.'

It was a quiet meal. Libby sat swirling the cauliflower cheese into the gravy, creating a sludgy mess. James wolfed his food down and then sat impatiently waiting for everyone else to finish so they could start on the apple crumble. As they stacked the dishwasher afterwards, Emma said, 'I'm sorry we didn't get the chance to chat earlier, Libs, but let's sit down after this. I think it's important we talk properly about the other night.'

'We talked about it on Friday,' Libby said, picking up a dirty plate.

'I mean more than a two-minute conversation. You can't just leave the house in the middle of the night and be in the state you were in and expect there not to be consequences,' said Emma, hands on her hips.

'Stop making such a bloody fuss about it, Mum, it's not a big deal.'

'Not a big deal.' Nick, who had been quiet up until now, suddenly shouted. 'Are you actually serious, Libby?'

'Nick,' Emma said, her hand on his arm. 'This isn't the way.'

'Well, your way clearly isn't working,' he said. 'You, young lady, are grounded for two weeks. I don't want you going anywhere apart from school. You won't be allowed keys and your mother will take you to and from school every day.'

How on earth am I meant to do that and get to work? thought Emma.

Libby laughed. 'How the fuck are you going to police that? Are you going to lock me in my room?'

'If I need to, yes,' said Nick. 'If you behave like a juvenile delinquent, getting out at night and taking drugs, then you'll be treated like one.'

'I'd like to see you try,' said Libby, and she walked out of the kitchen, slamming the door behind her.

'Come back here, right now,' shouted Nick.

They heard Libby run up the stairs.

'Let her calm down a bit and then we can speak to her quietly in her room,' Emma said to Nick. 'Shouting at her doesn't work.'

Nick shoved a glass into the dishwasher and swore as it cracked. 'She needs to learn a bit of respect, speaking to us like that.'

Emma turned to James, who'd been silently wiping down the kitchen surfaces. 'James, did you know about any of this?'

James looked at her. 'All the girls are like it, Mum. The girls in my year went through that too. Then they chill out and become normal again.'

'Really?' Emma said. 'And the drugs?'

The front door slammed, reverberating through the house.

'What the hell?' said Nick, opening the kitchen door and running down the hallway. He opened the front door and disappeared. Emma followed and stood at the front doorway, biting her lip. A few minutes later, Nick came back breathless.

'I couldn't find her. She literally just disappeared. I don't know how she could have got away so fast.' He bent over, gasping.

'Oh, Nick, we scared her off. What if she's actually run away?'

'She'll come back,' said James, standing behind them. 'She just wants to feel in control of stuff. She'll be OK. She'll just have gone to a friend's house.'

'I think we should go through her room, see what drugs she's taking,' said Nick.

'No, Nick, she deserves some privacy. Don't do that,' said Emma. She was glad she hadn't told him about the call from the school she'd received asking her to come in to talk about Libby's behaviour. 'Come on, let's sit down and wait. Like James says, I'm sure she'll come back.'

They sat on the sofa staring into space. 'I overreacted, didn't I?' said Nick after a while.

Emma nodded. 'Well, perhaps, yes. It's easy to.'

'She just pushes my buttons. I can't help myself.'

'I know.'

'Anyway, let's talk about something else. You haven't told me. How did you find Elizabeth?'

Emma explained about how Clare had found Elizabeth, and then how she had driven to her house and thought she may have seen her at the door, and then writing her the letter.

'You've already written her a letter? Christ, Em, what about talking things through, discussing it first? We're in this together, you know.' He looked hurt.

'I know, I'm sorry. But I just wanted to do it quickly so it would get to her as soon as possible.'

Nick sighed and held his head in his hands. 'Don't cut me out, Em. I'm here to support you, but I can't do that if you don't share it with me.'

◆ ◆ ◆

Emma woke in the early hours of the morning. The room was stiflingly hot. She sat up and looked over Nick's sleeping body at the clock. 1.43 a.m. The red neon light burned through the dark room. She fell back on the pillow, every muscle in her face tensed into willing herself to sleep. Libby had returned at 10 p.m. It was past her curfew but wasn't late-late. So why had Nick immediately gone nuclear? She slowly counted back from one hundred and her mind drifted again. She hadn't quite believed in Elizabeth until she saw her. Now she knew that a few miles away was her sister – and what could be a nephew or niece. A whole new family.

She swung her legs over the side of the bed and walked over to the radiator, expecting it to be belching out heat. It was stone cold. The clock read 2.03.

She pulled on her dressing gown and walked on to the landing, pausing to listen for the sounds of children breathing. Nothing from James's bedroom, but further down the landing resonated with Libby's snoring. It was reassuring now. She was home. Despite having her adenoids taken out as a little girl, she still snored. She briefly wondered whether they should put a baby monitor in her bedroom to alert them if Libby was trying to leave in the middle of the night. Then she realised how ridiculous that was.

She crept into Libby's room. She looked so young when she was sleeping, her arms thrown above her head, just how she'd slept as a baby. All the anger smoothed from her face. But there was something different about her, something biological had changed. It was the becoming-a-woman thing, Emma decided. She was no longer a child, but a woman now. It scared her. She just wanted to get into the bed with her, wrap her arms around her and hold her tight, protect her from the world. She wanted to breathe her in as she'd done when she was a baby and she used to cover her in kisses. What would Libby do if she did that right now? If she slipped under those plain white covers and held her? Libby stirred, drawing one arm down and laying it across her tummy.

Nobody warned you about parenting teenagers when you were pregnant. The National Childbirth Trust classes had focused on deep breathing and massaging the mother's back. Nobody told you that one day that little scrap of pink flesh would become an angry, sullen and withdrawn teenager, who one moment was desperate to talk to you and the next couldn't bear to lay eyes on you, and you had to scrape them drunk off the pavement. You were never as good a parent as you were the day before your first child was born – when you'd read all the books but not yet had the opportunity to put any of the advice into practice.

On the desk next to the bed was the thank you note Libby had written to Nick's mum for taking her out for the day a couple of weekends ago – just before they found out that Margaret had died. They'd gone shopping in London and had tea at Selfridges. Libby's very small, neat writing sloped across the page. Emma picked it up, squinting at the address in the half-light. Libby hadn't finished the letter. There was still a gap at the end of the page, and no name. What else had she been planning to say? She'd written out the envelope and added a stamp, but the words remained unfinished. So much seemed to be left unsaid with Libby at the moment.

Another memory pushed up through Emma's thoughts. Another envelope. A pile of letters. Emma looked at the envelope in front of her, struggling to remember. A pile of letters tied together with string. She'd almost thrown them out. Ration books. Postcards. And then she remembered the box in the boot of her car that she'd picked up from her mother's house. She'd completely forgotten all about it. Libby's drama and discovering Elizabeth's identity had taken over everything else. What was in it? Could it be something about Elizabeth?

The air was cold downstairs. She fumbled in the key bowl for her car key. It was a laborious job unlocking the front door – the two bolts and the deadlock – but she felt wide awake now. She loosely slipped on the pair of trainers and clopped out to her car, parked, for once, in front of the house. A fox at the top of the road turned and watched her, fascinated by a fellow inhabitant of the night. The box still lay in the boot, with a few other bits she'd brought back from Morecambe. She lifted it out and slammed the boot shut, the noise echoing along the silent street. She was beginning to shiver and hurried inside, leaving the box in the sitting room but taking her mother's owl mug out of the top and bringing it into the kitchen as she switched on the kettle.

Emma shivered again, looking suddenly over her shoulder into the gloom. She made herself tea, grabbed the full mug and some scissors, and went through into the sitting room. Emma opened the curtains, filling the room with the light of the moon and the jaded yellow of the streetlight. Cradling the hot mug, she sat on the floor, leaning against the sofa next to the box.

There were seven letters elaborately tied together with household string, the sort they'd had in the kitchen drawer for years. The thin envelopes had yellowed with age, their edges curling up like an elegant fan. A faint purplish bruise in the corner indicated a long-faded postmark. Spidery handwriting crawled across the envelope.

Emma recognised her grandmother's hand and pictured her sitting in the window of the London mansion block, where she had lived all her married life, looking into the gardens opposite, writing to her daughter.

Betty Bullman had been dead for sixteen years. Emma remembered the sparsely attended funeral. Her mother had refused to go, so Emma, a one-year-old James, and her father had represented the family, singing 'Praise My Soul the King of Heaven' a little too loudly to make up for the lack of mourners. Just a couple of old dears, who probably didn't even know Betty but were glad of the excuse to get out of the biting February wind into the warm crematorium, and the manager of the nursing home she'd died in. It was probably their protocol to attend all their residents' funerals. Professional mourners.

There hadn't been a wake, but her father had driven Emma back to her and Nick's Tooting flat and they'd stopped at a pub for a carvery, raising a glass to her grandmother. She had hardly drunk since having James, and there had been a certain excitement to a change in her monotonous routine of playgroup and afternoon naps. Lunchtime drinking, even when accompanied by drab food, flashing fruit machines, and a group of pensioners and the unemployed as fellow diners, had seemed quite fun.

'Betty and your mother never got on,' her father had said. 'Your mother didn't really talk about it, but I think Betty was too in love with Jack to pay much attention to her own daughter. She'd had her out of wedlock, which would have been a big deal in 1937, so it was quite a relief when Jack married her and adopted your mother and made them respectable again. Betty didn't want to rock the boat, so always took Jack's side in any family disagreement. That's what your mother told me. And they were too similar. Both argumentative, and too stubborn to make the peace.'

In the moonlit sitting room, Emma started to untie the stiff knots. Someone had tied the letters up very tightly. Because they didn't want to read them again? Or to stop someone else reading them? She opened the top letter, sliding a sheet of carefully hand-written text on to her lap. It looked as if it had been taken out and read many times – the text was smudged and faint, the paper well folded. She took a sip of the tea, and started reading.

> *Pullman Court*
> *Streatham Hill*
> *23 March 1953*

> *Dear Margaret,*
> *I hope you're having a lovely time at Granny June's. We both miss you here but are wishing you a very happy Easter and looking forward to seeing you after the holidays. I know things have been a bit delicate for the last few months. I think that a few weeks away will help you to put it all behind you. We both love you very much.*
> *Don't forget to go to church on Good Friday, I always think that's the most beautiful service of the year. And it's a Holy Day of Obligation. You don't want to get in trouble at St Hilda's when you get back for not having gone. Granny June will take you.*
> *Happy Easter.*
> *Love, Mother*

Emma started counting back on her fingers. In March 1953, her mother would have been fifteen and just pregnant with Elizabeth. Had she known she was having a baby? It was still quite early on. At that age, she might not have been aware. Had she told her mother and that was why she was sent away? Emma reread the letter again, but it sounded friendly, loving. Not like a letter to someone who was pregnant aged fifteen. What was the delicate thing that Betty had referred to? Perhaps they'd known her mother was seeing a boy and had insisted it ended – not realising it was already too late.

She refolded the sheet of paper and slid it carefully back into the flimsy envelope, setting it on the table. There were two sheets inside the next envelope, identical to the first. Emma could see the faint Basildon Bond logo beneath the text. It was from later that same year.

Pullman Court
Streatham Hill
2 December 1953

Dear Margaret,
Granny June just wrote and said that you telephoned her yesterday morning. I was so relieved to hear that you're alive and safe. Father and I have been so, so worried. We didn't even get a chance to wish you a happy sixteenth birthday. I've been going out of my mind for months. We thought you were dead.

What have you been up to for the three months? Where have you been staying? I'm not cross that you took the housekeeping money, even though I was sav-ing it up for something nice for all of us. I'm just glad you're safe. If that's what's stopping you coming home, then please don't worry. We just want you here with us.

I found the note you left. I wish you would just let all that alone. There are some things as a woman that one just has to learn to ignore. No good will come of it. I love you, Margaret, you must believe that.

It was just so hard at first. Granny never forgave me for having you without being married. She tried to make me give you up, but I wouldn't. I fought to keep you but it was such a difficult few years. All the disgrace, all the people looking at me and talking about me. I know that's hard to understand now that things are different. Then thank God Father came along and married me and adopted you, and it was all fine again. We are a proper family, which is what I'd always wanted for you. There may be ups and downs, but that's part of family life. I am just so grateful to him. Please try to understand.

I hope this letter reaches you, Margaret. It seems odd to send a letter to a shop in the hope you'll pick it up. I hope you're safe. I wish you would come home. You belong here with Father and I. You're safe here with us, not out there with no one. Goodness knows what's happening to you. Please write back to me. Granny said that you promised to call her again. Please do call. Please.

Love, Mother

So, thought Emma, her mum had left home abruptly – on her sixteenth birthday – without telling her mother and stepfather she was going. For some reason, Emma had always presumed that her leaving home was planned. But who would let a sixteen-year-old just leave? Emma's own son James was older now than her mother had been when she left home. He could barely make a sandwich for himself, let alone survive independently. What had her mum done when she left? Where had she gone?

Her mother's sixteenth birthday had been on 23 August 1953, so she would have been about six weeks from having Elizabeth – noticeably pregnant. She would have known she was pregnant by then, surely? Emma had read stories about girls who got pregnant but, through a mix of inexperience and a lack of education, didn't realise they were having a baby until they went into labour. What a shock that must be. A few hours' notice that you were going to be a mother. But Betty didn't mention a baby in the letter, so maybe she didn't know that her daughter had been pregnant. Her mother had managed to keep her pregnancy with Elizabeth secret from her own mother. Just as Betty kept her pregnancy with Margaret secret until she had her. The worst history repeating itself.

Emma remembered lumbering around in her pregnancies. Grumbling about morning sickness, then her size as she gradually outgrew every item of clothing she had. It would have been difficult to hide her pregnancy from anyone.

It was impossible to imagine receiving a letter like that from your own mother, having just had a baby and giving it up. She'd read that most of the girls at Birdhurst Lodge had to give up their babies within ten days. If her mother had done that, she'd have been desperate and miserable enough to make contact with her grandmother. Was it telling that she called her granny rather than her own mother? Emma counted on her fingers. She would have been without her baby for about six weeks by the time she got the letter. What must she have been going through?

She scanned through the letter again.

It was easy to see how relieved Betty would have been to meet Jack. To be given her respectability back. And how desperate she would have been to keep it. She'd never thought about Jack raising another man's daughter, but it must have been difficult.

Emma stood up stiffly and opened the cupboards under the shelves. There were numerous photo albums stacked higgledy-piggledy. Huge glossy tomes chronicled their recent holidays, but at the bottom there was a pile of much smaller albums. She started flicking through them and came across what she'd been looking for. Photos of Betty, Jack and Margaret together. The three of them standing in what might have been London Zoo, a giraffe behind them. Jack was in the middle, his arms around his wife and stepdaughter. It must have been a windy day because his hair was blowing across his face, obscuring his forehead but not the wide grin. Betty's hair was hidden under a head scarf, just a whip of blonde at the front escaping to dance in the wind as she held her hand on top of her head and smiled. She'd been a beautiful woman. Would her life have been different if she hadn't had those looks? Even Margaret was laughing, those dark eyes intense at that age – eight, nine?

In the next photo, Margaret was slightly older, almost as tall as Granny Betty. Her hair was longer and she was beginning to lose that little-girl look. The three of them were dressed smartly, standing in front of Buckingham Palace, Jack still in the middle with his arms around their waists. Their customary family pose. They all looked happy, carefree. A fun day out in London being tourists.

But in the next one that had changed. Jack was still in the middle, with his arm around Betty, but Margaret was noticeably separate, apart from them. And she was much older, almost as tall as Jack. The slim waist had gone and she looked like she was carrying a bit of weight. What Betty would no doubt have unkindly called 'puppy fat'. Margaret was staring blankly at the camera whereas Betty and Jack still had the same fixed grins. Behind them was a sea of hundreds of people, in front of what looked like the Mall. Everyone was dancing and smiling. It looked almost like VE Day, but her mother would have been a small child then. Margaret looked about fourteen, fifteen, so perhaps it was Queen Elizabeth's Coronation? She googled it. 2 June 1953. There were a whole series of photos of an incredibly young Queen Elizabeth and the Duke of Edinburgh and vast crowds watching the procession in London. And they looked identical to the picture in the album – even down to the same umbrellas. It must have rained. In June 1953, Margaret would have been about five months pregnant. Her face was contorted in a sort of anguish. She looked like the girl in the painting.

Emma glanced at the clock on the fireplace. It was now 3.30 a.m. Her tea was lukewarm. Suddenly she felt cold, and she picked up one of the blankets on the sofa and drew it around her as she opened the next of the four letters that were left.

Chapter 26

BETTY

AUGUST 1952

Jack was lying on the bed watching her undress, his face unreadable. He'd always done this and it made her feel relieved he was still interested in her but also self-conscious. She unbuttoned her blouse, slowly revealing her silk slip, trying not to hurry. She could hear him breathing heavily.

'What are you thinking?' Betty was smiling at him, her head on one side.

'Oh . . . nothing,' he stammered, looking away.

'Go on, tell me,' Betty urged. 'You haven't looked at me like that for a long time.' She moved towards him and sat down on the side of the bed where he lay, stroking his arm.

'Just thinking how much I miss you,' Jack said. 'We haven't made love for months.'

'I'm sorry, I know it's my fault.' Betty sighed. She'd known he was unhappy with that. 'I've just been so tired recently. All these women's troubles.' She went to rise from the bed, but Jack held her arm and pulled her towards him, kissing her hungrily on her mouth.

Betty laughed. 'Jack! Let me get my slip off.'

'I'll get your slip off,' he said, pushing her down on to the bed and tearing it slightly as he pulled it down.

'Be careful, this is expensive,' Betty cried out.

But Jack ignored her, laddering her stockings as he rolled them down her legs. Catching his thumbnail in them, he lost patience and left them around her ankles as he tackled her bra. Her breasts spilled out of it like cream. She knew he loved them, but he kneaded them too roughly, he always had. But she daren't say anything.

His hands were pulling down her knickers. At least he was still interested in her. She'd been worried that he'd go elsewhere. Plenty of men did. And it wasn't exactly attractive for him that she'd been in and out of hospital so much recently with her women's troubles. Betty studied the ceiling and started writing tomorrow's shopping list in her head.

Her focus was so far away from the bed with the pink counterpane that she could only presume she misheard him as he finished off, seconds later.

'What did you say?' she asked as he rolled off her.

'Eh?' he said, his eyes still holding that glazed look he always had.

'I thought you mentioned Margaret.'

He looked shocked. 'Betty! Why on earth would I mention Margaret? Good grief. What do you take me for?' He rolled on to his side and his breathing became slow and regular.

She lay still for a long time, staring up at the ceiling.

Chapter 27

Emma

February 2019

Light steps, treading the well-worn route to the bathroom above, echoed down the stairs. Emma put the next letter down on the table with the rest of the pile and drew her dressing gown closer around her and followed the sound. Libby was sitting on the loo, her eyes open but unseeing as the wee splashed against the sides of the porcelain. She often sleepwalked and talked. Her fringe flopped over her eyes as her head lolled forward. Emma leaned against the doorframe watching her pull up her pyjama bottoms. She stumbled towards her, and she caught her before she hit her head on the door jamb.

'Mum.' Libby opened her eyes slightly, and Emma realised she hadn't been asleep at all, just fighting the battle between sleep and the need to wee.

Emma wanted to pick her up and cuddle her like she had as a baby. But now, at fifteen, Libby was taller than Emma. She guided her back to her room, a hand on her shoulder and another on her back.

Libby climbed into bed and was fast asleep as her head sank into the pillow. But Emma still went into the routine of tucking her in, checking her water glass was close enough to reach but not close enough to knock over, that the light from the landing wasn't shining in her face. She kissed her cheek, closing her eyes as her lips touched the smooth skin. If only it was always like this.

Emma made another cup of tea and picked up the next letter in the pile. Same envelope, same paper – her grandmother must have used it all her life.

Pullman Court
Streatham Hill
1 July 1960

Dear Margaret,
Father saw the notice in The Times. *Do you have any idea how that made Father and I feel? To read about our own daughter's wedding in a newspaper?*

I imagine that you expect us to congratulate you. We do, of course. Although it would have been nice to have been invited, to meet your young man. Roger Goodman sounds like a fine name. I had so looked forward to one day being the mother of the bride, and to have that moment taken away from me has been hard. It's been worse for your father. After everything he did for you, he should have been the one to give you away.

I see that you're in Surbiton now. Granny June gave me your address. I'm not sure why you gave it to her and not your own parents. You're not that far from Pullman Court. Please do come home and

say hello, introduce us to your new husband. Father
wants to meet him. I'm worried you won't be a good
judge of men.
I wish you all the very best in married life and
hope you'll use the example that Father and I set you.
Despite our worry about you, we have had a very
happy marriage. Our one wish is to see you happy.
Love, Mother

Emma knew her mother had been married before. Her parents had been very open about it. But she couldn't remember asking anything else – about where they'd met or why the relationship had ended. How uncurious she'd been, accepting of what she was told. It would have been seven years since Margaret had given up Elizabeth. How was she feeling then? What did Roger Goodman think about it all? If this letter was anything to go by, then one thing was certain, and that was that there had been no warming in the relationship between Margaret and her own mother.

Emma folded the letter and put it back in the envelope and added it to the pile on the table. She drew out the next one. It was dated from when Emma was a child.

Pullman Court
Streatham Hill
15 June 1980

Dear Margaret,
I don't know why you have to constantly bring up
the past. Let bygones be bygones. Your father loves
Emma and he just wants the opportunity to spend
time with her, we both do. You never enjoy your

own children properly because you're so busy bring-
ing them up. We'd both like a chance to enjoy our
grandchild. Don't deny us that because of some silly
misunderstanding in the past. It's not fair that your
second husband's side of the family get to see her all
the time and we don't – only for a few hours when
you come for lunch a couple of times a year and never
on our own. You never invite us to see your house.
I'd love to see where you, David, and Emma live in
Sussex, it sounds idyllic.

I've called up Emma's school and I have the
dates for the summer holidays. We're free to have her
for any of the six weeks. Just let us know what's most
convenient for you all.

Love, Mother

Emma remembered the row. She'd so wanted to stay at her
grandparents' for a few weeks in the summer. Her mother had
never had much time for playing, she was always so busy with
something or angry about something else. And then after she disappeared, she was never the same again. And her father was always at
work. But the times they went to visit Granny Betty and Grandpa
Jack in their London flat were fun. She loved the journey up there
from the quiet Sussex countryside, then the motorway when she'd
stick her hand out of the window (and her head when her mother
wasn't looking) to feel the breeze against her skin, then the slow
trawl through the south London traffic where she'd look into all the
interesting little shops run by fascinating people who were nothing
like those you saw at home.

Grandpa Jack and Granny Betty's flat was interesting too. All
white and curved lines outside and then all the funny furniture
inside. Art Deco, she remembered Grandpa Jack telling her. He'd

once sat on the floor with her there and created huge farms of animals spread across the whole sitting room, using the legs of the coffee table as trees, the side of the brown leather chairs as mountains, and the green rug as a lake, the cows dipping their heads in to drink the fabric.

'What sort of things did Mummy play with when she was my age?' Emma had asked.

'I'll show you, come on. Granny Betty hasn't changed your mum's room since the day she left. It's still got all her old toys in it. And some of her sketches.' Jack had grabbed her hand to lever himself up from the floor and put his arm round her as they walked out of the sitting room, leaving the animals to fend for themselves.

'Where are you two going?' her mother had called out from the dining table.

'We're just going to your old room, Mummy,' said Emma. 'To see your toys.'

'No, I don't want you going in there. Just stay in here with us.'

'But . . .'

'No, Emma, you're to stay in here.' Her mother stood up and was almost blocking the way out of the room. 'Jack, don't push it.'

She had given Grandpa Jack a stern look – the sort she gave Emma when she was telling her off. Then Granny Betty came out of the kitchen and asked what was going on.

'I was just taking Emma to show her some of Margaret's toys in her room, but Margaret doesn't want me to show her,' said Jack.

A row had followed and they'd left quite hurriedly. Emma had cried on the way home, and her mother had reached behind her in the brown Austin Allegro, and smacked her leg hard. It had left a red mark which Emma watched deepening into a bruise as the car stuttered through the south London traffic back to Sussex.

Emma sighed and took a sip of tea. She wondered what had changed for her mother from 1960, when she was hardly in touch with her parents, to the 1980s when they were sitting down for lunch together, even if there were disagreements. Perhaps having a second child – one that she'd kept – had warmed the relationship between Betty and Margaret. Just as Emma's own relationship with her mother improved after her first child James was born.

All Emma's family relationships seemed to be so complex. No one – apart from her father and Emma – had ever seemed to get on. She put the letter back and extracted one sheet from the penultimate envelope. It was dated the following year.

Pullman Court
Streatham Hill
30 July 1981

Dear Margaret,
I think after what happened yesterday it might be best if you don't visit again for a while. That kind of behaviour is very disruptive to a family, particularly for a child of Emma's age. All we want is the best for you, David, and Emma, but it seems that all you want is to create merry hell wherever you go. You've deeply upset me and Father. I cannot tell you the impact it's had on him.

Emma is always welcome here. We've said many times that we'd love to have her stay for the holidays. But we don't want to see you again, Margaret, for a while.
Mother

What had happened that 'yesterday'? Emma would have been just six but she couldn't remember anything awful happening since the row after the time she'd played with Jack and the farm animals. But she'd clearly been there. There had been that funny time Granny had poured gravy all over the table, but that was just an accident. Had they visited again after that? She couldn't remember.

She picked up another old photo album and started flicking through it: past family Christmases, everyone posing awkwardly wearing Christmas hats around a table piled with food. Photos of a young Emma blowing out birthday candles at a table in a big garden – Greystones. Formal school shots of her with the pudding basin haircut – what had her mother been thinking? And then there it was.

A photograph of her, sitting between her grandparents at Pullman Court. The furniture was unmistakeable. She looked about ten or eleven. Certainly older than six. Who had taken it? It was impossible to say. She couldn't remember the specific visit, just that she had seen her grandparents after whatever awful incident had occurred. Had her mother been there or had her father taken her on his own? She struggled to remember.

She shuffled through the six letters. So much was said – and not said – across the flimsy sheets of paper. A relationship, or the destruction of a relationship – related over decades.

She looked at the table. There was just one letter left.

Chapter 28

Betty

September 1952

Betty laid the unopened copy of *Woman's Weekly* on the starched sheet and looked up into the ward sister's kind eyes.

'Good to see you sitting up at last, Mrs Bullman. Now I'd like you to try a little celery soup.' She placed a tray on the table.

Betty took one look at the congealing liquid, the colour of glue, and felt her stomach turn.

The sister put her hand on Betty's arm. 'You need to eat, Mrs Bullman, it's all part of the healing process. A lovely Lancashire Hotpot comes next. But you need to take these tablets first.'

Betty nodded and slipped the pills into her mouth where they stuck to her dry tongue. The chemical taste made her gag. The sister handed her a glass of water and she swallowed them down in one gulp. The tablets hardly seemed to touch the pain. It was like a knife continually turning inside her. But the pain was almost a relief. Something tangible to cling on to after years waiting for something to fill the empty place inside her.

The nurse touched her arm once more and walked away readjusting her apron.

Betty lifted the covers and stared at the long white bandage that sliced across her stomach. There was nothing underneath there now. Even her stubbornly empty womb had itself been taken away. She wondered what they did with it. Was her womb right now in the bottom of the hospital rubbish bin useless and discarded alongside the carrot peelings? Was what she'd tried to do visible – the marks from the knitting needle? Could the doctor have seen it, guessed at what she'd done?

She winced as she shifted in bed. The sterility of the ward reminded her of her parents' old bathroom scullery where Margaret had been born. What if things had been different?

Betty pushed on the dressing on her stomach and gasped as an arc of pain wrapped itself around her belly, like a circle of fire. She pressed again, curling inwards towards the agony. She deserved it. Jack had cried when she'd told him that the doctor said she needed a hysterectomy. No more chance of having children. Another failed pregnancy could kill her. All because of what she had done that day. What if . . .

'You look brighter. Feeling better now?' It was the woman in the bed next to her, her brows arched into a question. She'd gone in for the operation after Betty but looked ten times better already, her hair neatly curled, her cheeks rouged, her lips painted. Betty had seen her own reflection in the steel tea urn. Dark circles under her eyes on grey skin, framed by lank yellow hair.

Betty nodded and stared unseeing at the magazine that someone had brought. They were all so kind, but they didn't understand.

'Bet you're glad you're done now. When the doc said I could have it out, I almost danced around the room. No more babies. I've got ten and I'm done. My husband's happy, I'm happy, and the priest's happy.' The woman didn't look a day over thirty.

Betty thought of Jack at home, waiting to hear when he could visit. Mourning the child he'd never have, as he had every day for the past thirteen years. She didn't want him in this room.

'How many you got then?' The woman again.

'Just the one. A girl. Margaret. She's fifteen.' Betty forced the corners of her mouth into a smile.

'Only one. Bleedin' hell. How you get away with that?'

Betty thought back to the years and years of trying, from the night of their wedding. The cycle of waiting, her monthly arriving with depressing regularity, the trying again. The three tiny babies she'd held in her palm before they slithered into the lavatory bowl, washed out to sea. The one that died in the hospital when her stomach had grown to accommodate it and they thought they were safe. Arriving in a sea of blood and pain. That night in the maternity ward with the other mothers and their babies and her sitting there with nothing to hold but her grief.

'We wanted more, but it never happened,' she said quietly. 'I lost four babies.'

The woman nodded, her curls bouncing around her face. 'That's hard, isn't it? I lost two. You always count them as your own, don't you?' She tipped her head to one side. 'Still, must be easier just having the one. The three of you at home. Nice and cosy.'

Betty nodded and looked back to the magazine. Jack and Margaret got on better now, it was true. But there was something about the way he looked at Margaret. Hungry. Appraising. She pushed the thought to the farthest corner of her mind.

Chapter 29

Margaret

September 1952

Margaret liked it being just her and her stepfather in the flat. It made her feel more important, more grown-up. Before she'd left for the hospital, her mother had talked her through the supper menu for the week – where to buy what, how much to pay for it and how to prepare it. She knew most of it anyway – she'd been following her mother around for years helping her.

She knew exactly how long to leave the pork chops so they were just the way her stepfather liked them. She knew the brand of tinned fruit he liked, and how the evaporated milk needed to be on the side of the bowl. She knew what to do when the toilet blocked, which it had that morning. And when Mrs Wilson next door had her funny turn, she knew how to bring her round. Margaret knew how to use the heavy iron – she had a vague memory of helping with laundry when she was very little, her aunts teaching her how to fold a sheet. She was ready to be a woman, she decided.

She'd spent the morning cleaning the flat in the sweltering heat, getting the carpet sweeper right into the corners of the rooms just as her mother did. Her stepfather was watching her the whole time. He'd sat at the table with the newspaper in front of him, just as he always did, but not seeming to turn the pages. But he'd gone to his room now. Or perhaps he had gone out, though she hadn't heard the door.

Now she lay on her bed, the unseasonable heat making her sleepy. An Indian summer, they called it. The mansion block was stuffy, oppressive. The early evening air hung thickly, like a blanket, making it difficult to breathe. The windows were wide open but there was no breeze moving outside. She was waiting for her favourite skirt and blouse to dry, then she planned to go out to see Jilly. They'd talked about going into town, and meeting up with the boys again. She thought of *him* and smiled. He'd winked at her last time. Her mother always warned that a wink was the prelude to a kiss. Margaret hoped her mother was right for once.

Nat King Cole finished crooning 'Unforgettable', and she slipped off the bed in her underwear and walked into the sitting room to move the needle on the gramophone back to the beginning of the song.

Margaret hoped she was unforgettable to *him*, at least. She went back to her room and lay down on her bed and thought of him leaning over her, pressing his lips against hers. She kissed the back of her hand and wondered if it would feel the same. How hard would a kiss be? In the films, it seemed like the gentlest touch but Jilly, who had already kissed her boy, said it was rougher than that. That the film kisses were just for show. The thought of him that close to her.

She heard a creak in the hallway and opened her eyes. He was home after all.

Her stepfather was looking at her through the open bedroom door.

'What do you want?' she said.

'I want you to stop playing that song,' he said, wiping his hand across his forehead. 'And cover yourself up. You look indecent.'

Margaret turned on to her front, rolling her eyes at him.

He strode into the room, her room, grabbed her dressing gown and threw it over her. 'Cover yourself up.'

Margaret threw it on the floor, laughing at him. 'It's too hot. I'm going to get dressed in a minute. I'm just waiting for my skirt to dry,' she said, pointing towards the window ledge, where her skirt lay attached to the catch by its hoop.

Jack squinted towards the window. 'You know your mother doesn't want you wearing that. I thought she'd confiscated it.'

Her mother *had* confiscated it, but she always hid things in the same place – at the back of her wardrobe behind the shoe-boxes. Margaret had discovered this several years ago and would take things out to use or wear them and then later replace them so her mother was none the wiser.

'I'm fifteen, I can wear what I want, I can do what I want,' said Margaret. She got off the bed to walk out of the room, brushing against him as she walked past.

But he grabbed her by the wrist and threw her back on to the bed. 'I told you to cover yourself up,' he said slowly.

Margaret gasped as she fell back, but was cushioned by the mattress. Her left breast slipped out of the top of her bra with the impact and she adjusted it. She looked up at her stepfather and laughed. 'I'm not a little girl you can tell off any more.'

His eyes went dark – like they always did when he was angry. But there was something else there too, but she didn't have time to work out what it was. He strode towards her, flipped her over and smacked her hard on the bottom. He'd smacked her before, when she'd been naughty as a child, not laid the table or done what her mother had said. But not for several years. And this time felt different. Then he gripped her wrists and pinned her face down on the bed.

Margaret cried out. 'Stop, you're hurting me.'

But Jack didn't let go. She tried to wriggle up the bed to get away from him, feeling scared for the first time. What was he going to do? He grabbed her by her ankle and pulled her back down and hit her again. She cried out at the impact. Then she heard him unzipping his trousers and she realised what was happening.

'No, stop. Please, don't.' But her cries were muffled by the coverlet, his hand pushing down on the back of her head. The song on the gramophone was just finishing again in the sitting room. Unforgettable.

Chapter 30

Emma

February 2019

The milk van rattled past as Emma's hands shook opening the final letter and took out the two sheets of paper. This letter was more crumpled, the envelope more worn. It was dated September 1993, just after Jack's death. Emma remembered the phone call from the hospital to say that Grandpa Jack had died. It had been her final year of A-levels and she was living with her father David in Clapham, the tiny Sussex village. Her mother was already living alone in Morecambe by then. Emma was just getting ready to head off to school when the call came. She hadn't even been particularly worried when they'd asked if a parent was home. But once she'd told them she was eighteen, they'd told her the news. She remembered crying, the tears falling quickly, but at the same time part of her brain was wondering why she was crying. She hadn't seen Grandpa Jack for a long time.

He'd died in hospital – there was something wrong with his bowel. She'd asked if her mother had been told, but apparently Granny Betty had asked the hospital to call Emma and her father instead. She remembered thinking that was odd, but then Betty and Margaret had never got on. Betty was in a state and needed someone with her.

Emma had felt very important, aged eighteen, calling up her father in the office and explaining what had happened. The tears had been replaced by the brisk practicality of managing a crisis. She decided to go up to Streatham and see her grandmother that morning. Her father had been fully supportive and Emma was excited about skipping college and getting the train to London. She was at Pullman Court by lunchtime, and tailgated through the main front door.

'Granny?' Emma peered through the letterbox into her flat's dark, empty hall. There was no response, and Emma's heart started to beat a little faster. A tabby cat stood in the hall looking at her, mewing angrily. She'd seen men in films kick down doors, but she doubted she'd be able to do that, especially in high-heeled boots. She kept knocking and started shouting through the small gap. Eventually a door opened across the communal landing and a woman not that much older than Emma emerged wearing torn jeans and a dirty T-shirt, holding a baby, with a toddler peering out between her legs.

'What d'you want?' she asked, aggressively.

'Oh, sorry, did I disturb you?' said Emma.

The woman rolled her eyes.

'I'm just trying to get into my grandmother's. My grandfather's died and I'm here to look after her. Do you know Betty?'

'No. But you're going to wake the whole block up shouting like that. She works shifts,' she said, pointing her thumb towards the door next to Emma. 'And she won't be pleased you waking her up. Come here,' she called to the toddler who was starting to potter towards Emma.

'But I need to get in. She might be ill or something.' Emma started to wish she hadn't come all this way on her own. 'I wonder if anyone here has a spare key? They've lived here for years, someone might.'

'Try under the mat. All the oldies keep their keys under the mat.' The woman rolled her eyes again, dragged the child inside and slammed the door.

Emma lifted up the mat and sure enough a small single key lay beneath it. She slipped it into the lock and let herself into the flat. It was dark and quiet.

'Granny?' she called. The cat started rubbing around her legs. She didn't remember her grandparents having a cat before. 'Granny?'

Beyond the empty hallway, the place was a mess. In the sitting room, papers were strewn everywhere, a vase lay smashed. Emma bit her lip. Some of the framed pictures were face down. One was in pieces on the floor. She carefully picked it up, avoiding the shards of glass. It was of her grandparents with her mother, standing outside Buckingham Palace. They all looked so much younger and happy. Suddenly it was difficult to breathe. Had Granny done this deliberately? She carefully put the picture on the table and walked into the kitchen.

'Granny?' There was a foul smell – the cat's litter tray was over-flowing. Emma held her nose, breathing through her mouth, and walked back into the hallway, the cat following her mewling. The two bedroom doors were shut. She hesitated outside what she knew was Granny Betty and Grandpa Jack's room. She didn't want to know what was inside. She knocked quietly on the door.

Nothing. Her heart thudding, she cracked open the door. The room was dark, but she could just make out that the bed was made, a pink counterpane stretched across the mattress. She went in. In the corner, a wardrobe door was open and it looked like someone had taken all the clothes and dumped them on the floor. Grandpa Jack's clothes. Emma could see the stiff chef whites that she remembered him wearing when she was a child. She closed the door quietly, and walked down the hallway, glancing through the bathroom door. It was empty, two towels folded neatly by the basin. A toothbrush waited in a ceramic mug.

Emma stopped outside her mother's old bedroom door, looking at the flaking paint. The cat meowed loudly and stood looking at her expectantly. She shouldn't have come alone. She shivered, took a deep breath and opened the door slightly. The smell of stale alcohol seeped out, like an old man's pub on a Saturday morning. The curtains were pulled in this room too but in the gloom Emma could see Granny Betty lying in Margaret's single bed in the corner, completely covered by the sheet and blankets, only her blonde curls showing. Emma gasped, her heart hammering. An almost-empty bottle of gin stood on the bedside table, a tumbler beside it. The teddy bears and dolls were still lined up on the shelf above the bed. A charcoal sketch was tacked to the wall behind the bed – a girl crouched in a dark maze. It looked like an early draft of her mother's maze painting.

'Granny?' Her voice quaked. Emma walked over to her slowly, her knees feeling like jelly. 'Granny?' Emma's hands shook as she reached out to touch the covers. The figure in the bed below her started to move and Emma's shoulders dropped and she let out a long, slow breath. 'Are you all right?'

'Oh, Emma, dear.' Betty scrambled into a seated position, holding the blanket over her. But Emma could see that she was fully dressed. From today, or yesterday? 'I was just having a snooze.' Her eyes were bloodshot and her skin grey. She looked much older than when she'd last seen her.

'I'm sorry about Grandpa.'

Betty nodded slowly, looking down at her gnarled hands. Emma felt the eyes of the girl in the sketch on her. Somehow the starkness of the charcoal drawing made it feel even more sinister. Emma shivered and looked away.

'Granny, this drawing . . . Did Mum do it? It looks like an early draft of the painting she has in her flat now.'

Betty glanced behind her and nodded. 'She did it – and lots of others like it – when she was a little younger than you. Fifteen. I hated them at the time, I thought they were all so depressing. And then finally she painted that beautiful one – in oil. The painting that won all those prizes. I went to the West End to see it hanging in a gallery. I was so proud of your mum.' Betty looked down at her hands and her shoulders shook. 'We should bring it into the sitting room. It deserves more than being hidden away in here.'

Betty got out of bed unsteadily. Emma helped her up. The smell of booze was overpowering. She walked slowly through to the kitchen, stumbling occasionally. 'Do you want some tea?'

Emma followed her closely ready to catch her.

'It's okay, Granny, I'll make it.'

Betty nodded vacantly and went to sit down in one of the armchairs. Emma put the kettle on the electric ring and started to clean up the kitchen, emptying the disgusting litter tray into the equally revolting bin, feeding the cat, and tidying up. The fridge was empty, but a six-pack of long-life milk stood on top of it.

She went into the sitting room with two cups of tea on saucers, laid them on the little table and went to sit down next to Betty.

'Not there!' shouted Betty. 'That's Jack's chair.'

Emma jumped back. 'Oh, sorry, Granny.' She smiled and dragged up one of the dining room chairs and sat next to Betty. Her face seemed to have collapsed in on itself. Large black bags hung from her eyes. Without her false teeth, her mouth looked like a wrinkled baby's. 'I'm so sorry about everything. You must be devastated. Is there anything I can do?'

Betty nodded again. 'You need to go to the hospital and see him. I want to make sure that he's dead.' Her voice was quiet but angry. A tear was easing out of the corner of her eye, hanging on the edge of her puffy cheek before sliding into the wrinkles to her mouth.

'Granny! Of course he's dead, that's what the hospital said, didn't they? Do you mean to identify the body?' Betty nodded again, her head bowed. Emma gnawed the inside of her cheek. 'Of course I'll go, if that's what you want.' She thought of her father and wished again that he'd come with her. 'Do you want me to stay a bit, look after you until you're back on your feet?'

Betty looked up and smiled for the first time. 'You're a good girl, Emma. Yes, I'd like that.' She reached across and gripped Emma's hand, blue veins mapping her hands.

'Have you spoken to Mum? She should know.'

Betty shook her head. 'No, I haven't. Perhaps you could do that for me. I don't have a telephone here, but there's a phone box downstairs.'

'Of course I can . . . but don't you think it would be better coming from you?' Emma shrugged. 'If you don't feel comfortable calling her, then just write her a letter. She always got on well with Grandpa Jack, didn't she?'

Granny Betty looked down and said nothing.

Nick's phone alarm began to sound in their bedroom above. Emma heard the bed creak and then footsteps walking across the landing. She slipped the final letter back in the box and slid it under the sofa. She'd read it later. She didn't want it to spark another row between them. As he came down the stairs, Emma hurried into the kitchen and put the kettle on.

Chapter 31

MARGARET

SEPTEMBER 1952

Margaret got up early the following day, preparing her stepfather's breakfast and leaving for school before he woke up. She sat on the steps waiting for the school building to open. It was still horribly warm and she felt sweat down the back of her blouse.

'What happened to you last night?' said Jilly as soon as she saw her. 'We waited for ages. Your chap was really disappointed. I think he thought his luck was in.'

Margaret smiled and thought of him, but she couldn't picture his face. 'Sorry, I got caught up with chores at home. I couldn't get away.'

'We're meeting after school today. I promised I'd make sure you'd join us.'

'But I'll still be in my uniform – I won't have time to change,' she said.

'Oh, don't worry about that,' said Jilly airily. 'Some men love a girl in school uniform.'

Margaret tried to giggle, the sound odd in her ears.

◆ ◆ ◆

Later, as she slowly climbed up the steps outside Pullman Court, she thought how right Jilly had been. *He*'d been far more taken with her in her too-small uniform than he had when she'd worn her puffball skirt a few weekends before. But it was all different now. She felt different now. Like spoiled milk, gone off, discarded. He wouldn't want her if he knew. When he'd tried to kiss her earlier, she'd stepped back. It had been instinctive. She couldn't bear anyone, even *him*, touching her now. She swallowed and watched her feet walk into the building and up the stairs. She let herself into the flat and stood in the doorway listening. It was silent, waiting.

She hurried down the hall and into her bedroom and closed the door. On the bedside table was a small gift-wrapped box. Margaret sat on the bed staring at it. Eventually, she reached out and undid the ribbon, easing open the paper. Inside was a lipstick. Gala of London in Fire Engine Red. She and Jilly had seen these in magazines and she'd wanted one, but known they were far too expensive for them to buy.

Margaret put it in the drawer and lay down on her bed staring at nothing, waiting for her stepfather to come home. Only three more days and Mother would be back from hospital.

◆ ◆ ◆

Jack closed the bedroom door quietly, and walked across the hallway back into the kitchen.

'Is Mother going to be okay?' whispered Margaret, not wanting to talk to him, but needing to know all the same.

'She'll be fine, she just needs rest,' he said.

Margaret knew he was lying, just as he'd lied when he said he'd never touch her again. She was shocked by the change in her mother since she'd come out of hospital. She seemed grey and listless and had no appetite.

'What's for dinner?' Jack asked, pouring himself a whisky from the decanter.

Margaret consulted the menu, although she already knew. 'Corned beef hash. Shall I do some for Mother?'

Jack nodded, looking out of the window. 'Just a little bit. I'll give it to her when she wakes up.'

But her mother slept through the evening as Margaret watched from a chair near her bed. She felt safe in there, sitting close to her mother, even if she was asleep. Betty murmured in her sleep and tossed from side to side. Sweat glistened on her forehead. In the kitchen, her plate of food grew cold, the egg congealed. Margaret made her a cup of milky tea which also went cold and grew a skin. She could hear Jack turning over the pages of the newspaper in the sitting room.

Later in the evening, Jack started to make up a bed in the sitting room using his old army camp bed. Margaret watched him from the doorway. 'What are you doing?'

'The doctor advised that I don't sleep in the same bed as your mother,' he said. 'They said that she'll get a better night's sleep and recover quicker if we sleep apart.'

The sitting room was closer to her own bedroom than her parents' room.

'You're not wearing the lipstick I bought you,' he said, tucking in the sheet. 'Did you like it?'

Margaret nodded.

'What do you say when someone gives you a present you like?' he asked, looking up at her.

'Thank you,' whispered Margaret.

190

'Thank you, what?'

'Thank you, Father.'

◆ ◆ ◆

The following evening she was sitting at her mother's bedside when her stepfather came in and sat on the bed and took her mother's hand. He didn't look at Margaret as she moved her chair back. 'I've been thinking that with you so poorly, you really shouldn't have Margaret around bothering you. So I've arranged for her to come with me to the hotel at the weekends. It'll mean that you get a full day here to recover without Margaret interrupting you.'

Margaret stared at him, nausea exploding in her stomach.

Betty smiled back at him softly. 'It's kind of you, but surely she should be doing homework or housework?'

'Oh, it'll only be the occasional day. She'll have plenty of time for everything else.' He stroked Betty's hand with his thumb. Margaret got up.

'I'm glad to see the two of you getting on for a change,' said Betty weakly, her eyes darting between the two of them. She fell back on the pillows. 'I should stay in hospital more often.' Betty looked at Jack and smiled. Margaret walked out of the room and locked herself in the bathroom.

Chapter 32

EMMA

FEBRUARY 2019

After all the drama of the past fortnight, it felt strangely peaceful to be back at work, despite the worry over the letter to Elizabeth.

There was a sympathy card for her on reception. *Thinking of you at this difficult time.* The whole office had signed it, writing messages of various degrees of awkwardness.

She hated the impersonality of the new 'hot desking' system, but she found a spare desk next to someone she didn't know at all, which suited her just fine today, and stared blankly at her computer screen. She couldn't remember what she'd been doing before her mother died. The list of unread emails from the previous weeks stared reproachfully back at her. The calendar icon flashed up giving a fifteen-minute warning for the team meeting.

The woman next door raised her head and smiled over the desk barrier, that grim recognition of another prisoner of the nine-to-five.

Emma's diary was blank for the rest of the week, no other meetings. She was thankful for the monotony of sitting at her desk. She didn't want anything to spoil her pristine calendar. No reasons to suddenly have to leave, no dramas. Just coming to work, doing her job, going home, looking after the children – talking to Nick this evening . . . he'd come in too late last night.

Either today or tomorrow a postman would walk down the garden path towards Wisteria Cottage, take her letter out of his bag, and put it through the letterbox. Would Elizabeth write, or call? Emma hoped it wasn't a call. She shouldn't have put her number. A letter from Elizabeth would be much easier to deal with.

If it was an early post, she could be opening the letter at that very moment . . .

'Emma, team meeting.' Laura's voice cut through her thoughts. 'D'you want a tea?'

She sat through the meeting blankly, nodding and smiling when it seemed the right thing to do. When it finally all drew to a close, her boss Geoff asked her to stay behind.

'I was sorry to hear about your mother. It must be a very difficult time.'

She nodded and looked at the whiteboard on the wall, where someone had drawn half a Venn diagram in a permanent marker pen designed for a flipchart rather than a whiteboard before realising their mistake.

'Emma, are you okay?'

'Yes, I'm fine, sorry. It's okay. Just been a tiring couple of weeks, that's all.'

'Are you sure you're ready to come back? You don't look that well.'

'It's just the travelling and the sorting. It's been a lot.'

'Okay, well, take care. Do take more time off if you need it.' He put his pen down and looked at his laptop. She was dismissed.

As soon as she got back to her desk, Emma checked her phone, butterflies rising in her stomach. But there were no missed calls or strange messages. Just a text from Nick wishing her a good day back at work. She sent a heart in response and sat back down to stare blankly at her screen again.

'D'you want a coffee?' It was the woman next to her. She had introduced herself, but Emma couldn't remember her name.

'That would be great, thanks. Milk, no sugar.'

She was glad that the woman was away making the coffee when the call came. Her phone vibrated and she grabbed it, her hands shaking. It was a Worthing number. 01903. Safe. Her body relaxed. It must be something to do with Dad. She still got occasional calls about him. People not realising he'd died.

'Hello, Emma speaking.'

There was a pause on the line.

'Hello?'

Silence. She was about to end the call when the person spoke.

'Emma, it's Elizabeth. Your sister.'

Chapter 33

Betty

January 1953

Margaret hardly seemed to be home any more, thought Betty as she took the cleaning bucket into her bedroom. Exercise books were piled up on the small desk. She appeared for supper, did her chores at weekends and then made every excuse to leave the house. Betty had tried to ask her about boys – was there someone she was interested in, was she being sensible – but Margaret would just shake her head and walk off.

Betty picked up a green exercise book from the top of the heap. *Margaret Bullman* was printed very neatly but plainly on the cover. She flicked it open. It was all mathematics equations. The next, a blue book, had *I Wandered Lonely as a Cloud by William Wordsworth* written across the top of the most recent page. She was pleased that Margaret worked hard.

Her eyes darted to the teddy bears and dolls on the mantelpiece and then to the books on the bedside tables – *The Borrowers* and *The Catcher in the Rye*. The room was caught between childhood and adulthood, a little like Margaret herself. She opened the top drawer. A gold tube of lipstick lay on some tissue paper. Betty picked it up. Gala of London. Expensive. She drew off the lid to reveal the phallic red column. It hadn't been used. Margaret had never had lipstick before. Not of her own. Someone had bought this for her. Someone with money.

Chapter 34

EMMA

FEBRUARY 2019

She knew the station's intricate iron structure intimately. At one time or another, drunk or sober, she'd used every platform, waited on every seat. She'd bought hundreds of coffees from the station cafe, and a few dozen cans of gin and tonic from M&S. And the odd emergency ready meal when she'd run out of ideas or time to cook.

Now she scanned the arrivals board for the train from Littlehampton. Elizabeth had insisted on public transport rather than Emma picking her up. Maybe she didn't want Emma encroaching on her territory so soon. Emma hadn't admitted that she'd already visited Elizabeth's house.

She wondered what she and Elizabeth would talk about. Mum, obviously. But what else? Was it going to be a tell-all conversation where they went through each other's lives year by year? Wouldn't that be awfully painful for Elizabeth – hearing about Mum bringing one daughter up while the other searched for her. She just hoped it would be an easier conversation than the call.

It had been so strained. She regretted saying that she was at work and couldn't talk. What a thing to say after all these years. It had been mean. But she hadn't known what to say. Elizabeth had sounded nervous. In the end Emma had only suggested meeting up to get off the phone. But the following day was so soon. Still, better to meet quickly and get it over with. And her boss had been decent about her asking for another day off.

For once, Emma was very early. She checked the arrivals board again. Twenty minutes to wait. Emma queued up for a coffee, but as soon as she'd received her latte, she wondered whether it would be awkward having something in her hands. What if Elizabeth was a hugger? She'd spill the coffee. She wandered out through the arches towards the taxi rank and dumped the full cup in the bin. Then she saw a homeless man watching her and felt guilty. She walked over and put a pound coin in his empty plastic coffee cup. He looked young, late teens, early twenties maybe. Not that much older than James. Short brown hair, a young, trusting face but old, tired eyes staring back at her.

'Thanks. Have a good day.' He smiled. His teeth were grimy.

'Can I get you anything? A coffee? A sandwich?' Why had she asked that? Her hands were shaking.

He looked surprised, but smiled again. 'Yeah, I'll have a pasty, if that's okay. I'm freezing. Beef and veg. Or whatever they've got.'

Emma walked back to the station swinging her arms purpose-fully. She checked the arrivals board. Still ten minutes to go, but the queue at the Cornish pasty shop was long. Finally Emma got to the front and ordered a traditional Cornish pasty. The assistant seemed to go into slow motion as she reached for the tongs and carefully placed the pasty in the paper bag, turning over the top several times to secure it. Emma thrust a fiver at her and ran through the teeming concourse, scattering a group of foreign exchange students.

She ran up to the homeless boy, but as she was stooping down she realised it was someone different. An older unshaven man with long greasy hair sat smoking in the space where the young lad had been. She jumped away awkwardly, still holding the pasty.

Then a drone of tannoy announcements drifted out of the station and she heard Littlehampton among the jumble of words. Emma started to run into the station, her hand clutching the pasty bag. And there she was.

Elizabeth was already through the ticket barriers, standing still, looking around expectantly. She seemed different from when Emma had seen her outside her house last week. Younger, maybe. Her hair was styled. She was wearing lipstick. She looked so familiar, and not just from her photographs.

Emma had thought about this meeting from the moment she'd discovered she had a sister. A massive hug and then they'd walk through the station arm in arm talking about their childhoods and laughing at shared memories. Smiles and happy tears. But in the end, she found herself in a slightly awkward embrace, trying not to press the pasty into Elizabeth's coat.

'You're just like your Facebook picture,' Elizabeth said, holding her at arm's length, examining her in the way an elderly grandmother would inspect her grandchildren.

Emma half expected her to say 'look how you've grown', but instead Elizabeth just grinned shyly.

'So are you,' Emma stammered.

'Did you want to go for lunch, or have you already eaten?' Elizabeth gestured at the pasty bag.

'Oh no, that's nothing. Sorry. Yes, let's go for lunch.' Emma knew she was nervous and gabbling and tried to take a deep breath. 'Do you know Brighton well?'

Elizabeth shook her head, her soft grey bob swaying gently against her scarf. 'Not well. We come for shopping and the occasional night out, but not regularly.'

We. 'There's a little restaurant called Mange Tout, just down Trafalgar Street. A few minutes' walk. It does French food, Mediterranean stuff?'

'Sounds perfect. Let's go there.' Elizabeth smiled that shy grin of hers again.

They walked through the station, side by side, not touching. Elizabeth walked quickly with long strides and Emma found herself trotting along to catch up with her. Under the railway arch they were forced to walk single file. They self-consciously offered each other the chance to go first, but Elizabeth was the first to step forward. Emma watched her purposeful stride down the hill, the top of her boots catching on the back of her coat. As the pavement widened, Emma caught up with her and they walked on together.

Outside Mange Tout, a waiter was setting out metal tables and chairs on the pavement in the lukewarm winter sun. Inside only two tables were occupied. A young couple finishing brunch were deep in conversation, while a family with a baby in a high chair were drinking coffee as the baby shredded a croissant. The waiter gestured for Elizabeth and Emma to take a table near the family, but Elizabeth shook her head and walked towards a table in the window. Emma smiled and sat down. What would people make of them? Two old friends out for a catch-up lunch? Two sisters discussing their mother's latest health concerns?

It was only just noon, but the waiter gave them a wine list and the lunch menu. They left the menus among the cutlery, napkins, and glasses, and looked at one another properly for the first time.

Emma could feel Elizabeth's gaze on her as she took in her sister's firm chin and strong nose, offset by kindly eyes and that funny grin that she'd noticed from her car last week. Her face was lined, but it looked like by laughter, not sorrow. She seemed to be constantly smiling. The hands cradling the empty water tumbler were small with stubby fingers. Her unpolished nails filed short, her thumb with a line of dirt under the nail. Maybe she was a gardener. Her mother had loved her garden at home but had nothing more than a few window boxes when she moved to Morecambe.

'Do I look like her?' said Elizabeth.

'Mum?'

Elizabeth nodded. It was a stupid question to ask. Who else did they have in common? But it gave Emma time to think. Yes, she did look like Mum – scarily so. Those eyes. The hair. The hands. But there was also something else familiar which she couldn't quite place. Emma tucked her hair behind her ear. 'You do. So much. Your face is the same. I knew when I first saw your picture on Facebook who you were. Even before I saw your post about look-ing for Mum.'

The waiter came to take their order and they both made a show at looking at the menu.

'Maybe some more minutes for *mesdames*,' he said in such a strong French accent that Emma was convinced it was faked.

Elizabeth looked up at him. 'That would be lovely, thanks. Perhaps just some water for now.'

'Still or sparkling for *madame*?'

'Oh, tap is fine, thank you,' Elizabeth said.

Emma smiled. She always said the same.

'So, where do we start?' said Elizabeth. 'There's so much I want to know, but I'm sure there are things you want to know too.'

Emma nodded. 'I can't even begin to start. Three weeks ago I thought I was an only child. Now I'm sitting here, my mother's just died and I'm having lunch with my new sister.'

The waiter must have caught the last of the conversation as he returned, for he quickly placed the jug on the table and hastily retreated. The two women caught each other's eye and laughed as Elizabeth poured the water into the two glasses.

'Well, let's start with how you found out about me,' said Elizabeth. 'You said in your letter that you found my birth certificate and some other things in our mother's – it feels so strange to say that – flat. Do you have them?'

'I do.' Emma reached into her shoulder bag and withdrew a plastic bag with the shawl and the rattle. Elizabeth reached forward across the table and took them from her. She brought out the shawl and covered her face with it. Emma looked away.

When she glanced back, tears were easing down Elizabeth's cheeks.

'I don't have anything of hers you see, apart from the photograph that you saw.'

Emma smiled what she hoped was a sympathetic smile. What could she say? She had thousands and thousands of memories of their mother. Many of them not very good. But at least she had them. Elizabeth was fingering the rattle.

'I wonder where this came from? Did Margaret buy it when she was pregnant with me? Or did someone – my father . . .' Elizabeth looked up at Emma '. . . buy it for her?'

Emma shrugged. 'I don't know. It was in the box with the shawl and your birth certificate.' She hesitated as Elizabeth gazed at the shawl. 'I read in an article that babies born in mother and baby homes were typically adopted at around ten days old. Was that what happened to you?'

'Yes and no. I stayed with Margaret for ten days after she had me. My parents came to Birdhurst Lodge when I was three days old. Dad said it was the most wonderful and awful thing they'd ever done. Lines of prams set out in the garden, all the babies on show. But they could see behind the windows the anguished faces of the young mothers looking down, watching to see if their baby would be taken.' Elizabeth wiped her eyes with the corner of the paper napkin. 'They chose me because I was thrashing about in my pram. Dad said it showed I had spirit and they wanted a child with what he called "a bit of spunk". Funny, really.'

Emma could feel her throat constricting. It was hard to speak. 'I just can't understand what that must have been like for Mum. To watch a couple choose her baby.'

Elizabeth nodded. 'Yes. Not something you'd get over quickly.' She paused. 'After that, Margaret had a week or so with me and my parents went home to prepare for my arrival.'

'What are their names?'

'Philip and Maureen.'

'And do you have any siblings?'

'Sadly no. My parents met late in life – they're gone now – and they couldn't have their own children. In those days you couldn't find out why, there was no IVF or anything like that. So after a couple of years, they adopted me. They thought about adopting more children, but they ran out of time.'

'Did you have a happy childhood?' Emma blushed. 'I'm sorry, that sounds so intrusive.'

Elizabeth grinned the grin that was beginning to feel quite familiar to Emma. 'Yes and no. I think inside I always knew I was adopted. Even before they told me, I felt different, separate from them.'

'Really? I naively thought that because you were adopted at birth, it would've been fine.'

'Yes, you'd think that, wouldn't you? But I felt like our family was a plate that had been broken and then glued back together with one wrong piece. I never quite fitted. I remember always asking to go home and Mum saying that I was home. When they told me I was adopted I accepted it straight away. I don't think I understood what it meant at the time. It was only as I got older that I started to ask questions. But despite what you could consider was a bad start, I've had a good life. My parents were decent parents, maybe because they were so desperate to be parents. I met Justin, my ex-husband, when I was working for the civil service. We married in 1986 on the same day that Prince Andrew and Sarah Ferguson got married.'

Emma smiled. She remembered that day. They'd had a new carpet fitted and she'd been really annoyed because she wanted to watch the royal wedding on the TV but her mum had moved the TV out of the room.

The waiter took the gap in conversation to appear by the table. 'Have *mesdames* . . . ?'

'Yes, of course, I'm so sorry.' Elizabeth grabbed the menu and appeared to choose at random. 'The cheese and ham omelette, please, with fries and a salad.' It was just what Emma wanted.

'I'll have the same. Shall we have wine?' Emma hoped Elizabeth wouldn't be one of those people who never drank at lunchtime.

'Maybe we should. Red? White?'

'Red,' said Emma. She needed something to fortify her.

'The house red is Les Galets from the Rhône, or you can see the other options on our blackboard.' The waiter gave a typically French gesture towards the intricately written board.

'A bottle of house red then, please,' said Elizabeth.

'I'm so glad you ordered a bottle. I always think a glass is such a waste.' Emma grinned. They smiled at one other conspiratorially. 'So, sorry, you were saying. You got married . . .'

'Yes, in 1986. We had a daughter, Emilia, five years later.'

'But you're now divorced?'

'Yes, sadly. Our marriage coincided with a difficult time. Having Emilia unearthed lots of feelings about motherhood and started me on the quest to look for Margaret. Justin found it hard to understand what I was going through. I found it hard enough to understand my own feelings. It wasn't the only reason, but he left me when Emilia was about fifteen. I was devastated at the time, though it shouldn't really have been a surprise. He tried to reconcile a couple of years later, but I couldn't go back by then. The trust had gone. I've been on my own ever since.' Elizabeth paused, a little breathless. 'Anyway, Emilia's now thirty-one and she's due next month with her own baby. So I'm about to be a grandmother. You'll be a great-aunt!'

'Wow, that's exciting!' Emma was taken aback by Elizabeth's candidness. 'I'm a little way off that. I have two children. James is seventeen and Libby is fifteen.'

'What are they like?'

'Oh, typical teenagers. James is really into his sport and wants to go to uni the year after next – he wants to study astrophysics. Black holes and stuff like that.' She smiled at Elizabeth. 'Libby is more arty. I think she'll go on to the same college as James but to do art and photography. Some of her work is amazing.'

'And do you have any other relatives?'

'I had an aunt but she died a long time ago and my dad died a few years ago.'

'Oh, I'm sorry.' Elizabeth smiled, her eyes crinkling.

The waiter reappeared with the bottle of wine and went through the rigmarole of opening it and asking Elizabeth to taste it.

'So you always knew that you were adopted?'

'Yes. But I wasn't told the whole truth.'

'Oh?'

'They always told me that I was adopted, but Mum told me that I'd been left in the local church doorway and that she found me when she went to evensong. I wasn't even that well wrapped up and she said that I wouldn't have survived the night so it was lucky that she came by.'

'Christ, so you felt completely abandoned.' Emma leaned forward and put her elbows on the table.

'I hate that word, but yes.'

Emma gritted her teeth. She should have phrased it more carefully.

'But that's what it felt like,' Elizabeth said, fiddling with the cutlery and straightening her napkin.

'So how did you find out the truth?' Emma saw the hesitation in Elizabeth's eyes. 'If you don't want to talk about it, that's fine. I appreciate that it's going to be painful to open old wounds. We can talk about something else.'

Elizabeth looked up at Emma. 'Sometimes the only way to heal the wound is to open it up,' she muttered and took a sip of wine as the waiter brought their order. 'Mum died when I was twenty-six. She was only young herself really – she had pneumonia. I felt I was being left all over again. Dad tried to help, but he didn't really understand how I felt. From his perspective, I might have been abandoned as a baby but I'd been looked after ever since. I'd had a good life. He never really appreciated the emotional scars, I suppose, that I carried.'

'I know exactly what you mean.' Emma reached forward and touched her hand briefly. She realised she felt guilty. That however difficult a relationship she'd had with her mother, at least she'd known her.

'Things got worse and I ended up on carbamazepine. It's an anti-psychotic. There was a risk that I might be sectioned. I had all sorts of issues. Not ones to talk about over lunch.' Elizabeth cradled her right wrist, covered by her thick jumper. 'Dad was desperate. He had lost his wife and was now faced with losing his only daughter. And it was then that he told me that Mum had lied about me being left in the church doorway.'

'I guess he must have felt huge loyalty to his wife.'

'Yes. He said that he'd never wanted to go along with it, but she'd insisted they say that I was found so that I couldn't trace my birth mother. He gave me my original birth certificate – I'd always had a different version – and then the most amazing gift: the picture of Margaret holding me outside Birdhurst Lodge.'

Emma nodded. 'I can see your mum's point of view. She must have been desperate to have a child and didn't want to think about losing you if you tried to trace your birth mother.'

'Yes. She was a complicated woman too. Not being able to have children herself caused her all sorts of problems, I think. She felt she'd let my dad and her parents down. Anyway, I think it was just the sort of news that I needed. Suddenly, rather than being abandoned, I'd been born to an unmarried teenage mum with few options in a mother and baby home. Somehow, it felt a much better beginning. Almost romantic.' Elizabeth took a large gulp of wine. 'There were still difficult times. Since I've discovered how I was adopted, I've always found those ten days between my birthday and the day my parents took me home very difficult. Sort of helpless and empty. It's almost as if there's some sort of memory built into me about that time with Margaret. I'd never been keen on celebrating my birthday anyway – why celebrate a day on which I thought I'd been abandoned? Dad tried to help by celebrating both my birthday and then my adoption day – the day he became a parent, which he said was one of the greatest days of his life, and the day that our life as a family started.'

'But they kept your name? One of the things I was worried about when I was looking for you was that your adopted parents would have changed your name and we'd never find you,' said Emma.

'Yes, it's strange that, isn't it? Bearing in mind how my mother felt, I would have thought she would have come up with her own name for me. But they only changed my surname. I like having that link back to Margaret. She created me, and gave me my name, even though my parents then raised me.'

The way Elizabeth used her hands so expressively to make a point was very reminiscent of their mother. 'Is that when you started looking for Mum . . . for Margaret?'

'Yes. But it was much more difficult then – no Facebook, for starters. Dad gave me my adoption certificate too – again, Mum had said she didn't have it or always made excuses. I never thought to ask why. I approached the Adoption Contact Register to see if Margaret had left a letter there for me. She hadn't. It was really hard—' Elizabeth's voice broke slightly and she took a slug of wine.

Emma twirled the stem of her glass and watched the red liquid sweep around the glass, almost spilling out of the top. 'I'm so sorry.'

Elizabeth shrugged. 'Dad finally came into his own then really. He talked to me a lot about what it must have been like for Margaret having a baby at sixteen, especially in 1953. That she may not have felt she had a choice.'

Emma nodded. 'It would have been awful for her.'

'But I didn't care what sort of birth mother she was, or how bad my life would have been with her. She was my birth mother and I wanted to know her. I wanted to understand why she'd left me. There was a big, empty hole inside of me that only she could fill. I felt that I would never know who I was until I found her. I left a letter with the Adoption Register in case she ever got in touch and tried not to think about it.'

'But you did find her. You wrote to her?'

'Yes, how did you know?' Elizabeth looked up at her, surprised.

'We – Mum's friend Clare and I – found the letter a few days ago, stuck between the pages of a book.'

'Oh. So she did get it.' Elizabeth looked out of the window. Her eyes were full of tears.

'Yes. I guess she didn't reply?'

'No.' Elizabeth was still looking out of the window, through the condensation trailing down the glass. Emma followed her gaze but couldn't see what she was looking at. She spoke so quietly that Emma could barely hear her over the cutlery scraping plates, clinking of glasses and chatter. 'I went to the house, your house, before I wrote the letter.'

'Oh.' Emma tried to cover her shock. Elizabeth had done exactly what she herself had a few days ago.

'I don't know why. But once I got the address, I just wanted to see her. So I drove up to Clapham – Greystones – and parked outside. I just sat there in the car watching. Waiting for her to come out. And that's when I think I saw you. You were running around the front garden with a Labrador, trying to get it to jump over makeshift fences. I watched you for a long time, not really understanding who you were. And then I saw Margaret come out through the front door, wiping her hands on an apron and she called you. I knew she was my mother. She still looked like she had at sixteen. The same face. They say you can never recognise yourself in someone else, but I saw myself in Margaret that day. It was the only time I ever saw her. Ten days when I was born and then half an hour watching from a car years later. Not much of a relationship, is it?' Emma stayed very still. 'You ignored her and carried on with the dog, although I could hear her voice from the car—'

'Were you not tempted to get out of the car and say something to her?'

'Looking back, I think I should have done. But it was like I was frozen. Here was the woman I'd spent my whole life looking for. But I couldn't move.'

Emma remembered how she'd felt outside Elizabeth's own home a few days before, and nodded.

'You'd retreated up into the trees – some sort of tree house, I suppose, it was too overgrown for me to see – and she disappeared in there with you. I waited for ages and eventually the two of you reappeared. You dancing ahead of her with the dog. It just all seemed so perfect. So domestic. It was just like the life I'd had with my parents. It sounds so mean to say – and I'm not begrudging you your childhood – but I couldn't understand why she could be like that with you, but not with me. That she could play with one daughter and deny the existence of another.'

Emma took Elizabeth's hand across the table and looked her in the eye. 'I'm so sorry, it's just awful.'

Elizabeth looked at her wanly. 'So I came back home and wrote her a letter. I waited for weeks and weeks, rushing every morning to see if there was a letter from her. But she never responded. It felt like another rejection. She'd already rejected me once, when I was born, and then she was rejecting me for a second time.

'I was very low afterwards. Justin was cross at me for writing and going to see her and warned me never to go back. I was on antidepressants again for a while but gradually improved. It was an awful few years. Emilia was really young and, having my own baby, I struggled to see how Margaret could have given me up.

'I went back to Greystones a few months later and rang the doorbell. I just wanted to see her, to ask her why she hadn't responded. A lady answered and said Margaret had moved away. I couldn't find her after that.' Elizabeth picked at the side of her nail.

Emma thought back and it all clicked into place. Her aunt; boarding school; her mother's illness when she returned. 'Yes, Mum went away not long after receiving your letter. I wonder who you spoke to – maybe my aunt or our cleaning lady? Neither of them were a fan of Mum so they wouldn't have given you any extra information.' Her mother had disappeared from Emma's world not long after receiving that letter from Elizabeth, setting in train a whole series of events which had changed the course of Emma's life. If Elizabeth hadn't written that letter to their mother, would things have been different in her own childhood? Would her relationship with her mother have been easier? She sighed. It was impossible to tell.

'What's the matter?' Elizabeth asked, her head on one side.

Emma shook her head but didn't look up. 'Oh, nothing. It's not important.'

'You were saying that Margaret went away?'

'Yes, she went away for a while.' Emma swallowed. 'And then a few years after that, she and my dad split up. She changed her name back to her birth father's name of Chapman and moved to the north-west.' Emma glanced at her watch.

'Her birth father?'

'Yes, my mother's mother – our grandmother – Betty was pregnant with Mum before she was married. Our grandfather stood her up at the altar. It was a massive scandal. She never saw him again. She stayed at home with my great-grandmother and you can imagine the shame at that time – 1937. A few years later Betty met someone who then adopted Mum and brought her up. But Mum always seemed to have had romantic notions about her birth father.'

'What was his name?'

'The birth father? Chapman. I can't remember his first name.'

'No, her real father. The man who adopted her and brought her up.'

'Oh, her stepfather. Grandpa wasn't her real father.'

'He was though, wasn't he? He was the one who brought her up. In the same way that Margaret will always be my birth mother – she gave birth to me – but Mum and Dad – Philip and Maureen – are my actual parents because they brought me up.'

'Yes, I guess I've never thought about it like that, but you're right.'

'So, what was Margaret's father called?'

'Grandpa Jack.'

'Oh, that's a good name, my daughter wants to call her baby Jack if it's a boy. It could almost be after her – what would he be – her great-great-grandfather?'

Emma nodded. 'It's like a continuation of the family name.'

The waiter was hovering again and Emma realised she'd hardly touched the food but most of the wine had gone. 'Is everything okay with *mesdames*?'

'Oh, it's lovely. Sorry. I'm just not very hungry.' Emma picked up the wine glass and took the last slug of her wine. The waiter busied himself clearing the table while looking sadly at the two almost full plates.

Elizabeth caught Emma's eye and chuckled slightly. When he'd finally removed the wine glasses he left the coffee menu. 'I don't drink coffee, do you?'

'Not in the afternoon. But I'll have a tea.'

The waiter magically reappeared.

'A peppermint tea, please,' Elizabeth said.

'Same for me too.'

'So what about you? We've talked about my life but very little about yours.'

'It's funny, if you'd asked me that question a few weeks ago I would have said I'd had a happy childhood, and believed it. But I didn't really. Mum and I had a very difficult relationship. She was very up and down and maybe now I realise why. When I had James, we started to get on really well and for a couple of years we had a great relationship. But then Libby came along and all that changed.'

'Why?'

'Well, I didn't know at the time, but Libby . . .' Emma paused. 'Elizabeth.'

'Oh God. I didn't make the connection. How did Margaret react? That must have been awful.'

'Yes, it was very difficult.'

The waiter arrived with two tall glass mugs of hot water, with teabags at the side. Emma busied herself unwrapping the teabag and putting it in the mug, stirring it carefully. 'I guess that was the beginning of the end of our relationship. I was in Sussex with two small children; she was in Morecambe and was suffering from cancer. She made no effort to come down here, so I'd go up there all the time and it became too much. She was very anti-Libby – obviously, I know why now, but then I took it very personally, so after a while I stopped going to see Mum so much. And then after one particularly difficult visit, I didn't go again. When she died last month I hadn't seen her in some years.' Emma stared into her mug. 'That sounds awful, doesn't it?'

'Just because she's your blood relative, your mum, doesn't mean you have to get on.' Elizabeth looked out of the window.

'True, but sitting here with you, I feel I should have made more of an effort. There's you desperate to see her and not being able to. And me, deliberately not seeing her even though I could. It feels wrong.'

'But you didn't know about me until last week. There were times that I didn't get on with my mum. As a teenager I said some horrible things – about wishing they'd never adopted me, that my real mother – I used that phrase a lot when I was angry – was much better. Nasty, hurtful things. That's just growing up, isn't it?'

The waiter slid the silver plate with the bill on to the table.

'D'you think he's trying to get rid of us?' said Elizabeth. They both looked up and saw the queue at the door. Elizabeth rifled in her bag for her purse. 'Let me get this.'

'Are you sure? I'll get the next one.' They looked at each other and smiled. 'This is not going to be the best offer of a day out you'll ever have, but I have Mum's ashes. She requested that they be scattered from high ground, so I was going to scatter them at Devil's

Dyke. Would you like to come with me? I thought we could do it together.'

Elizabeth bit her lip and nodded. 'I'd love that. Thank you.'

'There's a nice cafe at the bottom of the dyke at Saddlescombe Farm. We could have tea there.'

'We should make a better job of it than we did this meal.' Emma laughed.

They walked back to the station together in a relaxed silence. 'I'm usually not very good at goodbyes,' said Elizabeth. 'I hate seeing people off at airports and that sort of thing. But this feels all right.'

'It's not goodbye,' Emma said gently. 'We're family now.'

Before the barriers they hugged, not the awkward squeeze of a few hours before but a full, long embrace. Emma watched Elizabeth stride along the platform, holding the bag with the shawl and rattle, heading for the front of the train. As she neared the end of the coaches she turned and waved – a tiny figure in the distance. Emma waved back. The figure could easily be her mother. If Elizabeth had her mother's mannerisms even though they'd been separated shortly after birth, would Margaret have had any of her birth father's gestures? Emma wondered. How did that feel for Granny Betty to see, knowing where they'd come from? It was all such a mess.

Emma turned away and reached into her bag for her phone. Her hands touched something soft and warm and she opened her bag to look. It was the flattened pasty. She took it out and started to nibble at the edges as she walked out of the station, the pastry flaking down her coat. Meeting her half-sister for the first time had somehow made her feel so much closer to her mother. Piece by piece she was beginning to understand her a little more, beginning to see her way out of the maze.

Chapter 35

Margaret

March 1953

'You're fifteen, you're not an adult yet. I do not want you wearing a top that shows your stomach. You look like a, like—' Her mother's face was puce. 'Just untie the knot and then tuck the blouse into your skirt, it'll look much nicer.'

Margaret didn't really know why she was bothering to argue. She could give in, tuck the blouse in and then take it out and knot it up the minute she left the flat. Just as she usually did. But her mother was so smug.

'Don't tell me what to do. I *am* an adult. Let me be myself.'

'While you're under my roof, you'll live by my rules.'

They stood either side of the dining table, their faces set. Her mother always pursed her lips when she was angry.

'You have no idea what goes on under your roof. You think it's all perfect. You're the perfect chef's wife. But you don't have a bloody clue,' she muttered.

'Please don't use that language.' Her mother's lips tightened.

'Oh for God's sake, stop being so bloody prim and proper.' Margaret's voice rose. 'You go on about me and how I dress. I wasn't the one who was easy before I got married and had a bloody child. You have a nerve going on at me.'

Betty's mouth slackened. Margaret smiled slightly. For the first time in months she felt a sense of power. Not just over her impossible mother but she knew her stepfather was in their bedroom across the hall, sleeping off an early shift. Even with the doors shut, he would be able to hear them.

'How dare you!' Her mother's chest heaved and she was struggling to get the words out. 'When you're grown-up, you'll realise that you don't know as much as you think. Relationships between men and women are very complex. As a child you can't possibly understand.'

Margaret snorted. 'I *do* understand. I'm not as innocent as you think.'

'Darling, the dalliances you have with boys are nothing in comparison to grown-up relationships, to loving marriages.' Her mother had adopted a simpering tone. She used it sometimes when Jack was angry.

'Loving marriages?' Margaret was incredulous. 'You think you know it all, that you're so lucky. You don't even know anything about Jack—'

'Margaret, that's enough.' Betty's voice was cracking. 'Don't talk about things you know nothing about. You're trying to be deliberately hurtful.'

'Really? You think you know everything.' Margaret's voice was suddenly hard, cruel. She could almost feel her stepfather in the room. But she couldn't stop herself. 'You have no idea what he's like.' Her voice broke and she sank down on to one of the chairs, the anger seeping from her like bath water down a plughole. 'What he's been forcing me to do to him,' she whispered, looking up at her mother's frozen face. 'How he touches me.' She closed her eyes.

The heavy silence was broken by the sound of glass smashing from behind the closed door of the bedroom. Margaret winced, her heart thumping. He'd threatened to punish her if she told anyone. But her mother would make him stop. Now she knew.

She slowly opened her eyes. Her mother was standing over her staring at her intently.

'You bitch,' she said slowly, then slapped Margaret hard across the face. 'How dare you! I've done everything for you. I never wanted you in the first place, not once your bloody father stood me up at the altar. I tried to get rid of you but you were too bloody stubborn. Like you always are. I wish I'd succeeded.'

'He forced me . . . He made me . . .' Margaret was sobbing properly now. But her mother stood there looking down at her, glaring. Margaret swallowed and then jumped up, running out of the sitting room and down the hallway.

Chapter 36

BETTY

MARCH 1953

Betty stood blinking, looking at the space where Margaret had been. She pressed her hands against her face, the sting in her right hand still smarting. Margaret's bedroom door slammed, shaking the whole flat. Her lungs felt tight and Betty struggled to draw breath. Was it true, what Margaret had said? She opened her eyes and caught sight of the photograph of the three of them at Buckingham Palace, sitting on the sideboard. Betty stumbled forward and picked up the frame.

She'd known that day at the palace that Jack looked at Margaret differently. Wrongly. She'd known then and she'd done nothing. Somehow she'd known when she saw the lipstick. Margaret and Jack. If it was anyone else. Another woman. But she was her daughter. How *could* he? How could *they?* Her stomach convulsed and the bile rose up, burning her throat.

Next to the Buckingham Palace picture was a photograph of Margaret on her first birthday, not long before Betty had met Jack. She touched her fingers against the plump cheeks, and remembered the promise she'd made on the morning of her birth.

Margaret had been such a beautiful baby. Betty remembered rushing back from the laundry or the factory and lying on her bunk bed with her, playing peek-a-boo. Her giggle had been infectious, making the whole family laugh.

Betty's smile slipped. But those had been hard years. The father never paid anything towards Margaret's keep. He denied she was his and there was nothing Betty could do to prove it, though she was the spitting image of him. Betty had seen him now and again, with a wife and other children. After she was sacked from the munitions factory, they'd struggled. The only laundry that would take her didn't pay as well, and everyone there knew about Margaret. Her sin was a heavy coat she couldn't seem to shed.

They'd have to go back to that. Betty a fallen woman, Margaret tainted by her illegitimacy and her mother's crimes. She'd be at the mercy of every snide comment – and worse. That was if her family would even take her back. She thought of her mother's smug face, her father's disappointment. Why would Margaret do this to them? Surely she was lying.

Didn't Margaret realise she would have to leave her school, that they wouldn't be able to afford it if Jack left them? Just as she was doing so brilliantly and she was about to take those important exams. Who else could she go to? She didn't have any friends of her own to speak of, they were all the wives of Jack's friends and they'd close their middle-class doors in her face.

So what if Jack looked at Margaret differently now? But he would never cross a line. No, Margaret must be lying. She was always trying to annoy her. Betty must stay with Jack. He was good; he was kind. Yes, sometimes she thought he looked at Margaret the way he should be looking at her, but Margaret was always wearing those provocative clothes. She thought of the lipstick. Perhaps Margaret had asked him for it. She was always after things from the magazines.

She walked into the hall, looking at the two closed bedroom doors. Betty quietly opened her bedroom door. Jack was lying face down, his head covered by the pillow. He never slept like that. She couldn't see how he could even breathe. Had he heard what Margaret had said? The vice gripped her chest until she thought she might faint.

On the floor by the bedside table, a glass had smashed, the shards scattering across the room and under the bed. Had Jack caught the glass in his sleep? Or maybe the wind had caught it? Betty glanced across to the window, which had been left slightly open. She bent down and mechanically started picking up the fragments, balancing them on top of one another in her palm, like prayer stone stacks.

She needed to pretend that this hadn't happened. For everyone's sake. Why was Margaret saying these things?

The tears came then and she stood pressing her fingers beneath her eyes to stem the flow. Betty felt betrayed. She didn't know who was telling the truth or what the truth even was. But she couldn't ask Jack – she might lose him. She couldn't go back to how her life was before Jack.

Betty picked up the final piece of glass, holding it up to the light. The sharp edges reflected the light a thousand times, casting a rainbow around the room. She brought it down against her thumb and a slice of crimson opened up along the top. She relaxed into the pain.

She needed to stop Margaret. Stop her from saying anything else and ruining everything. Betty turned and walked out of the room, closing the door quietly behind her. She dropped the glass shards into the kitchen bin, pressing down on her cut. She could hear Margaret crying behind her bedroom door at the end of the corridor. She looked at the framed school portrait of Margaret on the wall from the end of junior school. Still a little girl then, a confident gaze looking out from under a heavy fringe. How had it come to this? Betty reached out and touched Margaret's door. Her hand fluttered back and touched her face. Then she closed her eyes and took a deep breath.

'I don't want to ever hear another word about this nonsense. Do you understand?' Margaret was silent behind the door. Betty tried to steady her voice. 'If you want to remain in my household you will never mention such lies again.'

The tears came without stopping. She pressed her fingers under her eyes again but the tears kept on flowing. She dropped her head and walked back to her bedroom. She hardly glanced at Jack. The pain in her chest gripped her and she stood at the end of the bed waiting for it to pass, her eyes closed, her head bowed. A heavy silence smothered the flat.

Betty eased around to her side of the bed and lay down. Her whole body was numb. Even her mind was paralysed. After a while Jack grunted and rolled out, putting his arm across Betty. She stiffened but she didn't move. Then he opened his eyes and yawned.

'What's the matter, Betty? You look like you've been crying.'

'Nothing, Jack. There's nothing wrong,' said Betty, unable to meet his eye. She turned on to her side, away from him.

Jack lay still and then eventually turned to cuddle her. Betty flinched, but allowed him to hold her. He stroked her hair and she forced her breath into a regular pattern so he would think she was asleep. Eventually his arm stopped moving and she realised he was sleeping. How could he sleep after this? She lay stiff and wide awake in his arms.

Chapter 37

Emma

February 2019

Emma let herself into the silent house. There was a good hour until she had to be at Libby's school for the meeting. She made herself another cup of tea and went into the sitting room, mechanically picking up an empty drinks carton and crisp packet. Bending down to pick up a discarded sock, she noticed the box of letters she'd pushed underneath the sofa and remembered the final letter from Granny Betty. She'd forgotten it in all the excitement of going back to work and then meeting Elizabeth. She put her mug down and drew the box out.

This letter was more crumpled than the others. It must be the letter Granny Betty had written to Margaret telling her about Grandpa Jack's death, the one Emma had told her grandmother to write to her mother all those years ago sitting in Pullman Court after his death. Emma took a sip of the tea and started reading, curious as to how Betty had told her daughter about her stepfather's death. She couldn't remember her mother ever mentioning it.

Pullman Court
Streatham Hill
9 September 1993

Dear Margaret,
Please don't throw this letter away without reading it. I know I'm the last person you want to hear from, but I have something important to say. I want you to know how sorry I am for not believing you all those years ago. It must have taken a lot of courage to tell me.

I did believe you, deep inside, but I didn't realise how bad it was. I was afraid. Of what would happen to Jack if I told anyone what you'd said he did. Afraid of what Jack would do to me, and to you. And I was afraid for me. That he'd leave me. I didn't want to be alone and have people talking about me again.

I'm sorry I ignored the note you wrote when you left. I never told anyone about it. I wanted to think it was because you still wanted to cause trouble. I didn't want to believe what you said he was doing. My Jack.

When he proposed to me, they said I was the luckiest girl alive. Nobody could believe that he'd chosen me. A handsome chef from a good family with a twinkle in his eye, and me a nineteen-year-old unmarried girl with a three-year-old child.

It was so perfect, our lovely flat, all that space after living in that place for years. I don't think you realised at the time how lucky we were. Of course you didn't, you were so young. Without Jack, you and I would have been on the street. Granny June would never have taken us back – my mother hated me having you in the first place. I couldn't risk losing our lives. He gave us so much.

How could I believe that my perfect Jack was doing things that he shouldn't? Please understand how it felt when you came to me and said that, when you were just fifteen. I saw him looking at you. But all the men were looking at you by then.

I'm sorry to say this, but Jack died a few days ago. It was quick in the end. He was complaining for a few months of back-end trouble, and we went to the doctor's but they didn't find anything. But then he collapsed and when he was in hospital they found the tumour, the size of a grapefruit. There was noth-ing they could do except pump him full of morphine and wait it out, for six weeks in the end.

He was lucid even when he was dying, and that's when he told me, four days ago, what he'd done to you. He said he had lived with it all his life, that he regretted it, and he wanted to see you to say sorry. He didn't want to die without you knowing that he was sorry, that he wished it had never happened and he was sorry that you left us after that. But I couldn't call you. I didn't want you to see him like that, and I didn't want him to be upset any more. But he wanted you to know that he was sorry.

His funeral is next Thursday, the 19th. 2 p.m. in South London crematorium. I hope you can come, it would mean a lot to me. Emma has been a great help to me these last few days sorting out the flat. And I know David said he'd come, so you'd be among your family.

224

I know we haven't seen much of you these last few years. I am sorry, Margaret, I wish it had all been very different. I wasn't the mother to you that I wanted to be, that you needed me to be.

Love, Mother

Emma slowly stood to look out of the window. But she hardly saw anything. The sallow light reflected off her tears. Her mouth filled and she realised she was going to be sick. She dropped the letter and only just made it to the downstairs loo in time.

Emma stayed with her head over the bowl for a long time after she'd stopped retching, her eyes shut, the tears still falling. She'd loved Grandpa Jack, he'd always been fun, inviting Emma into the kitchen, showing her how to make the perfect scrambled egg.

'Just runny enough to spread but not to give you salmonella,' he'd say.

And how to whisk the perfect meringue. He'd had some sort of illness that meant he had to eat lots of egg yolks. Which meant plenty of leftover whites for meringues. She could picture him now, in his chef's whites in that flat in Streatham. He'd been so kind. But behind all that, he'd abused her mother, his own stepdaughter. And her mum had told Granny Betty and not been believed. Imagine that. She knew her mother had left home at sixteen, but she'd never asked why. And then suddenly she realised. Her mother had not had a teenage boyfriend with whom she'd accidentally got pregnant. Elizabeth was Grandpa Jack's baby. The thought curdled her stomach again. *Poor, poor Mum.* Eventually Emma got up from the loo floor and washed her mouth out in the basin. She caught sight of her reflection in the mirror – her dark eyes stared at her. She went into the kitchen and flicked the kettle on again, her hands trembling.

Chapter 38

BETTY

MARCH 1953

Betty knew something was wrong the minute she walked into the hallway. Jack was there waiting for her, his hair sticking up, his hands in his pockets. He couldn't look her in the eye.

'How was Mass?' he asked, examining his feet.

'Oh, you know, fine,' she said, her mouth dry, her eyes darting around. 'Where's Margaret?' She should never have left her alone with Jack.

Jack nodded towards the kitchen door but then barred her way. 'Let me take your coat.' His hand touched her arm as he slipped the coat off and she flinched. He bustled about in front of her, taking off her scarf and her hat. She stood stock still, finding it hard to swallow. When he'd put her coat, hat and scarf on the hat stand, she slipped past him and eased open the kitchen door.

Margaret was standing at the stove, stirring a pan. She didn't look up as Betty came in, but her cheeks were damp. 'Is everything okay, darling?' Betty asked.

Margaret nodded, but her hand seemed to shake on the wooden spoon. They were covered in charcoal from those sketches she was working on. A girl in a maze in the darkness.

Something had happened while she was at church. Betty set her jaw. She needed to get Margaret out of here. She touched Margaret on the shoulder and felt her flinch, and stopped herself pulling her into an embrace.

'I had a thought while I was at Mass. What if you went to stay with my parents for a little while? Over the Easter holidays? Give you a break from here. Grandpa would love to see a little more of you, I'm sure.'

Margaret nodded but didn't look up. But as Betty moved away, she felt Margaret staring at her. Betty busied herself clearing up the eggs that Margaret seemed to have dripped all down the cupboards.

Chapter 39

Emma

February 2019

Back in the sitting room, Emma took out the old photo albums from the cupboard and started scanning through the pictures of Betty, Jack, and Margaret.

Jack's high forehead and unusual ears were so obvious a feature in Elizabeth that she couldn't believe she hadn't spotted the resemblance before. She looked so like their mother, but also so like Grandpa Jack. Even now the resemblance was startling. How could Jack have stood with his wife and stepdaughter posing for happy family photos when he was abusing her? Did Jack know he'd fathered his stepdaughter's baby? Did Betty know? There was nothing about a baby in any of the letters. Maybe her mother had kept it all secret. *Poor Mum.* Emma covered her face with her hands.

And Elizabeth – should she tell her? All the people were dead now and the secret should have gone with them.

Suddenly she thought of Mr Eals and his warning to leave the past alone. She was certain he knew who Elizabeth's father was and had warned her to stay away as a result. But she'd dug around and found out the truth. She should have left it all alone. A sob rose up inside her. She had to talk to Mr Eals, and straightaway. It couldn't wait.

She called his office but there was no response. So she got into her car and started the drive north. The journey was a blur, a series of motorways merging into one another as Emma stayed in the outside lane, pushing the speed limit. After hours of straight driving she finally took the turn off the motorway to Lancaster and then to Morecambe where she pulled up outside the solicitor's office.

Her legs buckled slightly as she got out of the car, stiff after driving for so long.

The bell had hardly stopped trilling her arrival when the solicitor's secretary was on her feet, nervously twisting her hands. 'Can I help you?'

'I'd like to see Mr Eals, please.'

'Certainly, when would you like to arrange the meeting?' The voice was brisk, efficient.

'Now.'

'Oh, I'm afraid that Mr Eals is about to leave. He couldn't possibly have an appointment at such short notice. Perhaps one of our associates could see you tomorrow?'

'I need to see Mr Eals. Today. Please could you tell him that it's Margaret's daughter, and I know about Jack.' She could hear her voice break when she said his name, and she turned away from the secretary, focusing on slowly drawing air into her lungs.

'One moment.' She hurried down the corridor and reappeared almost immediately. 'Mr Eals will see you now.' The voice had changed. Softer, warmer.

'Thank you.'

'He's in his office. Go straight through.'

Mr Eals was bent over a huge pile of paperwork. He was slowly rising from his chair as she came in, levering himself up using the wooden arms. For a moment, she thought he was going to hug her, but he must have changed his mind and he instead grasped her right hand with his two hands in a strange embrace, the hairy knuckles stretched white.

Chapter 40

BETTY

AUGUST 1953

Betty came rushing into their bedroom screaming. 'She's gone! She's gone!' Tears were streaming down her face, her eyes wild. She turned on the light.

'Who's gone?' Jack asked, blinking.

'Margaret. She's not here.' Betty was twisting her dressing gown cord around her wrist.

'What d'you mean she's not here?'

Betty rushed out of the room and back to Margaret's room.

The wardrobe doors had been left open. Clothes spilled out of the chest of drawers. The depressing sketch of the little girl in the maze Margaret was working on was propped up on the floor near the bed which hadn't been made.

'Her jeans and two dresses have gone. Her nightgown. Some underwear. A couple of sweaters. Her winter coat. The weekend bag she took to Mother's at Easter. And Edward.' Betty's voice broke.

'Edward?'

'Her teddy bear.'

'Christ.' Jack rubbed his forehead.

'And on her birthday too.' Betty knelt by the bed, her head buried into Margaret's pillow.

Jack knelt down beside her and put an arm round her shoulders. 'Don't be silly, Betty. She'll be back. Could she have popped out for . . . Anyway, why are you up so early? Did you hear something?'

'No, I got up to ice her cake.' Betty sobbed even harder.

'Is there anything else missing in the house?' Jack asked, stroking Betty's back.

She nodded and turned round to him, tears spilling out of her eyes. 'That's what first made me realise something was wrong. The housekeeping money has all gone.'

They went into the kitchen. The tin had been taken down from the shelf and was on the counter. It was empty. He picked it up. 'How much was in here?'

'Twenty-seven pounds, five shillings, and three pence.' Betty hung her head.

'Bloody hell, Betty. Where on earth did you get that money from?'

'I've been putting aside what I could for years. For a rainy day.' She was crying again, using the bottom of her dressing gown to wipe her eyes. 'At least Margaret will have something to pay her way.'

Jack nodded. 'Did she, er, leave a note?' he asked.

Betty shook her head but avoided his gaze.

'I don't suppose she would have gone to your mother's?'

'I thought of that,' Betty said. 'They did get close at Easter when she stayed with them.' For the first time, she looked a little brighter. 'I'll get dressed and go down to the telephone box and call her neighbour.'

'Betty, it's too early.'

'This is an emergency, Jack. Our daughter has gone missing. You'll need to go to the police and report it. Get dressed and go right away.'

◆ ◆ ◆

That evening, they sat opposite each other at the dining table, Betty picking at her chicken. 'Why now? Why on her sixteenth birthday? It was supposed to be such a lovely day.' She was crying again. 'The things that Mother said on the telephone were so hurtful.' Betty sniffed.

'Oh, just ignore her, darling. She's always had it against us, and Margaret.'

'She still punishes me for what happened. As if it was my fault.'

'Your mother is just a bitter old woman. We shouldn't have anything more to do with her.'

'We have to, Jack, she's my mother. And Margaret might go to her.'

'True.' He speared a piece of chicken, popped it in his mouth and smiled. 'This is delicious. I love having the sweetness of the raisins with the chicken.'

Betty didn't smile back at him. 'Jack?'

'Yes?' He didn't look up and instead shovelled in another mouthful of food, chewing it slowly.

When he eventually looked at her, she stared right into him. 'You don't know why she left, do you? Things were okay between the two of you?' Her voice was soft.

Jack took a long time to finish his mouthful. 'Of course I don't, Betty. Margaret was my daughter too, remember. I've brought her up since she was three.' He looked her in the eye.

233

'Yes, of course.' Betty put down her fork, leaving her chicken barely touched. She said nothing else for the rest of the meal. Eventually Jack took her plate and finished off her chicken.

After dinner, she spent a long time in the kitchen cleaning and re-cleaning the surfaces. She stayed up much later than usual, pacing up and down the sitting room.

'It's dark now,' she said. 'I hope she's found somewhere safe to sleep. That she's not on the streets,' she said.

He looked up from his paper. 'With twenty-seven pounds in her pocket, she'll be in a nice hotel, Betty, there's no need to worry.'

'She's sixteen, Jack. Of course I'm bloody worried. My daughter is sixteen and on the streets of London at night when she should be home with me.' Betty marched across the room into the hall and slammed the sitting room door. She went into their bedroom, and thought he might follow her, but the idea of lying down with Jack made her want to retch. She couldn't face his hands on her. Not tonight.

Instead she walked down the hallway and opened Margaret's door. She got into the unmade bed fully clothed and took one of Margaret's teddy bears and hugged it. She lay there for a long time, thinking about Margaret and where she might be.

Eventually she heard Jack come out of the sitting room, and go into their bedroom. He must have been expecting her to be there because he quickly came down the corridor and opened Margaret's door. Betty stayed still and breathed slowly. When he eventually closed the door, she opened her eyes, swollen from crying. She hugged the bear a little tighter and burrowed into Margaret's pillow. It smelled of Margaret – that slightly sweet, unwashed smell. Where could she be? Apart from her parents, she couldn't think of anywhere where she could have just turned up announced. She squeezed her eyes shut and tried to imagine Margaret in a hotel somewhere safe and warm, but the image wouldn't come. What horrors was she facing? Betty pinched the bridge of her nose.

She sat up, drawing the blanket around her, and turned to look at the sketch by the bed. It was the best one Margaret had done by far; she was so talented. Her school was covered in her artwork. Betty sniffed. She wondered who the girl in the painting was. Perhaps it was Margaret. The hair was the same and she'd been very slight when she was that age. Not recently of course, she seemed to have put a lot of weight on. Puppy fat. Betty got on to her knees and touched the painting. There was something about the girl that made her feel a little uneasy. As if she was blaming Betty for everything.

Betty slumped back on the bed. It *was* all her fault. She shouldn't have ignored what Margaret had said in the winter. But she hadn't wanted to believe her. She didn't want to feel jealous of her own daughter for stealing her husband's attention. For nearly ruining their family.

Betty took Margaret's note that she'd left in the housekeeping tin out from the pocket of her dress and reread the few short sentences. Margaret was right. She'd let her down. She was a terrible mother. But Jack wasn't an abuser. Surely? A grope or two, perhaps. Not right, of course. But Margaret had always exaggerated, hadn't she? Betty would find her, bring her back, and then it would all be okay again.

She curled into a ball under the covers, and was unable to stop herself moaning quietly, like an animal dying.

Chapter 41

Margaret

August 1953

Margaret sat on a bench in Hyde Park watching the boats on the Serpentine. Couples rowing to and fro, sometimes a child sandwiched between them. Occasionally there was an outburst of laughter. Jack's old Navy duffle bag was squeezed between her feet. She hadn't wanted to take anything of his, but it was the only bag that was big enough to hold everything she'd needed. How strange, Margaret thought, that everything she had in the world was in one bag.

Margaret leaned her head back, closed her eyes and let the sun beat fully on her face. She smiled and took a deep breath. She was free. She'd felt it the minute she got out of Streatham, once she was certain that they weren't following her. He would never hurt her again. She might be homeless and probably expecting a baby, but she was free. The warmth penetrated into her and she felt it spread along her arms into her heart. She was happy. For the first time since he'd touched her. *Happy, happy birthday to me,* she thought.

She might walk up to Buckingham Palace later. It was a while since she'd seen the Changing of the Guard. And she'd never done it alone. She'd never even been outside Streatham on her own. Jilly would be impressed, if she knew. Margaret's smile faded as she thought about her best friend. She'd wanted to tell her she was leaving, to get her advice as much as anything, but she couldn't tell her just half the story. If she was pregnant, Jilly would want to know who the father was, and how could she have burdened her with that? It was better that no one knew. That way they couldn't bring her back. She would never go back.

She needed somewhere to stay, that was the most important thing. Somewhere safe and quiet, where they didn't ask too many questions. But where would that be? Margaret felt a prod in her belly and looked down. Her stomach was visibly rising. It must be a baby. Even the worst indigestion didn't do that. She stroked her belly through the fabric of her smock dress. It was just her and this baby – if it was a baby – in the world now. She would look for somewhere to stay after she'd visited the palace.

A man came and sat down on the bench, looked across and smiled at Margaret, his eyes then falling to her chest. She got up immediately, throwing the bag over her shoulder and walked away, her heart thumping. She knew that look and she knew where it led.

She made her way through Hyde Park into Green Park and to the palace and was just in time to see the Changing of the Guard. The familiar sight made her think of her mother. They would have discovered that she'd gone by now. Her mother would be angry about the money. She'd been saving it for as long as Margaret could remember. But if her mother had listened when she told her about Jack, if she'd stopped him . . .

Margaret took a breath and focused back on the bearskin hats. She was free. It was all going to be all right.

Once the ceremony was over, she picked up the bag again. It felt heavier against her back than she remembered. Her breasts and her bump felt hot and sticky as she walked away from the palace towards the maze of streets around Victoria. She'd not been in the area before. Signs advertised rooms to rent and Margaret walked up and down trying to pluck up the courage to ring a doorbell. What would she say? What should she ask for? And what was a reasonable amount to pay? She was hungry now, she needed to find somewhere.

One tall terraced house had wilting purple pansies in two window boxes, a cat sitting in the window watching her. The sign advertising rooms was written in a schoolmistress's hand – friendly, welcoming. Margaret had always wanted a cat, but her mother had refused. She walked up the three steps to the door and, before she could talk herself out of it, pressed the bell.

The woman who answered had her hair in a neat scarf and a shopping bag on her arm. 'Yes?' she said abruptly.

'I, err, that is, I've come about a room,' Margaret stammered.

The woman looked her up and down, her head on one side. 'I was just going out. You can come back later. After five p.m. We don't accept guests until then.'

Margaret tried to smile. 'Thank you.' As she turned, the cardigan she'd wrapped around herself fell open.

'Eh, what have you there?'

Margaret looked up at her. The woman nodded towards her belly.

'Are you expecting?'

'I think so,' said Margaret.

The woman shook her head. 'Sorry, love, you'll need to find somewhere else.' She rested her hand on Margaret's shoulder and gave it a squeeze. 'I'm sorry. People talk, y'know.'

'Oh,' said Margaret, a deep blush rising up her neck. She turned and walked quickly down the street, hot tears easing from her eyes. She hadn't thought it would be like that. The writing had been so welcoming. Would other places be the same? She soon found herself in an open square, a huge striped brick building in front of her. Some sort of church. It would be cool, and she could sit down quietly for a while and think about what to do.

It was dark inside after the brightness of the day and Margaret blinked as her eyes readjusted. Huge great stone arches rose into the blackness supporting the domes above. She'd never seen anything quite as big. Their local church was tiny in comparison. She slipped into a row near the back and watched as a group of nuns emerged from a door at the far end. They filtered through the church talking in low voices. As they passed her, several smiled at Margaret and she smiled back. Maybe they would be able to help her, she thought.

Chapter 42

Emma

February 2019

'Emma. May I call you Emma?' Mr Eals asked. She nodded. 'I hoped this moment would never come.'

'I think you knew that it would. One way or another. That's what you were warning me against, wasn't it?' She dropped into the chair on the other side of his desk and looked at him.

'How did you find out about your mother's *stepfather*?' He spat out the word.

'I think I was meant to find out.' She could see his untamed eyebrows rise up his face. 'There was a pile of letters in her flat which I took home last week. I only opened the final one earlier today. They were from my grandmother to my mother. The last one was written just after Grandpa Jack's death in 1993 – Granny Betty apologising for not believing my mother about what he did.'

'Ah, yes. I remember.'

'She showed it to you?'

Mr Eals eased one of the elastic bands off the file, carefully sifting through the various folders. He then opened one of the thin manila sleeves and carefully extracted a piece of paper, and laid it on the top of the file.

Emma leaned over the desk. 'Is that a photocopy of the letter?'

'Yes. On reflection, receiving that letter was helpful for Margaret. At last some recognition that what she'd been saying all along was true. And that Jack was sorry and had confessed. But what really got to her was that her mother put her own position in society, her own status and security, before her own daughter. It made her blind to the truth that was right before her.' Mr Eals looked sadly down at the photocopied letter.

'It would have been hard to forgive,' Emma said.

'And because Betty didn't speak up and stop what was happening,' Mr Eals spoke quietly and Emma fell silent, 'Margaret became pregnant by Jack. But she didn't realise for a long time that she was expecting his child. She knew she was gaining weight, but she just thought that it was normal, what we might call "puppy fat". Betty and Jack even laughed at her about her size.'

'When did she realise?'

'Very late on, a couple of months before the baby was born.'

'So before her sixteenth birthday, when she was sitting her O-levels. No wonder she failed.'

'Indeed. It was a terribly difficult period for her.'

'She started sketching ideas for *The Girl in the Midnight Maze* at that time, didn't she? I saw them after Jack died, when I went to look after Granny Betty.'

Mr Eals seemed to be examining something on the ceiling. 'I think your mother used her painting as a sort of therapy. To talk about how she was feeling, explain what was happening to her. Nobody would listen then and so it was her only way of sharing her story.'

'So she left home – on her sixteenth birthday?'

'Yes, she knew that she could legally leave then and there was nothing they could do. She left the first chance she could.'

'Where did she go? She was seven months pregnant. What happened between then and Elizabeth being born in the October? And what happened after she left Birdhurst Lodge? I know nothing until she got married for the first time in 1960, then after that she went to India and then there's another big gap until she met my dad in the early seventies.'

'Our parents' lives are a mystery, aren't they?' he said. 'We're not interested while they're alive, too busy with our own lives. We think that our existence is more interesting, that our parents are dull and have never lived. And then, too late, we often discover that we could have learned a lot from their example.' He smiled at her briefly, adopting his familiar pose, the tips of his fingers pressed together, his elbows resting on the desk. She waited for him to speak again, impatient for the silence to end, but not wanting to break his train of thought.

'Your mother wanted to get as far away from Streatham and Pullman Court as she could. She didn't want to risk her mother and stepfather finding her and bringing her home, or someone recognising her. So she went into central London and spent several nights in guesthouses. She sheltered in a church during the day and eventually some of the people there started to notice her and talk to her. Your mother was incredibly vulnerable and it wasn't long before she told them her story.' He sighed deeply and looked down at the file, stroking it slightly.

'She was moved to Birdhurst Lodge sometime in early September and spent six weeks there before she gave birth to Elizabeth. I know you've read about the place and your imagination has probably filled in the rest. There have been various films made of those types of institutions, and your mother told me they were true to life. It was a dreadful place to be. Brutal – both physically and emotionally. In many ways, it was far worse than the streets. Despite the circumstances of her parentage, Margaret wanted to keep Elizabeth. She loved that baby. She tried to run away when Elizabeth was just a few days old but the birth had taken its toll and she wasn't strong enough. She was brought back and punished. Elizabeth was adopted by a couple a few days later. And the day they came to take her, Margaret left Birdhurst Lodge as well.'

Emma realised she was crying, and rubbed her eyes. Mr Eals slowly opened a drawer in his desk and drew out a clean, pressed handkerchief and handed it across the desk. The initials GBE were hand-sewn into the soft white fabric.

She blew her nose noisily. 'Sorry. I just can't imagine what that was like. Living like that, being so heavily pregnant after everything she'd been through. Then thinking that she was somewhere safe in the church, and . . .' She blew her nose again, trying to quell the sob rising in her chest. 'I found a letter in the pile from my grandmother to my mother later that year. Mum had been in touch with her grandmother, Betty's mum – she was living somewhere in London. The letter was sent to a shop.'

'Do you have it?'

Emma nodded, and drew the letter out of her bag, handing it across the desk. Mr Eals read it slowly. He looked up towards the blackness seeping through the high windows and said nothing for several seconds.

'Can I take a copy? For the file?'

Emma nodded, watching his face soften and his hooded eyes drop again to reread the text. Eventually he rang a small bell on the desk. The secretary appeared almost immediately, as if she'd been waiting in the corridor, and silently took the letter. She reappeared within the minute with the original and a copy. Mr Eals eased the sheet into one of the manila sleeves.

'Your mother spent the next few years in London doing a—'
He swallowed noisily, and reached for a cup and saucer. Whatever
was inside made him grimace slightly. 'A variety of – jobs.' He
offered a tight-lipped smile. 'She then spent a year at art school.'

'But how did she fund that? Wouldn't that have been expensive? Where was she living?'

Mr Eals paused, glanced at the file, and then spoke deliberately.
'She was working, Emma, she did what she had to do to get by.
She'd always wanted to go to art school and was determined to
fulfil that dream.'

Emma absorbed the meaning of his words. She swallowed.
'And after that? You met her?'

'Yes, she was twenty-one, it was 1959. She'd left art school
and was working as a trainee window dresser at Liberty. She was
renting digs on Frith Street and the landlord was trying to raise
the rent to way above market value. There was no inside toilet,
no heating, no hot water, which wasn't that uncommon at the
time but the landlord was introducing certain . . . personal' – he
paused – 'requirements.' He took a deep breath before continuing. 'Which were illegal. I was introduced to your mother and
helped her write some letters and argue the case. She won and
stayed in the room for many, many years.'

'What was she like then?'

Mr Eals sighed, and drew his eyebrows together fiercely, audi-
bly breathing out. 'She was one of the most beautiful women in
London. Full of life, very passionate about what she did. But there
was an incredible vulnerability to her. It was a rather hot summer,
the year that we met, and we all sweltered in the heat and smog.
Ronnie Scott's opened that autumn and your mother loved to go
there and listen to jazz. Before I knew her background' – he waved
his hand at the file in front of him – 'I thought she was one of the

most carefree people I'd ever met. It was only as I got to know her that I learned the truth.'

'Which was?'

'She experienced a great trauma at a very young age and continued to experience challenges that affected her for the rest of her life. You have two children, I believe. To have a child forcibly removed from one as a child oneself was too big an event not to affect her deeply. Particularly when you take into account how she became pregnant.'

'Did she ever report what had happened to anyone?'

Mr Eals looked down at the paperwork and sighed. His shoulders dropped. 'Yes, she did. A few people.'

'Who? The police?' Emma leaned forward in her chair.

'Yes, she eventually reported it to the police.' Mr Eals was almost inaudible.

'And?'

The old man sighed deeply. 'I encouraged her. I was young, and I thought that the crime was so heinous that she should report it. That Jack should have been made to pay for what he did.' His hands were flitting around the files, alternately stroking and sifting through them. 'Sadly the authorities didn't believe her. You have to understand that this was the 1950s. Things are very different now. There was no DNA testing then. The' – Mr Eals seemed to struggle with the words – 'physical manifestations of the abuse – bruising, for example – had all disappeared. The only evidence was Elizabeth's existence. Nowadays they could DNA test Elizabeth and determine her parents and Jack would have been charged as Margaret was underage. But Margaret was determined that her daughter would know nothing about her father and the circumstances of her conception. She wanted her to be completely free of that knowledge.'

Emma nodded slowly. 'I can understand that. Give her a fresh start.'

'Yes, exactly.' His fingertips resumed their arched pose and he looked straight at Emma, making her glance away. 'I want you to understand what happened, Emma. I think it's easy to hear words like "abuse" and "rape" and not quite appreciate what it was like to go through that. Despite my advice, you've been determined to find out about your mother's past and—'

'I wish I hadn't.'

He held up his hand to silence her. 'Now that you have, I think you need to hear from your own mother what happened.'

Emma jumped slightly, almost expecting her mother to appear. She could feel her heart beginning to beat faster. 'What d'you mean?'

Mr Eals was sifting through his files, and eventually extracted two yellowed pieces of paper and slid them across the desk to Emma. It was headed *Metropolitan Police* and typed on an old type-writer. Emma glanced at the first few lines of text.

> *Metropolitan Police*
> *Marylebone Lane Police Station*
> *'D' Division*
> *8 June 1959*

'This is the interview with my mother about the abuse?'

Mr Eals nodded. 'Read it. It will help you understand what happened. How she was treated.'

Ten minutes later, Emma put down the report on the desk, her hands shaking and her shoulders slumped. 'It's so bloody unfair! Unbelievable.'

Mr Eals nodded. 'Yes, it is. But that was the law at the time. I was a fool – a naive fool – who thought I could challenge the legal

246

system and get some justice for your mother. But rape convictions were low then – they're still low now. The sergeant knew quite rightly that there was no chance of a successful prosecution. In the end, although it wasn't what we wanted, Margaret was relieved.'

'Really?' Emma sounded incredulous.

'Margaret was devastated at not being believed, but she had put down what had happened to her officially, on paper, and when the police didn't pursue it, it did mean that she didn't have to go through the rigours of a court case, which would have been very difficult.'

'Did the police speak to Grandpa Jack at all? Was he challenged about how he treated my mother?'

Mr Eals shook his head. 'I'm sorry to say that I don't think it ever went any further than the document here. I pushed and pushed her to do it because I thought that it would help. In some ways, maybe it did. Seeing it down on paper. But to not be believed. Or rather, not have it treated with the seriousness it warranted had a deep effect on Margaret. She rarely spoke of it again. It was as if she'd given the world the opportunity to put right this awful wrong and the world had shrugged its shoulders and looked away.'

Emma stared at the transcript again, wiping away fresh tears with Mr Eals' handkerchief. 'Did you know that Elizabeth tried to get in touch with Mum? In the early 1980s?'

He nodded slightly and the corner of his mouth stretched in a grim smile. He eased the file apart and started leafing through the individual manila sleeves, finally extracting a copy of the same letter that Clare had found. Emma recognised Elizabeth's odd handwriting.

'July 1981.' It was a statement, not a question.

'She never replied . . .'

'No, she was deeply, deeply shocked to get the letter. I remember the call – she was almost hysterical on the phone and couldn't read out the words. But I gathered what had happened. We met a week or so later and the change in her was extraordinary. It was if she'd been transported back to the earliest days after having to give up Elizabeth. You see, she'd tried desperately hard to ensure she was never found. After she was forced to give her up, she wanted Elizabeth to have a better life and not to know about her parentage and the circumstances of her birth. We put a note on the adoption register that she didn't want to be contacted and we changed her surname to make it impossible to find her.'

'We?'

Mr Eals shook himself slightly and positioned his fingers back together. 'I supported your mother with her legal affairs throughout her life.'

'In the summer of 1981 my mother suddenly disappeared, and shortly afterwards I was sent to boarding school and didn't see my parents for about a year. I think it was linked to her receiving that letter from Elizabeth.' Emma looked at Mr Eals searchingly.

There was a long silence. The old man seemed to be examining the tips of his fingers, the yellowing, but well-kept nails, the spindly fingers leading down to the wrinkled hands.

Mr Eals took a slow breath. 'The letter from Elizabeth reopened a lot of wounds for your mother. She had buried Elizabeth's existence underneath her new life with David and with you. I was concerned when she had you that it would bring her back to the circumstances of Elizabeth's birth. I think she was too. She certainly felt guilty having you.'

'Guilty?'

'Yes. In some ways I think she felt disloyal to Elizabeth, to her firstborn, to have another child which she kept. But although it did bring back some of those terrible emotions, the joy of having you – and knowing she would be keeping you – helped to dissipate some of the memories of that other birth, although for a while she suffered from post-natal depression, which was hardly surprising. Six years later, when Elizabeth got in touch, Margaret was not so well prepared and the realisation that her first daughter had tracked her down and wanted a relationship caused her immense problems. I suppose she had what we would call a breakdown, although it was termed differently then.'

'But where did she go? I didn't see her for almost a year and no one told me anything.' Emma could hear the shrill child in her voice.

Mr Eals separated some of the manila folders and shuffled them about carefully. He then opened one and drew out a piece of paper. 'She was admitted to Hellingly Hospital in August 1981. It was a difficult place and probably not the right environment for her. But at the time there was little else. Nowadays she would have been offered talking therapy. Back then it was all about locking difficult people away and giving them . . .' He hesitated '. . . treatment.' He paused uncomfortably and swallowed, reaching for his cup and saucer. After taking a noisy gulp, he continued. 'Unfortunately the similarities between Birdhurst Lodge and Hellingly were not lost on your mother and that hardly helped her recovery. She could have spent the rest of her life there – it was a difficult place to get out of – but your father battled quite hard to get her better again. In the end, she was an inpatient for nearly a year.'

'But I was at boarding school a lot longer than that.'

'She was a different woman when she came out. You may remember that?'

Emma nodded, recalling the quiet, dark house and her silent mother.

'You have to imagine what those places were like. It took her a long time to even begin to recover from it.'

'Did you go there? Did you visit her?'

Mr Eals looked at her over his glasses and nodded slowly, his eyes watery. 'I did.'

Emma shuddered and wrote down *Hellingly Hospital* on the edge of the envelope containing Elizabeth's birth certificate.

'So she never replied to Elizabeth's letter.'

'No. She never mentioned Elizabeth after that until much later.'

'When I called my daughter Elizabeth . . .' Emma closed her eyes and bowed her head remembering her mother's reaction to holding baby Libby.

'That was an unfortunate coincidence.' Mr Eals was watching her over his glasses, his fingertips pressed together.

'I thought she hated Libby.'

He was smiling slightly. 'But now you're beginning to understand.'

'Mum moved up here to Morecambe when I was about thirteen. So around 1988. Was that all linked too? I thought it was because her and Dad didn't get on.'

'Your parents' marriage suffered because of all of this. It's hard to keep this sort of secret and not—'

'Dad didn't know?' Emma heard her voice squeak.

'No, she never told him.'

'But why? Why on earth wouldn't she tell her husband something like that? Dad would have understood. He wouldn't have minded.'

'I suspect she thought it wasn't worth the risk. She'd told the police and they hadn't believed her. She'd told her first husband and he hadn't taken it well and it had led to the failure of that marriage. She couldn't face being rejected again. It was easier for her to bury it all. But as you know, that didn't work.'

'So what did Dad think when she fell ill and was admitted to the hospital?'

'I expect he thought she'd just had a breakdown.'

'He didn't know what had caused the breakdown, but he still fought to get her out?' Emma's eyes widened.

'Yes, he did. I only met your father once but he struck me as a good man. We worked together to secure her release. Not an easy thing, although we were both quite determined.'

Emma paused. 'There's just one last thing I wanted to know.'

'Yes?' Was it her imagination or did Mr Eals look very slightly apprehensive? What was he worried she was going to ask?

'We visited Granny Betty and Grandpa Jack a fair bit when I was a child. Not every week, or even every month, but we must have gone to their flat in Streatham a couple of times a year. And that was the flat where – where it all happened. I never remember them coming to us. Why on earth would Mum voluntarily go back there, see her parents, Jack, after all that happened?'

Mr Eals grimaced slightly and rubbed his eyes. 'It seems a strange thing to do, doesn't it? But you know, it's not uncommon for victims to voluntarily spend time with their abusers later in life as part of the family unit. I suspect there were a number of reasons. First, don't forget that your mother hadn't told your father David about what had happened. He was very much a family man and wanted to spend time with his wife's parents. He saw it as a normal part of life, especially when they'd had you.' Mr Eals smiled at her. 'They both wanted a normal life for you, and Margaret didn't want you or David to feel there was intrigue within the family. I suspect also she felt it gave her a sense of power, to go to Pullman Court, having made a success of her life despite everything that had happened, and show it off in front of her mother and stepfather. She knew Betty resented her presence, was jealous of the perceived relationship she had with Jack, and Margaret enjoyed winding her up. But that's just my opinion, I don't know that as fact.'

Emma nodded. *Made a success of her life.* She'd never considered that her mother had made a success of her life. She'd just been her mother. Distant and difficult to get along with. But perhaps she had made a success of it. By whose measurement is a life successful? Despite everything that had happened to her as a child, her mother had made it through. Maybe that was success enough.

The secretary reappeared with a pot of tea and two cups. Emma poured milk and then tea into her cup, decorated with roses, watching the white liquid disappear into the blackness. She remembered the card attached to the white roses at her mother's funeral. She was certain they'd been from Mr Eals.

'Why did you move to Morecambe?'

'What do you mean?'

'When you met my mother, you said you were living in London. But now you're here in Morecambe, and so was she, which seems a bit of a coincidence. Morecambe's hardly the centre of the legal universe.' She could hear the slight accusation in her voice and tried to relax.

'Ah, but there's far less competition here than there was in London.' The old man looked down and shuffled his papers again, then scratched his ear.

'And you were with her when she died?'

The solicitor looked up quickly. 'Who told you that?'

'Clare did,' Emma said simply, oddly pleased to see the normally unflappable old lawyer look uncomfortable. 'Why were you there? Surely you're not there for all your clients?' She waited for him to speak.

He swallowed noisily again. 'Your mother had some last-minute legal issues to tie up, that's all.' He stroked the file and looked up at her, his eyes watery. 'The more we speak, the more you remind me of your mother. So very direct.'

'I never really think of myself as being my mother's daughter. I suppose because she wasn't around in those early years, and then she left to come here. I never feel I spent that much time with her as a child. It's easier seeing my father in me.'

'True, but blood and genes mean a great deal. It's difficult to escape them. You must see that in your own children. In James and Elizabeth.'

'We actually call her Libby, that's the irony. Almost from the beginning, so she was never really an Elizabeth at all. She's okay, going through the typical teenage challenges.'

'And James? Margaret always talked so fondly of him.' Mr Eals was looking at her questioningly.

'Oh, he's fine. A typical teenage boy. Doing his A-levels at the moment. He locks himself away now and again and plays loud music but nothing too bad. I've been so caught up in all of this, that I haven't spent much time with either of them over the past few weeks.' Emma slurped down the rest of her tea. She needed to be home. 'Thank you for seeing me this evening and for being so frank. It helps to understand what happened to Mum. She was always so angry, so difficult. And now I can see why.'

Mr Eals nodded slowly. 'I completely understand. I am sorry that you have found all this out, but now that you have, at least you can appreciate what she went through. And you now understand why I counselled you not to contact Elizabeth. Being given up at birth by a single mother was a difficult enough start in the 1950s. Finding out that your father is also your step-grandfather would be devastating. Margaret wanted that kept secret.'

The knot of worry unravelled and spread through her stomach. Emma hung her head and sighed.

'Emma?' Mr Eals' voice was querulous.

'It's too late,' she whispered, her eyes still closed. 'I've already met her.'

Mr Eals' mouth formed a perfect circle. 'And will you tell her?'

'I'm not sure what to do,' Emma said quietly.

◆ ◆ ◆

Outside the solicitor's office, Emma drew out her phone. It rang almost immediately.

It was a breathless Nick. 'Oh, thank God. Are you okay?'

'Yes, I'm fine, why?'

'You haven't picked up Libby. You were due in for a meeting too. The school said they called you numerous times, but got no answer. I'm at home. I've got her and done the meeting and dinner for them but I was so worried. Where the hell are you?'

'Oh, Christ. Shit. I'm sorry. I just . . . forgot.' How could she have forgotten?

'Where are you?' Nick's worry had been replaced by anger. 'I called everyone I could think of.'

'I just needed to see Mr Eals . . .'

'Who the hell is Mr Eals?'

'Mr Eals, my mother's solicitor. You met him at the funeral.' It sounded ridiculous that she'd driven all this way just for a meeting. But he hadn't answered the phone, she'd had no choice.

'Oh, for fuck's sake. Is this what this is all about? Again! Your bloody mother? You need to forget about all—'

But Emma didn't hear what she needed to forget about. She took the phone away from her ear and pressed the red button, ending the call, then turned the phone off and got into the car. She was desperate to get back home but felt that while she was here she had to drop in on Clare and share what she'd learned. Without her help, she would never have found out as much as she had, and perhaps she'd have something to add too. She took her phone out of her bag again, sent Nick a short, apologetic message saying she was on her way back. Then she drove to Clare's, determined to be as quick as she could.

Clare looked surprised to see her but welcomed her with a hug. 'What are you doing up here? I didn't expect to see you. How are things?'

Emma gave her a shrug and a grimace and followed her into her kitchen. There was something different about the room but it took a moment for her to realise what it was. There was a gap on the wall where *The Girl in the Midnight Maze* had been. She walked towards the space.

Clare must have seen her looking. 'I've taken it down,' she said, coming to stand next to her so they were both staring at the empty wall. The memory of the painting hung in the air. 'This is going to sound crazy, but I thought I could hear the girl at night. Rushing around the maze in the dark, crying.'

Emma glanced at Clare and then looked away. That night at her mother's flat she thought she'd heard the girl twirling in the maze.

'It didn't feel right me having it here,' Clare continued quietly. 'It's a beautiful painting but it's part of Margaret's history, your history. It should be with Margaret's family.' Clare looked down at her hands. 'Weirdly, I've come to think of it as some sort of estrangement. That the little girl is separated from her family. It's been playing on my mind. She needs to be with you.'

The smile spread across Emma's face. She threw her arms round Clare's small frame and hugged her. 'Oh, Clare, thank you. Thank you so much. That means the world to me.' She couldn't wait to show it to Libby.

Clare patted her on the back. 'It's packaged up. I was going to courier it down to you but you can take it with you now. I'll miss her though, just like I miss Margaret.' She stared vacantly into the room.

Clare missed Margaret. Of course she did, they'd been friends. But in all this time, Emma had never thought of her mother as being missed. Her mother had been too difficult a person to miss. Emma had been intrigued about everything that had happened to her mother and had spent hours following it up and thinking about her. And she'd wanted her to be alive so she could talk to her. But she'd never actually missed her.

Emma was still staring at the gap on the wall when Clare handed her a cup of tea. Emma told her about everything that she'd learned from the letters and the solicitor. The tears came easily again, for both of them, as Emma talked about her mum being forced to give up the baby Elizabeth.

'Since we last talked, I've been reading about those places.' Clare shuddered. 'There's this really good book about a mother and baby home in Sussex. The way they treated the girls was just awful. Beyond comprehension.'

'Mr Eals said that she was punished by the people at Birdhurst Lodge when she tried to run away with Elizabeth.' They both looked at each other. Emma closed her eyes.

'I just wish I could have found out all about this before meeting Elizabeth. Let sleeping dogs lie, as my father would have said.'

'The damage is done now,' said Clare. 'And it sounds as though the two of you got on well.'

Emma nodded, it was true.

'You're not going to tell her everything, are you?'

Emma shrugged. 'Who wants to hear that they were conceived by child abuse?' Emma could feel her heart begin to thud at the thought of saying something so terrible. 'She is already quite fragile about her background and parentage. This would be devastating. But I also feel that she deserves to know the truth.'

Clare looked at her. 'I read an article once about family dysfunction. It described it as rolling from generation to generation like a fire in the woods, taking down everything in its path. It said that you need one person in one generation to have the courage to turn and face the flames. And that person will be the one to bring peace to their ancestors and spare the children who follow them, and their children.' She looked Emma in the eye. 'That's what you need to be. I know what you've discovered is awful. But you need to be the one to face those flames – you already have in so many ways – and make sure that you don't let it burn your children and their children. And Elizabeth.'

◆　◆　◆

Emma stopped at a service station on the drive back to Brighton, and suddenly she felt compelled to rip the brown paper covering the painting just to check the little girl. She was still there, trapped in the centre of her maze. Laughing. Crying. Confused.

'You're coming home,' Emma whispered to her, leaving the torn paper open so the girl could see out of the darkness. Emma's dry eyes itched and she had to stop three times, once to sleep in Stafford service station car park for half an hour, before she made it home. She struggled through the front door with the painting and carried it into the kitchen. It was past midnight. Nick was locking up.

'Oh, there you are. Please don't tell me you've been all the way to Morecambe and back.'

Emma nodded.

'This is just ridiculous, Em. And what the hell's that?' he said, indicating the package.

'It's Mum's painting. *The Girl in the Midnight Maze*. D'you remember it from her flat?'

'No, but then we haven't been there for years. Funny that.' He turned his back and finished stacking the dishwasher.

'I thought you could put it up above the fireplace. Move the Downs view one somewhere else?'

Nick grunted.

'I'm sorry about missing Libby's meeting.'

'It's not just the meeting.' Nick turned round to face her. 'You just disappeared. You can't do that. We go on at Libby about telling us where she is going, about being a family and not disappearing and you did exactly that. Some sort of role model. I couldn't explain to her where you were, what had happened. I was going to call the police. Libby took it as an opportunity to disappear herself and only got home thirty minutes ago, decidedly worst for wear. I've just got her to bed with a bowl next to her. She needs you too, Emma. *I* need you, but you can't be bothered. You're too fucking busy with this whole thing about your mother and long-lost sister.'

Emma bit her lip. 'It's not that I can't be bothered. I found out some stuff earlier. I just had to talk to Mr Eals. It's serious, Nick, really bad.'

'D'you know what? I really don't give a damn. Margaret was a twisted woman who made your life hell in her lifetime and is managing to fuck up our family now she's dead. Focus on your kids, our kids, and forget that bloody woman.' He looked like he was about to slam the door, but instead pulled it to quietly and walked down the hall and upstairs.

'She had good reason to be twisted,' Emma muttered as she dropped her bag on the kitchen counter and followed him up. She cracked open James's door. He lay sprawled across his bed on his back – half boy, half man – his mouth open, fast asleep. When he was a baby, she and Nick used to stand over him, watching him sleep, checking that he was still breathing. Emma closed the door quietly and walked down the landing. She edged open Libby's door, the landing light piercing the deep gloom. Libby was on her side, curled up like a baby, lightly snoring, the plastic bowl Nick had got for her on the bedside table. Emma sat down next to her, the dip in the bed tipping Libby towards her and she stroked her hair. Libby's face looked like she had as a child – all the anger wiped away. Emma smiled and moved down to stroke her arm. She leaned over and lay down next to Libby, spooning her. The girl moved slightly in her sleep to accommodate her. Outside, clouds moved away from the moon, allowing it to reach through the blinds and touch Libby's sleeping form. Within seconds Emma was also asleep.

For the first time since her mother had died, Emma slept deeply and dreamlessly. The emotional and physical exhaustion overwhelming her. It was Libby who woke first the following morning.

'Mum, what are you doing?' she exclaimed.

Emma tried to drag herself up through the weight of her sleep. 'Darling.' She pulled Libby down and cuddled her again. Libby let herself be held and gripped Emma's hand. They lay like that for a few minutes as Emma's consciousness gradually surfaced.

The sun was beginning to penetrate the thin curtains. It was the unusual brightness that made Emma ask.

'Libby, what's the time?'

Libby shifted to look at the clock. 'Mum, it's eight o'clock.'

'Shit.' Emma was instantly awake and out of bed, racing in to Nick to wake him and screaming at James through his closed bedroom door. 'Come on, everyone, we need to get up. We're all really late.'

Chapter 43

JACK

JULY 1981

Jack was dreading Margaret and her husband David coming – he always did. Although it had been almost thirty years since *all that*, seeing her brought back the guilt. But Betty insisted they come round at least twice a year to maintain the illusion of happy families. And he liked seeing his granddaughter Emma – she was a sweet thing and growing fast. When had he last seen them? Six months ago?

While Betty prepared the lunch, he paced up and down the sitting room and along the narrow hallway. He opened the door to Margaret's bedroom, untouched since the day she left, avoiding the gaze of the girl in the charcoal sketch that Betty insisted must not be moved and now hung above the bed. Then he turned into the bedroom he'd shared with Betty for more than forty years. His hip ached again but walking seemed to help.

Out of the window the sky was darkening despite the summer heat. Dark clouds were gathering over the square, stifling any breeze. Even with the windows wide open, the air in the flat was clammy. He leaned his head outside. The grass in the square was parched brown. The large elms sagged, their trunks still decorated by bunting from the royal wedding. Charles and Di's engagement poster stared out from the railings and was still taped to the inside of some of the windows in the square. Diana's blue eyes seemed to stare at him seductively.

Jack heard the car before he saw it, and shouted over his shoulder to Betty.

'They're here!'

The brown Austin Allegro stopped directly in front of Pullman Court. Jack could see Emma inside on the back seat. Her thighs must be sticking to the plastic in this heat. The doors slammed and the three of them were suddenly on the pavement, Margaret and her husband David stretching their arms and legs. Margaret shielded her eyes against the sun which had briefly appeared, and looked up towards the flat. Jack stepped back from the window.

The entry bell went in the hallway, and he dutifully buzzed them in, not bothering to speak into the receiver. Jack went into the kitchen. Betty was leaning over the stove, her face flushed, loose hair sticking to the back of her neck. He liked watching her cook. Over the sound of the bubbling pans, Jack could hear voices on the stairs outside the front door. He walked down the hallway into the bathroom, silently sliding the lock across just as the doorbell rang.

'Jack? Jack, can you answer that? I just need to blanch these pears. Jack?'

'I'm on the loo,' he shouted, as he looked into the mirror. An old man stared back at him.

'For God's sake.' He heard Betty moving down the hallway to the door, and the sound of the latch being drawn. Emma's lively voice quickly filled the space and he could hear her bounding down the hall. He imagined Betty welcoming her daughter with a quick, stiff embrace, their eyes not quite meeting, and her much warmer hug for her son-in-law David, who she adored. Jack flushed the chain unnecessarily, slid the bolt back across and walked out of the bathroom, a smile stretched across his face.

'Welcome, welcome,' he said to everyone gathered in the small hallway, careful not to meet Margaret's eyes. Emma ran towards him crying, 'Grandpa Jack!' and he reached down, swinging her up into his arms. Her small hands clasped round his neck as he walked her through into the sitting room where Betty had laid out a crocheted cloth on the drinks trolley with the small bottles of squash and water. Jack busied himself holding the decanter steady while Emma vigorously pumped its siphon. Both were transfixed by the jerky stream of pale liquid slowly filling the glass.

'What is it, Grandpa?'

'I think this one is barley water, poppet, but Granny Betty bought you lots of different types for you to choose from. Look.'

Margaret's husband David had wandered over and his damp hand touched Jack's shoulder. 'How's your hip, Jack?'

He looked up at his son-in-law, his tie immaculately straight despite the heat. 'Not too bad, thanks, David.'

'And what's the state of play with your balcony tomatoes? Still keeping the neighbours in salads?'

'Yes, doing well as always, thanks.'

'Perfect weather for them this year, I suspect.'

'Yes, we've been lucky.' The man was an expert in small talk.

David wandered over to the open window looking out across the park. Margaret joined him.

'Jolly hot, isn't it?' he said, his back to the room.

How much did David know? Jack wondered. He always seemed perfectly friendly in that City sort of way of his, but you never knew what he was thinking.

Emma's glass was now full, and Jack carefully wiped it with the tea towel before handing it to her. Her hair was drawn back into two plaits, each threaded with shiny blue ribbon. Betty had done that to Margaret's hair. Before things had changed.

Betty came bustling into the room. 'Are you taking drinks orders, Jack, or are you just going to stand there staring into space?' Why did she always have to put him down in front of Margaret and David? It was like she was trying to score points.

Jack's automatic smile came back. 'Of course, of course. David, G&T?' The figure at the window nodded. 'Margaret?'

'I'll have a whisky and soda.'

'Really? I've never known you to have whisky.'

'Well, perhaps it just goes to show how little you know me.'

Jack started mixing more drinks. His hands trembled as he used the tiny tongs to plop the ice cubes into the glass tumblers. The sound of them hitting the glass seemed to echo around the still room. He left the G&T on the window ledge next to David, and the whisky on the dresser where Margaret was now looking at the shelves stacked with books and games. He gazed at her back. He went to the trolley and poured himself a triple whisky.

'Oh, I'd forgotten all about this.' The rare enthusiasm in Margaret's voice made him turn in surprise. She was clutching the old chess board that they had regularly played on when she was a child. The overhead light reflected off the polished surface, temporarily blinding him. He smiled, remembering her sitting at the same table, with the same short plaits that Emma had, while he taught her the different moves.

Through the doorway to the kitchen, he could see Emma standing on a stool stirring something on the hob while Betty looked on. Margaret rummaged in the dresser, looking for the chess pieces. She found the old Quality Street tin and started to lay them out on the board.

'Do you want to play?' Jack asked her uncertainly.

Margaret looked directly at him for the first time, her eyebrows raised. 'Why not, while Mum finishes lunch?'

Jack sat down opposite her at the table, the board separating them. They laid out the pieces, opposing armies preparing for battle. Margaret started, quickly moving her queen into an aggressive forward position. It wasn't one of the standard moves Jack had taught her, and he was puzzled. She left her rook vulnerable, and Jack took it, but was confused by the slight smile on her face as he put the wooden figure back in the tin. He manoeuvred his queen and bishop into a set piece.

'Do you really think I'm going to fall for that?' She smiled, looking straight at him again. 'I knew that move when I was seven.'

Jack smiled back, disarmed by her relaxed charm. Usually she was so tense when she came for lunch.

She slid the glass across the table, empty except for two shrunken ice cubes. 'I'm empty, Jack.'

'That was quick.' He slid his chair back from the table and mixed another drink for both of them. He could see David still clutching his full glass at the window, looking at them, deep lines etched across his forehead. Jack slid the glass across the table. Margaret's was slightly too full and the amber liquid sloshed out on to the polished wood, creating a tiny pool. He wiped it up with his hand. They continued playing rapidly, in silence. It must have been the whisky on an empty stomach that made him miss her trap for his queen. She smiled as she took it and added it to her growing bounty.

Betty poked her head out of the kitchen door into the sitting room, her face red from the cooking. 'Can you lay the table, Jack?'

'Yes, Betty, just give me a minute.'

'The food's almost ready, Jack, I'll be serving any moment.'

He looked at Margaret, who had her back to Betty, and smiled, raising his eyebrows with a slight roll of his eyes. He knew Betty could see him. Margaret, unseen by Betty, smiled back. Jack stayed still, pondering his next move. Betty stood in the kitchen door, hands resting on the faded apron on her hips.

'Jack, will you please stop playing with *her* . . .' Her voice rose.

He ignored Betty, as he slowly moved his rook to take Margaret's bishop. Betty turned back into the kitchen as Margaret said, 'Checkmate.' Jack looked at her in shock, her mocking smile seeming to enjoy his disbelief, before studying the board. He was just thinking he'd found an escape route, when a scorching stream of gravy hit the back of his hand. Jack screamed and leaped up from the table.

'What the hell are you doing?' he yelled, cradling his burned hand against his chest.

Betty was standing by the side of the table with the last few drips of gravy trickling from the empty gravy boat. He could feel the liquid soaking into his shirt and burning his chest.

'I'm sorry, I just slipped,' said Betty calmly. 'Silly Granny,' she said to Emma who had come out of the kitchen. Betty smiled at Emma and took the gravy jug back into the kitchen. 'I'll refill this. You'd better clear up that mess,' she added to Jack, pointing at the chess board. 'And then lay the table. I'm ready to serve up.'

Margaret remained at the table, watching the gravy drip off the chess board on to the table and then pool on the floor. She slowly drained the last of her drink, set the glass down and got up. Jack looked at her transfixed. She was almost smiling.

Chapter 44

EMMA

FEBRUARY 2019

One of many challenges of having teenagers was laundry, thought Emma later that day, as she trudged upstairs with a basket full of sorted washing. Four members of the family. Four piles of laundry. Now James and Nick were the same size, it was impossible to tell some of their clothes apart. Emma dumped the basket on Libby's bed and put down Libby's teetering pile of washing. The smell of old incense hung in the air and she opened the window, letting in the chill afternoon air.

Despite the regular chores that needed doing it was good being home after everything that had happened over the past few weeks. The house felt soothing, as if it was wrapping a warm blanket around her. She was trying to put Elizabeth out of her mind. It had been wonderful meeting her, but she couldn't face deciding whether or not to tell her about Jack.

For now, she needed to focus on her own children. Be the mother that her own mother hadn't been able to be. Emma closed Libby's door and dumped the remaining clothes pile in James's room, kneeling down to put it all away in his chest of drawers.

Mashing potatoes later for dinner, Emma remembered a book they'd had when the children were small and wouldn't eat their food. James had read it to Libby. They'd pretended that mash was cloud fluff from the pointiest peak of Mount Fuji. And they weren't peas but green drops from Greenland. How simple life had been then. She and Nick had been exhausted and thought it was all so hard but it hadn't been really. She'd been a better mother then, she was sure, when she wasn't working as well. There'd been more time.

'Kids, dinner,' she shouted upstairs.

They all crammed around the table, James's friend Deaglan squeezing in next to Libby.

'How was your day, Libs?' asked Emma, handing around the plates.

'Same as always,' said Libby, helping herself to baked beans.

'What subjects did you have?'

'All of them.'

Emma dug a spoon into the mash and tried to heap a pile on to Libby's plate. Libby moved her plate away. 'I don't want any mash.'

'It's not mash. It's cloud fluff from the pointiest peak of Mount Fuji.'

Libby rolled her eyes.

'You staying for the Seagulls–Arsenal match, Deaglan?' asked Nick.

Deaglan nodded. 'If that's okay?'

'Yes, I reckon we have a good chance.'

Emma yawned.

'That's disgusting, Mum, I can see your food,' said Libby, her eyes narrowed. 'You're always telling us to put our hands in front of our mouths and you don't bother.'

'Sorry, it's been a long few days, meeting Elizabeth and all that.'

'It's been a crazy time for you,' said Nick levelly. 'I'm looking forward to meeting Elizabeth at some stage.' Emma heard the unsaid apology for his harshness the night before.

'Yes, that'd be lovely. We were talking about getting her family and us together.'

'That'd be good. And she's got a daughter too, right?'

'Yes, though she's thirty-one. About to have a baby herself.'

'Nice. An extended family.' Nick smiled at Emma. 'Is it tomorrow that you're scattering your mum's ashes? Do you want me to take a day off and come with you? I said I might not be in when I left today.'

'That's kind, but it's all right. Elizabeth and I thought we'd do it together at Devil's Dyke and then we're going to walk down to Saddlescombe Farm and go to the tea shop there. But you could pick Libby up from school? I might not quite be back in time.' She smiled at him gratefully.

Nick nodded.

'I really don't need picking up from school.'

'I think we've agreed that you do for now,' said Nick quietly.

James had finished and was looking round for seconds. 'What's it like having a sister, Mum? Must be so weird after all this time.'

'Yes, it is a bit weird. But all we really share is DNA. She has no memories of Granny.' Emma shrugged.

'So Granny Margaret had her before she met Grandad David?' James asked.

'Yes, that's right.'

'And how old was she, sixteen?'

Emma's mouth was dry. She fixed her gaze on her sausages. The gravy had congealed and was lumpy. She wanted to retch. 'That's right, sixteen.'

James raised his eyebrows. 'Wow, that's so young to have a kid. Who was the dad?'

Emma tried to stop her foot tapping on the floor. 'We don't know. I don't think we'll ever know.'

Nick reached forward and covered her hand with his.

'There's a girl in our year who's pregnant,' said James.

'Really?' Nick asked. 'Who?'

'Victoria – you know, the one who broke her leg in Year Eight.'

'Oh, yes.'

'Imagine having a baby now,' said James. 'Your whole life is ruined.'

'Oh, shut up, James. Like anyone would care about your sad little life.' Libby rolled her eyes at him.

'Libs,' said Nick. 'Enough.' He stood. 'Come on, let's clear up. Em, you have a sit down, you did the prep.'

Emma yawned. 'Thanks, darling.'

Lying on her and Nick's bed, Emma mechanically checked her emails on her phone. Mr Eals had sent her an email that morning repeating what he'd said to her yesterday. That she shouldn't talk to Elizabeth about Jack. He seemed to be the guardian of her mother's secrets even after her death. It must be more than just professional curiosity. She was sure he must have been in love with her mother. Had she loved him back? Perhaps that was why they were both in Morecambe together. Maybe she would never know.

Emma heard a light tread on the stairs, and looked up expecting it to be Nick. But it was Libby.

Emma went to ask her in, to sit with her, maybe just to chat, but Libby was through her bedroom door and inside, the door shutting before Emma had a chance to open her mouth. She sighed and her shoulders dropped as she lay back on the bed.

Was this what middle age meant? Trapped between the pain of the older generations while trying to deal with the younger ones?

Chapter 45

Emma

February 2019

It was a companionable silence. The sort they would have had as sisters who had grown up together, intimately involved in each other's lives, on their way to scatter their beloved mother's ashes. Rather than virtual strangers, meeting late in life, to scatter the ashes of a woman neither of them had really known.

Lying on her side on the car's back shelf was their mother, her ashes incarcerated in a thick plastic pot. Like the Maxwell House coffee jars her father had bought, Emma thought. She could see it every time she glanced in the rear-view mirror, wedged between the battered tissue box, and the travel blanket sticky with discarded sweets. She wished she'd put it in the boot now, but that had seemed disrespectful. This was the only journey the three of them would make together, she thought. A mother with her two daughters. Emma sighed.

In summer, the car park at Devil's Dyke was bustling with activity – people, children, and dogs swarming between parked cars, the ice cream van doing a steady trade, hang-gliders dipping towards the horizon. But today there were only two vehicles parked outside the pub. The patchwork of muddy paw prints on the outside of the boots gave them away as dog walkers. It had begun to spit with rain.

Elizabeth jumped out of the car as soon as it stopped, slamming the door. Emma slowly turned to look in the rear-view mirror. Elizabeth's face loomed at the side window. Emma eased out of the car, going round to the boot to collect the ashes.

Emma handed the pot to Elizabeth. She clutched it to her chest.

'Did you have a place in mind?' Elizabeth asked.

'Not really. Just somewhere high. And private. But there's hardly anyone here today anyway. Let's head over there. We can walk down towards Saddlescombe Farm and get a cup of tea when it's over.'

As soon as they'd left the safety of the gravel car park, Emma's low-heeled boots sunk into the churned earth. She watched Elizabeth stride confidently ahead in her stout walking boots. How alike Elizabeth and her mother were, she thought. Her mother had loved walking across the Downs when Emma was little, and then on the beach at Morecambe once she'd moved north. She would have appreciated her last journey being across the hills.

The clouds were a resolute grey, unchanged by the blustery wind. The drizzle trickled down their faces as they walked along the edge of the Dyke. Emma trailed in her sister's wake, as she had behind her mother as a child. After walking for a few hundred metres, she cupped her hands and yelled, 'Elizabeth, if we go much further, we'll lose height.'

The figure ahead stopped and turned, nodded. She was still hugging the pot to her chest, her hair and cheeks streaked with rain. Elizabeth walked back uphill and joined Emma, and handed the pot to her. 'You do it, you knew her better than me.'

Emma shook her head. 'No, we'll do it together.' She paused. 'This is going to sound a bit weird but before I knew about you, I'd planned to listen to some music that Mum used to play on the piano when I was little while I scattered her ashes. As a sort of tribute to her. D'you mind if we do that now?'

'Of course.' Elizabeth's voice broke.

Emma fiddled with her phone, tucking their mother under her arm. As the first faint funereal chords of Beethoven's 'Moonlight Sonata' drifted out, Elizabeth began to cry. Emma's hands shook as she unscrewed the cap to the urn. She opened the top of the bag within and looked at the grey ash inside. No more than from a good fire on a Sunday night, she thought. Their mother must have lost more weight before she died. The music became darker, heavier.

She offered it to Elizabeth, who hesitated and then dipped her hand in and brought it up to her wet face, as if to drink it in. In one gesture she threw the ashes away from the wind, the air carrying them up, arcing over the small copse, and sprinkling them across the tree branches like grey sleet. Elizabeth plunged her hand in again and again, scooping the ashes out, making them fly over the grey hills. The stormy arpeggios grew more ferocious, intense. The rain pelted their faces.

Emma thought back to the funeral and tried to picture her mother happy, content. But the images wouldn't come. Instead, her mother was playing 'Moonlight Sonata' on their old, battered piano, her hands so like Elizabeth's, thundering out the chords as the music reached its peak. Emma was a child, standing behind her, asking for something but being ignored. Her mother refused to turn round, she wouldn't show her face, she just kept playing. The music slowed and grew quieter.

When there was no more ash left, Emma took out the plastic bag and emptied it into the breeze. She realised she too was crying and sniffing. As the music softened towards its sombre conclusion,

Emma turned to Elizabeth and hugged her. The rain streaming down their faces, they held each other, shaking, as the pianist played the few final low chords. Elizabeth's soft coat absorbed Emma's tears. When the last note had faded out, they drew apart and looked at one another.

'I love that piece of music,' said Elizabeth simply.

Emma nodded. 'It was one of her favourites. She used to play it a lot.'

'I want to know everything like that. I want you to tell me all the things she liked, and didn't like.'

Emma nodded again.

The rain and ash had left black sludge on Elizabeth's hands and she stood looking at them transfixed. Emma turned away. She wished she'd brought the wipes from the car. She slid the bag back into the pot, screwed on the lid and handed it back to Elizabeth. Elizabeth's smudged mascara had left dark circles under her eyes, making her look almost ghostly. Emma wiped her fingertips under her own eyes, smearing the tears away. Without saying anything, they continued to walk down the side of the dyke. Elizabeth lingered now, the pot under her arm, still trying to wipe the ash away. Emma matched her own pace with Elizabeth's.

After a while Emma pointed out the farm. Elizabeth nodded. They continued in silence. Her mother was gone now, and something in Emma felt a sense of release. It was over. Her relationship with her mother had been stormy, difficult, hurtful. But it was now over and her mother could rest.

After the bitter wind, the warmth of the cafe steamed up Elizabeth's glasses. They looked at each other and laughed, breaking the tension of the previous hour. Elizabeth went straight to the loo to wash the remains of the ash off her hands.

After ordering at the counter, Emma sat down, the steaming mugs of tea arriving before she had discarded her wet layers.

Elizabeth returned, her hands no longer streaked with the grey ash. Emma was glad. She hadn't wanted to look at them like that.

Their hands cradled the mugs, and they looked at each other and smiled. Emma started. 'It was a fitting end, I think.'

Elizabeth nodded, looking directly at her. She reached forward to hold her hand. 'Tell me more about her. Am I really like her?'

Emma put her head on one side, examining Elizabeth's damp silvery bob, dark intense eyes and concentrated frown. Her mother had worn the same frown almost every day of her life. But it was hard to ignore the wide forehead. 'You look so much like her. And so many of your mannerisms are the same.'

'When you were doing your research, and found me, did you have any inkling of who my father was? There was nothing on the birth certificate.'

Emma's mug paused mid-air. She looked at Elizabeth through the steam, at her high forehead and pointy ears. Grandpa Jack. The man who everyone had worshipped for being willing to adopt another man's child. The grandfather who had seemed so kind to Emma too. Then she remembered Mr Eals' words and suddenly she knew that her mother refusing to acknowledge her first daughter, was less about not wanting to meet her – what mother doesn't have a biological need to feel and touch and know her own flesh and blood? – and more about protecting her daughter from the knowledge of who her father was, and the circumstances of her birth. Emma felt her eyes well up again. Much of her life she'd thought of her mother as heartless, selfish and cruel, but this showed another side of her. Would her mother have wanted Emma to keep the secret that she herself had so successfully kept hidden? But, in that case, why had she left behind the birth certificate and letters? She would have known that Emma would find them and would discover the truth. Eventually.

Elizabeth was looking directly at her, the glasses enlarging her questioning eyes. 'I guessed it was a boy at school,' Elizabeth said.

Emma's hand shook slightly as she put the mug slowly on the table, causing the liquid to spill over. She reached for a paper napkin from the metal dispenser on the table, a whole handful coming out in a rush, and she slowly mopped up the mess, carefully wiping the bottom of the mug, before putting it down again and looking up past Elizabeth. She recalled Mr Eals' words spoken in his dusty office. Her mother was determined that her daughter Elizabeth know nothing about her father and the circumstances of her conception. She wanted Elizabeth to be completely free of the knowledge of her father's identity. This was not Emma's secret to share. But at the same time, if Emma denied knowing who Elizabeth's father was, how could she have a relationship with her sister built on such a lie? Wasn't that simply perpetuating the secrets of the past? Didn't Elizabeth deserve to know? If Elizabeth were somehow to find out, and discover that Emma had known all along, then their relationship would certainly be lost.

Emma put the soggy napkins to one side and reached across to take Elizabeth's hands. The calluses made her think again of their mother. But she wasn't here now. Nor was Grandpa Jack. It was down to Emma to decide what to do.

'I wonder if he could still be alive?'

'What?' Emma's heart started to pound, and she released Elizabeth's hands.

'My birth father. I wonder if he could still be alive. If he was the same age as Margaret, he'd be in his eighties now. He could be alive. I wonder if there's a way we could trace him. There might be records from Birdhurst Lodge, or the Adoption Service. I never thought to ask because his name wasn't on the birth certificate. But he might be listed somewhere.'

But Jack had been dead for more than twenty-five years. His funeral had been a big affair. It felt like all of Pullman Court had come. Only Margaret was conspicuously absent. But Emma's father David had made a big deal of saying they were representing the family. They'd been glad they came because Betty had been inconsolable – as if she'd never dreamed that Jack would die.

'Or maybe there would be school records.'

'Sorry?' Emma looked up at Elizabeth, her mouth dry.

'School records of Margaret and a boy. We could trace him that way. Or maybe we could get a list of her friends and see if any of them are still alive and talk to them to see if they know his name. I'm sure she would have told someone. Someone will know and be able to tell me. Us.' Elizabeth was leaning forward, her eyes wide.

Emma picked up a spoon and carefully stirred her tea. Had her mother told any friends about her stepfather? Surely if she had, then that person would have reported it. Maybe she plucked up the courage to tell a friend but the friend didn't believe her. She had told her mother and was accused of lying. Why should anyone else believe her?

Elizabeth was looking at her intently. 'Do you know something?'

Emma laid the spoon back on the table and sighed. She wanted to warn Elizabeth – just as Mr Eals had warned Emma – to keep away from the past. But she didn't have the words.

'Are you okay?' Elizabeth was looking at her, her head on one side.

Emma closed her eyes and rubbed them, running her hands through her hair. She glanced around the cafe but the waitress was standing behind the counter busy on her phone and the other couple were some distance away, absorbed in conversation. She reached forward and took Elizabeth's hands again. 'I know who your father is Elizabeth.'

Elizabeth's eyes widened and she stared intently at Emma.

'He's no longer alive. He died when I was eighteen.' She let out a slow breath.

'You knew him?' Elizabeth held her gaze.

'I wasn't sure whether to tell you. I feel certain that one of the reasons Mum chose not to meet you was not because she didn't love you, and think about you constantly – I now know that she did. It was because she didn't want to reveal who your father was. She wanted you to be free of that knowledge.'

Elizabeth took her hand from Emma's and pressed it against her heart.

'Who?'

'When I found out about you, I didn't know who your father was either.' She thought back to the conversation she and Nick had had – that it had somehow been a romantic liaison. 'Like you, I suspected it had been someone at school. There was no Pill, no options for young women then. She would have had little choice but to give you up.'

Elizabeth nodded, but there was a deep frown between her eyes.

'When I was clearing out her flat, I found some letters between Mum and her mother, Granny Betty.' Emma swallowed, remembering how she'd felt opening that final letter – when Betty had begged for her daughter's forgiveness for not believing her about the abuse.

'This is an impossible thing to tell you. But I now believe your father was her stepfather Jack.' Her hands shook, and she placed them carefully on her legs under the table and focused on breathing.

'Margaret's stepfather is my father?'

Whatever Elizabeth had been anticipating, it hadn't been that. Emma dipped her head slightly. 'Yes. The letters showed that Jack had been abusing his daughter, been abusing Margaret and that's why she left home – on her sixteenth birthday.'

'I can't believe this.' Elizabeth's mouth sagged.

Emma reached forward again and took Elizabeth's hands, stroking them gently. 'I know this is terrible.'

'Poor, poor Mum,' said Elizabeth, gripping Emma's hands.

'Yes,' said Emma. 'I'll give you the letters next time I see you. Mum told her mother – Granny Betty – but wasn't believed. It seems that she was sent away to be with Betty's mother for a time. Maybe after she first spoke to her mother about Jack's abuse.' Emma swallowed. 'The final letter I have is just after Jack died. Granny Betty wrote to Mum apologising. Apparently Jack had confessed what he had done on his deathbed. Granny Betty was shattered by the revelation apparently.' Emma rolled her eyes. 'But the signs were all there according to Mr Eals, Mum's solicitor. He says Granny Betty wilfully ignored what was happening to Mum because she was afraid of the repercussions.'

A tear rolled down Elizabeth's cheek. She took a hand away from Emma's and wiped it away. 'Poor, poor Mum.'

Emma sat silently, holding Elizabeth's tear-stained hand. Her face seemed to display a range of emotions and Emma remembered how she'd first felt. Shock, anger, sadness.

'Do I look like him?' Elizabeth said eventually.

Emma thought about a white lie – she could easily save Elizabeth from further pain, but she knew Elizabeth would eventually see the old family photo albums and realised she'd been lied to. She took a breath. 'A little,' she said. 'But you look far more like Mum. I knew who you were from the moment I saw your photo. Your face shape, your eyes, your mannerisms are all Mum.'

Elizabeth gave a small smile. She took a napkin out of the dispenser and wiped her eyes. 'Excuse me a minute.' She got up and went back to the loo.

Had she done the right thing? Emma wondered. What would her mother say if she could see them now? What would Mr Eals say? But it wasn't just her mum's secret, Emma reminded herself. The knowledge could have died with her mother but she'd chosen to leave behind a trail for Emma to follow. And for Emma to decide what to do.

Outside the rain was easing and the dog walkers were out, determined to scale the dyke before the sun failed. Emma watched them through the condensation, wondering whether they would walk the route she and Elizabeth had taken, past their mother's ashes. She was free at last. Her secret was free at last.

Elizabeth emerged from the loo just as Emma was wondering whether she should check if she was okay. Her face was composed but her eyes red. She slid into her seat opposite Emma, caught her eye and grimaced.

'Are you alright?' asked Emma.

'Not really. It's quite a lot to take in. I think I need to sleep on it and then perhaps we can talk again.'

Emma reached across the table and cupped Elizabeth's hand. 'I know. It's completely devastating.'

'Does anyone else know in your family?'

'No,' said Emma. 'I haven't even told Nick yet, though I will do. But I don't want my children to know.'

Elizabeth sighed. 'It's been a strange time. Wonderful in some ways' – Elizabeth smiled at her – 'and terrible in others.'

Emma nodded slowly.

'I'd love to introduce you to my daughter Emilia one day. I've told her about you, and your children.'

'I'd love that.' Emma smiled, relieved at the change of subject. 'My children are keen to meet you too. They're very curious to see their new aunt. I'd love to show you some of Mum's things too. I can't remember whether we talked about it in the restaurant, but she was a really good artist – well, at least, I think so. I have some of her pieces – a couple of paintings and some sculptures.'

Elizabeth had tears in her eyes again. 'I'd love that. To be able to see and touch the things she created would be wonderful.'

'There's this one painting that she painted not long after she had you – a girl in a maze. It's beautiful. I think it might be based on you.' Or maybe it was of Margaret herself, she suddenly thought.

'Really?' Elizabeth's whole face flushed.

'You'll have to come over and meet the whole family. How about this weekend? Sunday lunch?'

'That would be wonderful. I've always wanted to feel part of a bigger family, my own family.'

'And I always wanted a sister.' Emma grinned.

Chapter 46

LIBBY

FEBRUARY 2019

Mum always slams the front door so loud. She goes on about being noisy but she's the first to shout and slam doors. Libby swivelled her laptop on the kitchen table so Emma couldn't see the screen.

'Hi, Mum,' she said, glancing up. 'How was it, scattering Granny's ashes?'

'It was a little sad,' her mum said, sitting down opposite her. 'Particularly for Auntie Elizabeth who only spent ten days with Granny. Actually, it was really emotional.' She looked around, blinking. 'What are you up to?'

'Homework,' Libby lied.

'When you've finished, would you like to watch a film? Perhaps we could get pizza.'

Pizza mid-week. Mum looked uneasy but perhaps it was to be expected with the scattering of the ashes and everything. Libby closed her laptop. 'I'm done.'

'How about a cup of tea?' Emma asked.

Libby nodded. 'I'll put the kettle on.'

Emma and Libby took their mugs into the front room. The painting above the fireplace had changed. Libby realised that must have been the banging last night.

'I remember this from Granny's flat,' Libby said, standing in front of it.

'*The Girl in the Midnight Maze*,' Emma said.

'It's beautiful but I always thought it was quite scary because the girl is so frightened and crying. And what's she doing out at night anyway?'

'That's strange. I always thought she was laughing. It's only recently that I came to see that she's crying.'

Emma and Libby stood looking at the painting for what felt like ages. There was something hypnotic about it. Libby couldn't look away. It was so beautiful – you felt you could reach out and touch the maze. All the different shades of green lit by the moonlight. And yet there was also something so otherworldly about it, something unknowable. She couldn't imagine painting something as layered and full of hidden meaning.

'It just goes to show how difficult it is to interpret someone's emotions,' said her mum.

Libby nodded. 'Yes, you could say that. There are times when you're a bit scary and a bit hysterical when you're screaming and laughing at the same time.'

Her mum laughed. 'I've felt like that quite a bit since Granny died. Maybe you have too recently.'

Libby allowed herself to think her mum might finally be right about her.

'Who d'you think the girl in the painting is?' Libby asked.

'When I was little, I thought it was me. I had a dress like that. But now I realise it was painted long before I was born, so it couldn't have been me. Granny did early sketches for this painting

283

when she was about your age, which were in the flat where she grew up. She painted this when she was nineteen.'

'So I have four years to get this good,' Libby said.

'You're well on your way to being just as good as Granny,' Emma said. 'You just need to pay attention more in class and study at home rather than always going out.'

Libby ignored the double-edged compliment. Her mum could never just be nice; there always had to be a complaint attached to it. Or some 'advice'.

'Maybe it's Granny then,' Libby said.

'Yes. Or I wonder if it's Auntie Elizabeth. Granny would have painted this just after she had her.'

'Yeah, maybe. My new aunt.' *Or maybe it's all of us,* Libby thought. All women were trapped to some degree – definitely her mum and granny's generations. Trapped by tradition and expectations of what women could and couldn't do. Trapped by marriage, lack of money, by children. Libby looked at her mum. Did she feel trapped by having her and her brother? Would she have wanted it differently? She was always miserable.

Libby decided she wasn't going to be trapped. She would forget having children and getting married. As soon as she finished school, she would travel, explore the world. Work in bars and paint everything new she saw. She wasn't going to be a girl stuck in a maze. Or even stuck at home in a dead-end job.

Her mum put an arm around her shoulders and they stood looking at the painting together. The girl looked down at them and, for the first time, she seemed to smile.

ACKNOWLEDGEMENTS

The inspiration for *The Girl in the Midnight Maze* came when I was clearing out my late mother's house in 2016. I didn't discover anything that helped to explain our difficult relationship (and the one that she'd had with her own mother), although I wish I had. But writing this story was a form of therapy in itself, and I now feel at peace with our relationship, which is why this book is dedicated to her. And that she'd nagged me since I was a young girl to write a book. It's ironic that it took her death for me to finally put pen to paper.

Motherhood comes in many forms. Some of us are biological mothers and are fortunate in being able to raise our children. Sometimes mothers have to give up their children, but they still remain mothers. Some of us are adopted mothers, stepmothers, foster mothers, surrogate mothers, godmothers, mothers-in-law, or grandmothers. Sometimes we are mother figures, playing a motherly role with other family members, or in our wider communities.

Like motherhood itself, mother and daughter relationships are endlessly complex – as I'm always learning as the mother of two young women. The relationship between the women in *The Girl in the Midnight Maze* reflects just some mother-daughter emotions – endless love and joy but also deep fear, regret, jealousy, and even revenge. I once read that motherhood is your heart forever walking around outside of you. I can't think of a better way of describing the great love and deep worry that comes with being a mother of any kind.

While my mother's death inspired *The Girl in the Midnight Maze*, this book could not have happened without countless other people.

Rosie Chard, who read the first and second drafts and helped to shape what the book became. And who suggested I enter the Lost the Plot writing competition, which introduced me to the lovely people at Agora Books who published a first version of this book, called *The Girl in the Maze*.

My agent Sam Brace at PFD who took a chance on me and believed in the characters in this book as much as I do.

The Creative Writing Programme in Brighton. It was on their two-year course that I realised that I was writing not a series of separate stories, but one story, which eventually became *The Girl in the Midnight Maze*. And the wonderful group of writers I met there who gave such great feedback on the early ideas for this book – Imogen Avsec, Natasha Baker, Victoria Benstead, Rose Dykins, Holly Fitzgerald, John Hebert, Judith Horth, Laura Maloney, Emily O'Brien, and Toby Slater. Special thanks to Catherine Smith who guided me through those first few scary terms so well.

The #WritingCommunity on Twitter for inspiration, ideas, and always providing a perfect distraction from actually writing.

The Motherless Mothers group on Facebook, who were so supportive after I lost my own mother.

Jackie Bennett Shaw who gave me a reason to visit Morecambe and introduced me to the beautiful Midland Hotel (and their rather fabulous cocktails) where I later spent two intense weekends writing the Morecambe sections of this book.

The Jubilee Library in Brighton for providing the perfect place to write. And a space away from the temptations of the fridge and snack cupboard. It's rather wonderful to now see the book I wrote there on their shelves.

Lucy Jeynes for providing me, at extremely short notice, with a couple of lines of beautiful poetry for this book. And for being a fabulous role model as both mother and writer.

Richard Wilson for the support, encouragement and for always being ready to answer random questions about what a surveyor would actually do.

The November mums for the endless supply of Prosecco and helping me along the motherhood journey. And to Mel, Davina, and all the Brighton mums who have shared the highs and lows of motherhood with me over the past twenty-two years.

Rachel Martin and Jo Sutherland, my beta readers. Thank you for your time, encouragement, and ideas. It was so scary sharing that first draft with you back in 2020 but I'm so glad I did.

My late father, a single dad before that was even a thing. I wish you were here to see this book published. I know I wasn't always the easiest child to raise, but I'm so glad we shared those last few difficult months together before you died. Everything I do is down to the person you helped me to become. Your memory is truly the wind beneath my wings.

Jude, Zara, and Katy: thank you for guiding me into becoming a mother – the best, and sometimes the hardest, job in the world – and for continuing to delight and challenge me. You are a never-ending source of joy and pride.

SOURCES

I read widely about mother-daughter relationships and adopted mothers and children to write this book as well as using my own experiences. Sources I found really useful include:

Boughton, J. (2019). *Municipal Dreams: The Rise and Fall of Council Housing*. Verso Books

Edelman, H. (1994). *Motherless Daughters: The Legacy of Loss*. Hodder & Stoughton

Jamelia. (2011). *Shame About Single Mums*. Documentary on BBC3: https://bit.ly/3uvRUCp

Morris, C and Munt, SR. (2019). Classed formations of shame in white, British single mothers. University of Sussex: https://bit.ly/3xXT6k8

Morton, S. (1992). *Women on Their Own: Single Mothers in Working-Class Halifax in the 1920s* Acadiensis: https://journals.lib.unb.ca/index.php/Acadiensis/article/view/11916

Newton Verrier, N. (1993). *The Primal Wound: Understanding the Adopted Child*. Gateway Press

Penfold, RB. (2006). *Dragonslippers: This is What an Abusive Relationship Looks Like.* Black Cat

Thane, P and Evans, T. (2012). *Sinners? Scroungers? Saints? Unmarried Motherhood in Twentieth-Century England.* Oxford University Press

BOOK CLUB DISCUSSION POINTS

If you're choosing to read *The Girl in the Midnight Maze* in your book group, then a massive THANK YOU. I obviously love the idea that people are reading my book, but far more exciting is that you're sitting around talking about it with cups of tea or glasses of wine.

Here are some pointers for your discussion which I hope are helpful. If you haven't yet read the book, then stop reading this now. There are spoilers ahead!

1. How did *The Girl in the Midnight Maze* make you feel?

2. Motherhood is a key theme throughout the book. All of the mothers in the story are flawed to some extent. Who did you have most and least sympathy for as a mother? Betty's mother June, Betty, Margaret or Emma? There is also Elizabeth's adoptive mother to consider.

3. The solicitor Mr Eals advises Emma to leave the past alone. Would she have been happier if she hadn't uncovered her mother's secrets? And do you think she will be a better mother to her two children as a result?

4. Mr Eals himself is a mysterious character, the guardian of many of Margaret's secrets. Do you think he and Margaret had a romantic relationship? Does it matter that the reader never knows?

5. After Margaret and Emma become estranged, Margaret erases all references to her daughter from her life. Why do you think this is?

6. The painting of the girl in the midnight maze is a key character in the story and many characters perceive it in different ways. Why do you think Margaret gifted the painting to Clare in her will? And why do you think everyone interprets the painting differently?

7. Margaret spends pivotal parts of her life in institutions – the mother and baby home and then the mental hospital. How do these spells impact on her life?

8. Was Emma telling her half-sister Elizabeth about her father's identity the right thing to do? Or should she have kept it secret?

9. Do you think trauma can be passed down from generation to generation? How do you think traumatised families can break the chain?

10. In the UK today, women have more choice around pregnancy. Do you think this story could take place now?

11. If the book was to be made into a film, who do you think would play the key characters – Betty, Margaret, Emma and Elizabeth?

ABOUT THE AUTHOR

Cathy trained as a journalist and wrote about everything from accounting and supply chains to football finances and port strategy before moving into public relations. In 2022, after having spent a lifetime pottering around bookshops, she bought Kemptown Bookshop in Brighton, where she has created a community hub that supports local authors and aspiring writers. In 2023, she took on management of The Creative Writing Programme, the leading independent centre for creative writing teaching in the south-east of England—the course that set her on track to be a writer. When she's not writing (or reading), Cathy loves pottering in other people's bookshops. She lives in Brighton with her three children and two rescue cats.

Follow the Author on Amazon

If you enjoyed this book, follow Cathy Hayward on Amazon to be notified when the author releases a new book!

To do this, please follow these instructions:

Desktop:

1) Search for the author's name on Amazon or in the Amazon App.

2) Click on the author's name to arrive on their Amazon page.

3) Click the 'Follow' button.

Mobile and Tablet:

1) Search for the author's name on Amazon or in the Amazon App.

2) Click on one of the author's books.

3) Click on the author's name to arrive on their Amazon page.

4) Click the 'Follow' button.

Kindle eReader and Kindle App:

If you enjoyed this book on a Kindle eReader or in the Kindle App, you will find the author 'Follow' button after the last page.